Maggie Nora Liza
Mhór

Paul K. MacNeil

 FriesenPress

One Printers Way
Altona, MB R0G 0B0
Canada

www.friesenpress.com

ISBN
978-1-03-912214-7 (Hardcover)
978-1-03-912213-0 (Paperback)
978-1-03-912215-4 (eBook)

1. FICTION, ROMANCE, GOTHIC

Distributed to the trade by The Ingram Book Company

TABLE OF CONTENTS

Maggie Nora Liza Mhór is a fictional love story about a young lady, now in her mid-twenties, who was raised by her grandmother until the age of thirteen. She believes she is a miracle baby and is searching for her family identity, her own sense of person, place, and being, along with proof of the mystical tales related to the conception of life. She finds them in the Iona area of rural Cape Breton where spirits have been known to pass between the two worlds. Maggie meets with many interesting characters and places, and falls in love along the way.

CHAPTER 1
A Morning After

Oh, to sleep: perchance to dream, and I had slept all night for the first time since I didn't know when. There was no way to explain it—it simply was, the night before.

That was too easy, but it was pretty special and every now and then things just fall into place. Fate, if you like. Luck, if you believe in that. You can't deny you make your own luck sometimes—and maybe all the time.

Regardless, the thought of a bright new day had me thinking it could be. It could be everything.

Her light butterscotch skin looked like delicate velvet you needed to wrap yourself in. I felt beautiful standing beside her, as if caught up in her luminescent glow. She moved like the wind. Wild at times, and then gentle like a whisper through the trees. She weaved, as if through openings in the forest or an alleyway. A gust that would make you grab your hat, back to that gentle breeze that tickled your neck Could I handle it? And my mind flashed back to the evening before.

Wow, I felt it again or maybe I was wishing, but the thought of that moment itself had me spinning. I didn't know what to think.

Did she know what she was doing? She seemed to—or was it a bit of poor judgment on her part? It didn't matter and I tried to enjoy it for what it was. It had been so long since I had that much fun and it felt so good.

I struggled to believe it really happened and questioned if I talked too much or sounded like a child. She had a coy way of flirting with me that told me she liked me. Why wouldn't she like me? And I knew in my racing head I needed to stop.

I was enjoying my feelings so I closed my eyes and her image floated for a few more minutes. Oh my God, I heard birds singing, spring birds with a thousand stories to tell. I hoped I wouldn't start birdwatching after this because I always found that sounded a little odd.

I'd delayed long enough and knew I needed to get my feet moving. She told me to touch base in the morning and that we'd make a plan but she didn't say what time. I wondered if she was awake and decided to wait a while before sending her a text.

I'd give her a chance to get out of it, if she was having second thoughts. I shouldn't be too surprised if she did—and who knew what her friends were saying to her. Thinking of which, what was the story on that Zoe girl? I couldn't remember meeting anyone with that name who I ever really liked. It might be OK for a cat, but even I wouldn't do that.

Funny about that but there were some names that rubbed me the wrong way. We were pretty old-school growing up, so it had to be my roots. As odd as she was, she was nice to me—or at least it seemed that way.

I shook myself, made some coffee, and nervously anticipated what could be a great day. After all, it wasn't that long since the Easter season so something had to be working in my favour.

All of those trips to church and I still didn't get it. Hour after hour after hour and how much my parents said they loved it. Oh God, I can't go there since I tortured myself enough over the years. I'm not sure what I would've said if she had suggested we go to church, but it probably would have been yes.

She didn't really talk about church for that matter, it was just a trip she had always wanted to make. She said it was a little pilgrimage or *camino*, whatever that is. I wondered what her religion was, but why would I care? I wasn't religious. In fact, I was pretty indifferent to it all.

She must have had some connection to it and what was the thing about the Judas Kiss? Should I have known that? I should look it up. Regardless, whatever it was, she didn't say it about me. It was that friend of her old boyfriend who was there last night, who I don't think she liked very much.

It was hard to know at the time. She may have been having fun with me so word would get back to her old boyfriend. I shook my head, poured the coffee, and knew I needed to stop grinding my mind on it.

I thought about the car and if it needed to be cleaned. The outside was OK but I was pretty sure the inside needed a little wipe. I wanted to make sure I had lots of gas since I didn't know where we were going. She said she had been there before. Actually, she said she hadn't been there but had been trying to get there for years. No one would go with her and her old boyfriend wasn't interested enough. Maybe he wasn't listening or maybe he just didn't care?

I also knew there was no point in my trying to analyze a guy I didn't know. I knew if he felt the same way about her as I did, he'd have taken her every day and any day, and from the little she said about him, it sounded like he only cared about himself.

It was actually Zoe who brought him up, so I'm not sure if she was messing with me or just having some fun. It kind of blew by me at the time and I certainly didn't get it, if it was meant to be a joke.

I looked at the time. It was 8:15, Saturday morning, and I wondered again if she was awake.

Soooo the forecast told me sunny with cloudy periods and a chance of rain, or thundershowers later tonight. Wasn't that the safe way out, the chance of the sky falling or worse? There was nothing wrong with a little rain, and at least they weren't talking about snow, so it was very manageable.

Rain was nice. In fact, I enjoyed a little thunder and lightning. Not sure why, but I always liked being out in it. Perhaps it's facing the elements and feeling like you're at their mercy. Was that more religion sneaking in?

Was it a chance to show off my masculine side, even though I didn't sense she was looking for that? I thought women liked to have someone strong beside them, even if they didn't say or act it. If I was a woman I wouldn't want someone weak and soft hanging off me. I'd rather just swim the river by myself if those were my choices.

I struggled not to text her and checked out the news to see what was going on in the world. We'd have something to talk about if there was dead air between us but I couldn't imagine that happening. Our conversations last night just kept going and going as if we'd known each other forever.

We could have written a book last night. It seemed so effortless, as if we were supposed to fall into each other. Yet I wondered if she was regretting the whole thing this morning.

Wait now, hold on. I needed to get a grip. If she had wanted to make that trip for so long and now had someone to take her, she wasn't going to be calling in sick or making up any other excuse. We were going on a trip, baby! Oh, it was bigger than a trip. It was a pilgrimage or *camino* or something like that.

I thought about calling her but if she was asleep that would suck so I sat down and backed away from that idea.

I thought about checking in with my friend Dougie to see if he had something to add. But the more I thought about that, the more I knew it wasn't a good idea. He had taken off before Maggie and I got together so he wouldn't be much help. I should have checked on him, but not right now. There was a pretty good chance if something had happened, I'd have heard from him and I hadn't. So he was probably OK.

All those things kept creeping into my mind. Like that line about Passover, which was really meant for her job and being passed over. She laughed about it and said she didn't care, but I sensed there was more to that story. Maybe I needed help and toast always helped. I cooked it up, wolfed it down, and hit the drops.

The shower ran for a while until it got hot, so therefore this day was just like any other. I guess today wasn't going to be the day everything changed. Oh, well, there was always lots of it when it got here; you just had to wait for it.

I remembered when I was a kid, we were lucky to have hot water. If the stove was going you'd have a chance at warm water, but there were a lot of days when it didn't seem to matter. I don't know how my mother survived all that. Waiting a few minutes was nothing for me. She waited half the day if she had the time.

There were always a hundred things that needed to be done and she hardly complained. I remembered her talking about how hard her mother worked.

It was probably the same with every generation. But it seemed like kids today had everything and I didn't see them working nearly as hard as we did. Kids, children—I needed to stop thinking about that. If she wanted to bring that up it was OK with me, but I was not starting it.

So much has changed, even from when I was a kid. I must have smelled like the barn when I was growing up but then again most of the kids were in the same boat. We were all kids from farmers or fishermen, so I don't think any of us thought we were better than the next.

I was enjoying my shower when I thought of my uncle, who used to say, "If it rained hot water, it would be pretty cool." I chuckled to myself and started a fresh shave. It'd been a few days and I had the time so I took a layer off, which felt pretty good.

I was dressed and cleaned and it was only 9:05. I'd waited long enough and struggled with my words but found these and texted Maggie.

> *I had a blast last night. Are we still on for today?*
> *Elvis!!!!!*

I wondered if she would find that funny today. She had called me Elvis last night and was very amused. It was comical, I guess, and I wondered if she remembered my real name. I wasn't giving it away as I sent the note and wondered what would happen.

With nothing else to do, I poured another cup of coffee and thought about cleaning the car. At least it would be fit to be in and it would pass some time. I should have paid more attention to what she was saying instead of gawking at her because I couldn't remember where this place was. She mentioned a couple of places and said she thought it took a couple of hours to get there. She was trying to find some people and, if nothing else, we'd go on a hike.

I thought about taking some food but when I looked through the cupboards I didn't have much for snacks. I had a bottle of wine that was looking to breathe and a couple of bottles of water. That was a good start, but I figured I'd stop somewhere and grab some sandwiches just so we had something.

I almost called Doug but decided to send him a text. There was no need to bother him if he was in bed, enjoying the day off.

Hey, Doug, did you get home all right?
Any news on the night?
Just checking in.

A few minutes passed and my phone chirped. Who was it, Dougie or her? It was her…Shit, it was him.

All's good…No news…What are you up to today?

What could I say to that? Why was he up and Maggie wasn't? I wanted her to write back.

Not sure yet.
Maybe something big.
I'll let you know.

What do you mean big?
What did I miss?
I'm coming over.

Shit!!!!

Nothing yet, just maybe something.
I'll let you know when I do.
I'm not home. Come over all you want.

You are so home.
Give me a clue.

I couldn't tell him in case nothing happened and why had I said big? That was a mistake and I wished she'd text.

OK, maybe big was the wrong word.
I'll let you know when I do.
What are you up to besides torturing me?

My phone chirped again. What was it now? Oh, it was her!

I had fun as well.
Yes, I'm on…I can't believe I'm going.
I can leave at any time.
What about you?

WA hoo…Today was my lucky day—and yesterday and tomorrow!!!! I wrote her back right away.

> *I'm good to go any time.*
> *Did you say 3rd and Central or Sentinel?*
>
> *Central*
>
> *OK. How about around 9:45?*
> *Is that OK?*
>
> *OK, meet me at the deli on the corner.*
> *I'll go there now and grab a coffee.*
> *Do you want one?*
>
> *No, I already had a couple here this morning.*

I didn't want to tell her about the wine, so I just said:

> *Can you grab some bread or something sweet to eat?*
> *I have some bottles of water just in case we get off the*
> *beaten path.*
> *Whatever you like.*
>
> *Sure. Sounds nice.*
> *See you soon.*

My mind was racing as I grabbed the bottles and some wipes for the car. I leapt down the stairs and flew out the door into the warm late-spring day. It was a Hello World kind of day.

There was no wind and the sun had been up for a while so things were all heated up. I heard the birds singing again and I hadn't noticed them yesterday. Whatever, birds were nice and the car wasn't in that bad a shape. I cleaned off the seat, wiped the door and the dash, and she was shined up to code.

The tank was full so I didn't need to stop and I talked to myself the whole way there, thinking of things to say to her. I was thinking this must be what it would feel like if I was going to Mars. I had no idea what was going to happen and the phone kept chirping. I was about to panic and getting very frustrated so I pulled over before I got there and checked it. Frig! Doug, I forgot to write him back.

> *What's up, bud?*
> *I'm coming over.*

Next text.

> *I mean it. I'm coming over.*

Next text.

> *What's going on?*
> *I'm on my way!*

Next text.

> *Where are you?*
> *You really aren't home.*

I needed to reply.

> *Oh, hey there.*
> *I told you I wasn't home…I'm going for a drive.*
> *A little adventure. I'll be in touch.*

Then Maggie texted.

> *What kind of car are you driving?*
> *Wouldn't want to jump in with the wrong guy.*

Then Doug texted again.

> *Can I go for the drive, as well?*
> *I like going for drives.*

> *No, you can't… That would make three.*
> *An odd number. Have to go.*
> *I'm late.*

I finally got there and was about to send her a note when I saw her. I touched the horn and waved my phone and she waved back, smiled, and opened the door.

"Well, hello there, nice to see you again," she said.

"You, too."

"Are you sure you're up for this?" she asked.

"I wouldn't be here if I wasn't. Although I'm not sure I know what *this* is all about."

"Well it's a bit of a mystery in itself, so I'm not sure what to tell you. Are you sure you don't want a coffee or anything before we leave? You know, they've got good stuff in there."

"No, no, I'm good."

"I grabbed a loaf of their olive bread and a lemon loaf—do you like that?"

"Sure, sounds great, I'll eat just about anything."

"You know they make a great smoked meat sandwich if you're ever looking for one," she said.

"Perhaps another day. So where exactly are we going?"

"Well, we'll start by going north on the big highway and take the 223 after that. I have a map so I don't think we'll get lost. What's the worst that could happen? We get stranded in some quaint little town and have to spend the night?"

Shit, I hadn't thought of that—I didn't pack anything. Then again, what if I got caught with a bag? She'd think that was weird.

"Aahhh, I didn't pack anything for overnight, did you?"

"A girl always packs for overnight, and I'm sure you could pick something up if you needed to. They have stores in the country, you know. Maybe not the same as the big city, but you'd find something."

"I'll be OK, I guess," I said sadly.

We drove through town onto the highway and it was pretty slick. There wasn't a lot of traffic this time of day—or any time of day, for that matter. The city wasn't as big as I thought it was when I first got there, plus I knew my way around pretty well.

"I haven't lived in the city for long," I said. "How about you?"

"No, I've only been here for a few years. I grew up in a town that's about a third the size. Or maybe a quarter would be closer."

"So you're not a big city girl?"

"No, not at all."

"That makes two of us," I said.

"I like it here. It's just really different and sometimes I miss my old friends. I had to make a change, you know, I felt like I was going nowhere and having a lot of uncomfortable feelings. Blah, blah, blah, enough about me. What about you?"

"No, no, no. I'd like to know more, but I guess we've got all day. Or maybe a little longer," I chuckled, then continued. "Well, I grew up in a small town and came here to go to college and ended up staying. That was five years ago now. My parents have passed since I've been here and there's not much left back home, as they say."

"Gee, your parents must have been young when they…I'm sorry, by the way."

"Thanks, but it seems like a long time ago now. They were in their seventies, which *is* pretty young, I guess. They got sick around the same time and died within a year of each other after fifty years together. Everyone said they couldn't be separated—and perhaps that was true."

"That's a long time," she said. "Maybe they're still together."

"I like to think they are, but I probably won't know till I get to the other side. It's all a mystery, just like you said, and I'm in no rush to find out. I've got a few things I'd like to accomplish first."

"Oh, yeah? Like what?" she asked.

"Really?"

"Yeah, why not? Like what? What are your goals? I should know these things before travelling off into the wilderness with you," she said with a grin.

"Wilderness? Who said anything about the wilderness?"

"Goals, please." She frowned as she tapped her index finger against her opposite knuckle.

"Well, I'd like to spend time with you," I said.

"Aaaahhhhhh, that's sweet."

"And I'd like to make you breakfast someday," I said.

"Aaaaahhhhh."

"Just kidding. Kind of serious though," I stuttered. "I've always wanted to go to Europe and see Italy, France, and Germany. You know, places like that. I'd also like to see northern Europe, I guess they call it that. Nordic countries like Finland, Sweden, and Norway. And Scotland. And Ireland, of course. You know, I'd like to see something different than what's around here. There's so much history in those places and I feel as though there's a connection of some sort. I'm getting a bit more interested in history lately, how about you? Do you want to travel at all?"

"Well, I am now," she said with a laugh. "And I would like to travel, but I had a warmer climate in mind. You know, something a little further south or Australia. But Europe sounds nice. And, yes, the north, for sure. Some of the pictures seem so primitive and risky, I think it would be tough living in some of those places. The northern thing would be fun for a few days, like the whole concept of being bundled up in an igloo while the wind howls outside. That would be pretty cool to me."

"I wonder if it's really like that," I said.

"What do you mean?"

"The igloo idea is nice, but a lot of the images I see on TV don't make it look very cozy. But then again, most of what you see on the news is the bad stuff, no matter where the story is coming from. Don't take that the wrong way. I hope I'm wrong."

"Well, we'll have to go there to find out for ourselves, I guess."

"You never know," I said.

"But, yeah, I am interested in that whole Norse adventure, for sure. That's right up my alley. What else?" she asked.

"Well, to travel, you need money, so I'd like to make more money. I always thought I'd invent something and become rich and famous—you know, the easy route."

"How's that going?"

"Not very well so far. I've had some ideas and we've got some prototypes on the go. We're still moving forward and it's not eating up a lot of money, so it's OK. That's one of the tricks, you know. Don't invest too much unless you're sure you can get it back."

"I'd love to hear about them if you want to share them with me. And, I promise: I won't steal them."

"I don't think we need to discuss them right now. You might think I'm crazy and get out."

"They can't be that weird, can they?"

"They're not, but what about you? What else do you want to do?"

"Well, I'd like to have a family someday—you know, babies. And I'm hoping today will solve a few things."

"OK, so what's this trip about? I still don't know the whole story."

"Well, you might think I'm crazy and throw me out if I tell you the whole story."

"It would have to be pretty strange."

"OK, so did you ever think about having kids? You know where they come from, how they get here, and all that?"

"Well, I've thought about making them more than having them—practice and all that. Wait, now, don't you know where they come from?"

"Ha, ha, very funny. That's not really what I mean. Are you scared?"

"No."

I thought to myself that she was moving kind of quick or maybe she was joking around? And then these words jumped out of my mouth before they could be stopped.

"I don't think we have to drive to the country to make a baby." Oh, geez, I said that.

"Ha, ha," she sort of giggled. "That's not exactly where I'm going with this."

"OK, OK, there's more to your story. I'm sorry. What is it?"

"There are lots of different beliefs out there that when people die they're born again and come back as different people, birds, or animals. You've heard about this sort of thing, right? It could be anything."

"Yes, I've heard of it and I think it's a big part of the Indian culture. By that, I mean India, not Native American."

"I think most people know it as reincarnation. Coming back as another animal or person or some other life form."

It sure felt like another Easter connection to me.

"I think it is connected to Hinduism and other cultures like that," she said. "They believe you come back time and time again until your soul becomes one with God and then you live in peace for eternity. It's all part of the conception and the re-entering of flesh in a mother's womb. I'm no expert on it by any means, but it's something like that.

"There is an ancient Norse belief that carried over to the Gaels—Scots and Irish, in particular—that some babies are conceived the same sort of way, or through some mysterious way like that."

"Is this common knowledge? Because I've never heard of it," I said.

"No, it's not very common anymore, but it was at one time. I know that Christianity and science have a different outlook or presentation of how these things happen. Mam—that was my grandmother—used to say that the church, as much as they believed in and loved it, took a lot of the old beliefs and customs away from the people. You know, they've been converting people and cultures for a few thousand years now, so they need to drive the old beliefs out to get the new ones in.

"Mam said that all the time, 'You have to get the old ones out before you get the new ones in.'"

"Yeah, I guess that's true," I said.

"Now, part of the folklore goes like this: when a person dies and that person's soul is about to rise, conception is possible for a woman who is trying to have children or for one that couldn't get pregnant through the usual means. You know what I mean there, don't you?"

"Ahh, yes, I have a pretty good idea what you are talking about," I said.

"Now the other interesting thing about this is that only the souls of the cleansed can be part of this. It's kind of the same idea as the Hindus, but different. Sort of a judgment day where the pure souls pass to the other world and the evil ones are left behind. It's kind of heavy, eh?"

"Yes, it's a little more than I was expecting, but keep going."

"Well, I'm hoping to learn a few things today. Some of it is who I am and where I come from, but I also want to know if these old people have heard of this and believe in it.

"I think it was a fairly common old belief that when you die your soul would pass from this world to the next. Some say the souls could come back if they couldn't pass and that's why we have ghost stories and stuff like that."

"What do you mean?" I asked.

"Well, I don't know what it is but it was considered the day of new life or a new beginning. I guess it's the time when spirits can pass to the other world or come back if they've left some unfinished business behind. It was also when this magic of conception would occur."

"Well, there sure is a lot going on," I said.

"I've seen it in several different cultures, where people will dress up to scare off the bad spirits and stuff like that. I think it's all related."

"I suppose there's more?" I asked.

"Oh, there's a lot more, but I'll just add a few more things for now. Mam used to say that she heard from the old people that this happened in the forest and near water at the same time and it would affect many women at the same time.

"Did you ever wonder why some people have the same birthday?" she asked. "They may be the same day but years apart."

"I always found it, I don't know, ironic," I said.

"Well, I know one family that had nine different people born on the same day."

"Wow."

"Now they were spaced over 100 years, but what are the chances?"

"Well, I'd say they weren't very high."

"You must know someone who has the same birthday as you," she said.

"As a matter of fact, I dated a girl who had the same birthday as me and her brother had the same birthday, as well. I know a brother and a sister who are seven years apart with the same birthday. Their cousin and uncle on their mother's side has the same date, as well. So I get what you're saying, I just never thought of it like that."

"See, there you go. I know it's a bit of a stretch by normal ways of thinking, but I think it's all connected. How many couples do you know that want to have children, but can't, and then out of the blue, they are pregnant? So these are just parts of the story. Do you want to hear more?" she asked.

"Yes, sure," I said rather timidly.

"Are you scared?"

"Yeah, yeah, I am, but keep going. But before you do, I think this is our turn off—or should I say turn on? Ha, ha, get it? Babies, turn on?"

"OK, turn on, turn off, I got it. Let's go this way and see what happens."

"So where are we going from here?" I asked.

"Well, there are three stops that I want to make and just see where that takes us. Does that sound OK?"

"Sure thing. It's an adventure, isn't it?"

"So the first place—and I think the easiest—is just getting to Iona itself. It's just a little town but it's on the map so we should be able to find it easily enough."

"Iona? I never heard of it."

"Well, it's there. Mam talked about 'Fiona from Iona' and that's one of the other pieces I'm trying to sort out. I believe she was my great-grandmother and there are a couple of old ladies I want to try to track down. The other is an old cemetery or celebration site in a place called Skye Glen or The Glen. This part is a bit of a stretch, but they had old church grounds or something like that so I'm hoping these ladies might be able to help with that, as well."

"Do you mean like a pioneer cemetery? Because we had one in our town."

"I'm not sure. There's nothing like that on the map—at least I couldn't find any information on it so I'd like to see if that goes anywhere."

"Oh, well. That seems like plenty to start with."

"The other thing was something about Magic Mountain or a harbour that I'm connected with. It could have been a cove or bay—I just don't know. And then there's some sort of clue or combination of clues from all of these places that will lead us to a ceremony of some sort."

"A ceremony? You didn't mention that. I didn't bring anything to wear—you know we talked about that already."

"Hey, this is what I'm working from, and I know it sounds a little nutty and may not exist. But do you want to keep going? 'Cause if you don't, I understand completely. But that's the story. Sooooo, it's up to you," she said.

"Ach, sure, why not? It does sound like a bit of a stretch, but I've heard crazier tales so I'm up for it. Carry on, Canada, as they say. It will be fun and, besides, no one knows us up there."

"Well, that's part of it. I do have a connection up there and I'm curious to find out as much as I can. So I guess I have more than folk tales to figure out. But I'll take what I can get."

"Right on, that's probably the place to start," I said.

"I did find a place called Skye Glen on some maps, but it seems to be too far away from the Iona area, so I don't think that's it. But doesn't that just say it all? It's like sailing every ocean and going to the moon all on the same trip. Do you know what I mean?"

"Yeah, that sounds like an interesting place. It's like big sky country in the West, I guess."

"I never heard of it until just lately, but it just sounds really cool," she said.

"I knew a guy from Glen Street one time. I wonder if he came from there?"

"You don't quite get it, do you? You told me your last name was MacLean, right?"

"Yes, is that what I told you? Just kidding. It's MacLean."

"Well, that could be Irish or Scottish but most likely it's Scottish. And Patrick, well, I don't think there's any doubt that it's Irish. So you have a connection to both countries in both names. So your parents or grandparents or someone in your family probably came from there."

"Oh, I guess I've heard some of this before and I know my family came from there a long time ago."

"Did you take any history or geography courses in school?" she asked.

I paused to think about an answer and she said, "Did you even go to school?" Then added: "I'm just kidding."

"Yes, I went to school."

"Look, I'm just learning about this myself and it's not something I was into until recently, but now I find it interesting."

"Well, I never expected to find myself heading on some history crusade searching for magical babies, but it sounds like fun."

"Well, good. Now *crusade* is a bit of an old word, but all right. Now let me ask you this: if I told you all this last night, would we be going there now?"

"Yes, I'm pretty sure we would."

"Well that's great. Now let me ask you this: when I say Skye, what do you think of?"

"The sun. And I guess the colour blue. Maybe storms. Why do you ask?"

"Well, there's more to it than that. I was thinking of the Isle of Skye, in what they call the Outer Hebrides on the west coast of Scotland. It's one of about sixty islands in an archipelago and where a lot of the original settlers came from.

"So, Patrick MacLean, if in fact that is your real name, your people probably came from one of those islands some 200 years ago. Does any of this ring a bell?"

"Well, no, not so very much. Is Wales one of those islands?"

"No, it's not. It's in a different area but you are generally in the right part of the world."

"So anyway, back in the day—or century, as they say—around 2,000 years ago, these Norse guys were like, the bullies on the block. They used to have their way with the island people and most anyone. Stealing, beating, killing, enslaving women and men, you know, raping and pillaging, to put it in pirate terms."

"I never heard of this."

"Well, the story goes that at this particular time, the Norse ruler, Noron, was attacking the area around Skye. I believe it was a place called Glenelg and there was a young girl living there named Boronia, who was said to possess great powers."

"What kind of powers?" I asked.

"Well, they say she had medical powers to cure and protect people. She was the seventh daughter of a seventh daughter and was becoming notorious throughout the islands for her special powers. Do you know about that?" she asked.

"Sadly, no, I don't."

"Seriously, nothing?"

"No, not really," I said.

"OK, how about lucky number seven or maybe the seventh son of the seventh son? That's pretty much the same sort of story. Still nothing?" she asked.

"No, sorry. It's not ringing any bells."

"They say that the seventh child born into a family is supposed to have an advantage over all the rest. There is some ancient folklore here but it comes from, well, I forget them all, but the moon has four phases and each one of them has seven days, or nights, however you want to look at it. And in ancient times there were only seven planets and you must know this one, the world was created in seven days."

"Yes," I said, raising my finger. "I've heard about this."

"Ok, how about seven days in the week, and oh yeah, how many colours are there in the rainbow?"

"Let me guess, there must be seven."

"Very good. What are they?"

"Oh, geez, I don't know."

"Oh, it doesn't matter, at least not that I know of. It may be very important but it's not something I know about. Oh, there's something else," she said.

"What is it?"

"Oh yeah, how many notes are there in music?"

"Well it must be seven," I said.

"Correct, and there's a whole pile more, but anyway, you get the idea. Oh, I love this one. How many lives does a cat have? Well, it's nine but if it doesn't get to seven first the last two are useless. Oh, that's funny, isn't it?"

"Yes, very funny. So anyway, back to your story."

"OK, so Boronia's village was attacked year after year along with many others, and when the Norse men were coming, the Celts would just scatter into the forests and hide. But there would always be people caught or someone sick that couldn't get away and they'd be taken and sold like slaves or killed. Pick your poison—they weren't treated very well.

"So at this time the Celts weren't able to defend themselves at all and they'd run to try and survive. There were hundreds of these communities and all were in the same state and living under this fear on a pretty regular basis.

"So it's said that Boronia, who was not that old, could communicate with the fairies and the fairies taught her how they could defend themselves.

"The first was to make weapons, the second was to build structures they could live in for years, and the third was to make food they could store for long periods of time. They must have had some kind of magical powers because she soon started building this structure called a broch. Any idea on that one?" she asked.

"Aah, no."

"They're stone structures with an inner and outer wall about four feet apart and a wooden roof. They built them in a circular shape roughly forty feet high and forty feet wide, although there were many different heights and sizes.

"They say she started building this structure with the help of the fairies at night and the first structure went up in no time at all, like in a week. As time went on all the people in the small communities started building these stone structures to harbour everyone and keep them safe. They could survive in there for a long time, defend themselves, and didn't have to run and hide.

"So after returning to this village, which most people think is Glenelg—seven letters, by the way, and it's a palindrome—this Norse leader Noron, another palindrome, returned to pillage again but they couldn't do anything and, in fact, some of his men were killed.

"This did not please him at all so they left only to return some weeks later with people they'd captured from other communities and threatened to kill them if Boronia didn't help him. He had become aware of her powers and knew she was the one who was responsible for these brochs. They were seeing more and more of these structures all the time and feeling a little threatened. She was now a young woman and a leader who was becoming quite famous for her powers and wisdom."

"So what did they do?" I asked.

"Well, the first thing he needed to do was release his prisoners before she would even talk to him. Once he did this she agreed to help him, and this is where it gets interesting if it wasn't already.

"You see he was having a problem fathering a child, for no woman that he was ever with was able to have a child. It seems as though he was firing blanks or something like that. Are you following me?"

"Yes, I think so."

"In those days, this of course was very important, and perhaps somewhat embarrassing as well. But he thought if Boronia, once again seven letters, was in his court, she would have the powers to fix his problem."

"Are you making this up or what?"

"No, no, it's the story that was told to me," she said. "So Boronia said if I can help you with this problem, you must return all the people you have taken from here if they wish to return and you must never attack us again. For if you do, we will become stronger, become the aggressor and we will start attacking your villages. So he agreed to this."

"So did she have to give birth, sex scene in the movie?" I said.

"What movie?" she asked.

"This is playing out like a movie."

"It's just a story. Anyway, it doesn't matter, but no, it wasn't her that gave him a child. This is what is said to have happened next."

She asked me if I ever watched an ant in the sand on the beach. I couldn't remember the last time I was at a beach, let alone saw an ant there. She then asked me if I knew why ants never got sick, about which, again, I had no idea. Her joke was that they have little antibodies that had nothing to do with the story but she found it amusing.

"It seemed they never stop moving and we may not know where they're going, but they sure did. So Boronia took Noron to the beach and they walked the beach until they found an ant and they sat down across from each other and held their hands together.

"She called to the spirits and fairies for help as the wind increased, blowing to the west. She picked up a handful of sand with her right hand and told him to hold out his right hand. She dumped the sand into his hand and told him to dump it onto the ant. He did that and a few moments passed and the ant dug its way out. The sand had taken a very unusual shape as the ant kept going toward the west.

"She picked up another handful in her other hand and dumped it into his other hand and told him to dump it on the ant again. He did this and some time passed and the ant dug itself out again. Once again, the mound of sand took on an unusual shape and the ant kept on moving to the west. She did it again with her right hand, the sand, his hand, and a shape appeared. Now the ant was looking very weak but kept going. One more time with the left hand and the ant was buried. The sand took on a shape but the ant did not come out."

"So what does this all mean?" I asked.

"Well, I guess they both stood up and looked at the four piles of sand that now resembled four islands on the beach and she looked right into his eyes and said, 'You know where this is, don't you?' He said he knew where it was and she said, 'You must go there and I need to go with you.'"

"Where was it?" I asked.

"It was fringing Cape Breton before it was Cape Breton. The four shapes were Iceland, Greenland, Newfoundland, and Cape Breton."

I questioned it all but she was convinced and told me there had been numerous discoveries that pointed to the Norse people being there long before the English and French. They found what would have been settlements in Greenland and Newfoundland that had to have been built by someone. Nearly all of the evidence from those settlements pointed to the Vikings being here more than 1,000 years ago. Maybe even 2,000 years ago and that was long before the English, French, and Spanish explorers landed in North America.

I had read something about this, or saw it on TV, but still questioned if it could have happened this way. She went on about where the American Indian came from. It may have been Russia, but she believed it was from one of these early Viking settlements, though she certainly couldn't prove it. And just how long were they coming here before we even guessed they were here?

"Well, it all sounds possible to me. But what about the fertility issue?" I asked.

"Well, now, the folklore is that they came here and landed on a shore-line here on the island, and the powers she had and the powers of this place started this whole new conception of life. Mam said something about the spirits needing a place to cross over. She said something else about the work of the fairies that would allow this to be released to the world and these kinds of miracles could then take place.

"Are you sure you want to keep going?" she asked.

"Let me think about that for a minute. YES!"

"So this doesn't sound like a quick field trip to me anymore. Do you have this all figured out or are you just getting started?"

"Gosh, no, I don't know what we're going to find. We may have to make a few trips if you have time and are interested."

"Let's just see where it goes today," I said.

"Like I said before, I may not get anything from this at all and we may be going nowhere. But it's an adventure and you said you didn't have anything else to do today, right?"

"Oh, yeah, for sure, it's been fun so far."

"This is an old story that my grandmother told me. She said she heard it from her grandmother, so that goes back at least 200 years, around the time people were coming here in ship after ship and the countryside was full of people."

"It's not like that now," I said.

"No, it's not, but Mam said that most people just passed this off as some crazy old story. I've been thinking about it and then learning that the Norse people were in Newfoundland. Well, they had to have been here as well. I mean think about it, if you sail across the Atlantic Ocean and get to Newfoundland, are you going to stop there or keep going when you can practically see PEI and Cape Breton from there? I mean it just makes sense to keep going. Does it make sense to you?"

"Well, when you put it like that, yes, it makes complete sense," I said.

"Good, because I think all that history stuff is pretty well documented. It's the mystery of Boronia's powers and miracle babies that I want to get a handle on."

"You know if nothing comes out of this, it will be nice to see the country-side. I've never been out this way before—have you?"

I couldn't remember being this far from town before. I had no idea it was so pretty and the size of the lake was what was surprising me most. We'd been driving for a long time and there was a ton of water ahead of us.

We were both taken by the beauty and I lamented that I'd not seen a store since we left. She assured me I'd be OK and reached for my hand.

Between the bright blue shimmering lake and her glistening lips that looked like roses you'd want to lick and taste, I could hardly keep my eyes on the road.

Every now and then a house or old farm appeared and another stunning view came into sight along with it. I was starting to realize why so many people lived here because it was beautiful if nothing else.

She was talking for a while, but for some reason, I wasn't hearing her. She was looking at me and her hands were weaving all around but I was zoned out completely, and then I heard her say, "Do you know what I mean?"

It was like hearing someone say: What are you thinking right now? Well, not exactly the same, but close. All I could think of was: "I think so." And out of my mouth came: "Do you believe in fairies, as well?"

"Yes, of course I do. I know they're real, they have to be. Mam said she saw them, but she used to make shine back when they lived in the country so maybe I shouldn't be so sure. I don't think I've ever seen one but sometimes when I shouldn't be seeing anything at all I think I see something move and I think I may have seen one."

"Does this happen very often?" I asked.

"Well, every now and then, so maybe I *have* seen them. Mam used to say they move so fast you have to slow your whole life down to see them. Twice the speed of a hummingbird's wings, she used to say. They would make a hummingbird look old. I'll always remember that."

"That's pretty fast for sure," I said.

"So I guess she moved to the city after her mother died and I don't think she saw many of them there," she said.

"What do you mean, hummingbirds or fairies?"

"Both. Mam's father stayed in the country and I guess he was brewing and drinking as long as he could. I guess he worked hard and played hard right to the end. She said he was one of the last people on the mountain and you couldn't take him out of there. It was where he belonged. Mam always talked about it as if she was still there, and in many ways, she always will be."

"I'm thinking we could be at this for a while. And I know I said that before, but there seems to be a lot of pieces to put together."

"Yes, there's a lot of loose ends," she said.

"So, if this keeps going on, is it like a date—you know, if, in fact, this is a date?"

It was a bit awkward but I think she blushed a bit and I wasn't sure I should have said that but she didn't seem to care.

"Well, today's going very well so far, so let's just take it one mystery at a time and see where we end up."

I was thinking to myself: did you ever have an hour melt right in front of you? It was like playing a game of hockey or ball. You waited all day for the game to start and the next thing you knew it was over. It was like waiting in line for a roller coaster ride and you got on it and it was over.

Well, that was two hours that just fell off the map, like water falling off a mountain. Like it was all dammed up and had been waiting to be set free and now it was flowing like endless time, flying freely through the air and landing safely in the arms of the pooling pieces of itself. That was what the last two hours had been like.

She was talking again but I was just dreaming away, thinking about what I was just thinking about. I was trying to make some sort of sense of it all and then realized I should just stop thinking about it and enjoy it.

"So do you have a place to start when we get there?" I asked.

"Well, I know we're going in the right direction, but we'll have to stop and get some help or at least ask some questions. Mam used to always talk about 'the rear.' There was the rear, the mountain, and the front. But for some reason, she always talked about the rear, or at least that's what I remember.

Anyway, I think it means off the main road, the back, or the other side of the hill. And she was always talking about Iona and these two sisters, I can remember that, as well."

"What kind of name is that anyway?" I asked. "Iona car, Iona donkey."

"Hey, now, it's another piece of the puzzle, as far as I'm concerned and it's another link to Scotland. I know that area was all settled by people from Scotland and I'm pretty sure it's a mostly Catholic community. So I think there's another link to a saint or something like that.

"There used to be a ferry there but now there may be a bridge."

"Seriously, a fairy? This is over the top. We were just talking about this and now I get to see one. I can't believe it's that easy to see one."

"Oh for heaven's sake, it's a boat that will ferry you from one side of the strait to the other. This has been a mainstay of transportation for the people of the islands for centuries and they brought a lot of that here with them. Of course, the government runs it now."

Maggie continued, "I'm sure they are MacNeils, and their names are Margaret and Sadie or Isobel and Sally. They were two sisters that were living out in the rear by themselves. My grandmother spoke of them often and she talked about some sort of miracle that connects them to me. There was some kind of unique mysterious story about special babies being born."

"Special like what?" I asked.

"Well, it goes back to the story I told you earlier about Boronia and the miracle babies. There were a few of them in that area and more stories like that around the island. My great-grandmother—or great- great-grandmother—was supposed to be one of these, as well.

"So am I scaring you off or anything? Are you scared of a little baby? Wah, wah."

"No, I'm not scared, but I am starting to feel a different kind of pressure. I just thought we were going for a drive and looking for some old place. Not planning a family or anything like that."

"Don't worry, I won't make you do anything you don't want to do.

"Do you want to turn around so we can pick up some diapers," she said, devilishly.

"Yes. I mean no. I don't think we'll need diapers today, so, yes, we'll need to go home at some point in time and, no, I want to keep going."

"Yes, no, yes, no, now I'm confused," she said, and smirked the whole time.

"But let's make this perfectly clear: this is now a date. We are on a date," I said confidently. "Oh, and you know how dates are supposed to end?"

"Oh, how's that?"

She looked at me as if there was no correct answer or certainly none that I could find.

"Well, with a kiss, of course."

"A kiss, that's it, is it?" As if to say: you should have asked for more.

"Yeah, at least. I don't know."

Once I said that she popped her seatbelt, leaned over and kissed me on the cheek.

There you go, date's over!

Oh, that smile. Her lips and teeth—they were the most luscious I'd ever seen. It wasn't right. Why did the girls get all of the cards?

"Very cute," I said. "But…"

"But what?" she asked.

She was playing me for sure. Oh, great, the eyes were batting while she was smiling and tossing her hair.

"You are very attractive. Do you know that?"

"Do you think so? You're OK, I guess. You can drive me around for a little while longer. I'm just kidding and thank you. You're very handsome yourself and I'm not trying to scare you off."

"You're not at all. In fact, it's the opposite. I'm enjoying myself quite a bit."

She was smiling again and said, "I had a great time on our date, by the way."

Oh, she was a piece of work.

"If you feel like it, well, you know, you have my number."

I could see where I was going to have to sharpen my game.

"You are very quick," I said.

"I can be. Most men don't like smart women, at least that's been my experience. Oh, and what about you?"

"Oh, no, I'm not one of those guys. The smarter, the better, especially when they're as good-looking as you are. It's a perfect storm.

"So how come you don't have a boyfriend?"

Shit, why did I say that?

"How come you don't have a girlfriend?" she responded.

"Well, I've been saving myself for the right girl," I said, smiling back at her.

"Really? Maybe you *are* different."

"No, I'm sorry, I shouldn't have brought it up. It's just that your friend talked about your old boyfriend last night, and I just sort of spit it out. You don't have to talk about it if you don't want to."

"I don't want to talk about it, but I will give you the *Reader's Digest* version. We were together for a year-and-a-half and broke up about two months ago. So you know it's been different but I feel a lot better about myself. I like having someone to hang out with but he was very controlling and it was getting worse, so this is better. I'm happier, I know that, and I don't miss him, if that's what you're thinking."

"No, no, I wasn't thinking anything and it's not really my business. I just thought you might want to talk about it. Your friend Zoe brought it up last night. That's her name, isn't it?"

"Yeah, that's her name, but I'm not sure she's my friend, if you know what I mean. She was probably trying to confuse the issue even more if she was talking to you about him. You see, I met her through him, and he was telling her that he wanted to get back together again. But I'm not the least bit interested in having anything to do with him. He's a bit messed up and he's got her telling me we're a perfect match."

"So you broke up with him?" I asked.

"Yes, is that important to you?"

"No, I just thought I'd ask, but maybe that's enough of that."

"We can talk about it some other time," she said.

"Maybe on another date," I said.

"Sure, but I think we can find something better to talk about."

"I agree, and—again—I'm sorry."

"No worries, it had to come up sooner or later and, besides, now I get to pry into your past and see what's hiding underneath."

"Hey, what's that ahead? It looks like the end of the road and a dock so I can avoid that conversation for a little while longer," I said.

"Well, that was convenient," she said with a smile.

Keltic Drive

Paul K. MacNeil

Jig

CHAPTER 2
Ferrymen's Hall

66 **I** don't see a boat or a ferry," she said.

"No, me, neither, but there's a train bridge, and is that another bridge behind it? You know I veered off the main road back there a little piece and perhaps I should have stayed on it, but I got a little nervous with the conversation."

"Oh, did you now?" she said. "What is that over there? The Wheelhouse Café, Grand Narrows, the name sure does suit the place."

"Do you want a coffee or drink or something?" I asked.

"Well, I could use the bathroom, that's for sure. Let's go in and ask for directions, if nothing else."

I parked the car and we walked toward the café as I gazed around. It was quite beautiful, with mountains and hills on both sides of this wide stretch of water that looked to be flowing more like a river than a lake. It had to be part of the lake we'd been driving beside all morning and felt like two different worlds connected by the bridges. There were newer homes nestled along the hillside and some older ones that were in decline. There was no activity around the area but I pictured it as a booming little place in its day.

When we stepped inside we met a short lady who was standing behind the counter. She had a round, smiling face surrounded by black and grey hair.

"Hello, hello, how are you today?" she asked.

"Just great," I replied.

"What can I get for you?"

"We're not sure yet," I responded.

"That's OK. Take your time."

"I don't think I want a big lunch but I wouldn't mind a little snack. What do you think, Maggie?"

"There are lots of choices, but I don't need much either. Maybe whatever kind of bread it is I'm smelling."

"Those biscuits look awfully good. Do you make those here?" I asked.

"Usually, yes. But sometimes my co-worker up the road will make them at home and drop them down. I just made these and I think you'll love them, especially with our beautiful local jam."

"Well, if that's what I'm smelling, that's what I'm buying," I said.

"Me, too," Maggie said.

"So, would you like a drink, as well?"

"Coffee," we responded at the same time and grinned at each other.

"So, two coffees and two biscuits with jam. It'll just take a couple of minutes, so have a seat anywhere at all and I'll bring it over when it's ready."

"I'll pop into the washroom," Maggie said.

"Fine, I'll be OK, I won't leave you here."

She turned her head toward me and smiled that look.

That was my chance so I pulled out my phone, found her number, and texted her:

> *I really enjoyed our first date.*
> *Would you like a second one this p.m.?*

The café was a newer building with many pictures of ferry boats and scenery shots, I assumed from this area. There was another room connected to the café called the Ferrymen's Hall that had more seating and a stage. A few more minutes passed and I asked the lady for the Wi-Fi password.

"Yes, it's right there on the board, BARRA123."

I heard a door open and my phone chirped. I looked at Maggie and checked my phone.

Yes...Sounds like fun!

"Where's my food?" she scowled with a jesting smile as she sat down at the table.

"Coming right up, honey. And did that feel better?" I asked.

"Sure did."

I saw the lady heading toward our table with our order.

"So, these are nice and hot, or I can bring you cold ones, if you prefer."

"No, no, that's fine," I said.

"I brought you some butter and rosehip jam. Let me know if you need anything else. Enjoy."

The biscuit looked like the top of an ice cream cone, the soft kind that just keeps rising and rising. It was golden brown—oh my, it looked like it shouldn't be eaten, but I started eating it anyway. First with no butter, then with butter, then with butter and jam. Every bite was incredible. It was simply delicious, coupled with the fact that I was a little hungry and having a great day.

Maggie looked equally content and impressed with the choice and said, "This biscuit is the best I've ever had."

"Well, you haven't had mine yet," I said.

"Oh, so you bake as well, do you?" she asked.

"Well, I don't like to brag, but, yeah, I know my way around the kitchen. How about you?"

"It's not one of my better skills, but I've managed to keep myself alive."

"Maybe this lady will know these sisters you're looking for. You should ask her before we finish up—and do you want anything else, by the way?"

"No, I'm good for now and that's a good idea. Excuse me," Maggie said.

"Yes, dear, would you like something else?"

"No, we're good for now, but we could use some information or some help finding someone."

"I don't think anyone around here is lost," she said gently.

"No, I didn't mean that," said Maggie. "Would you know of a couple of older ladies around here?"

"I know quite a few," she said, smiling once again. "No, no, I'm just kidding with you, go on. Do you have any names?"

"Well, I'm pretty sure they're MacNeils."

"Well, there are lots of them around these parts," she said, smiling again.

"I'm pretty sure they're sisters," Maggie said.

"OK, so we're narrowing it down," the lady said.

"I think their names are either Margaret or Isobel or it might be Sally or Sadie. I'm sorry I don't know much more than that. You see, we're on a bit of a wild goose chase."

"Now that doesn't ring a bell with me. There are several Sadies but not many Sallys. There are quite a few Margarets but not so many Isobels. There used to be a lot of Isobels at one time, just like Flora, you know, but those names kind of went out of style. I still like those names, you know. They're nice and old sounding."

"Yes, for sure," said Maggie.

"Do you know where they might live around here?" the lady asked.

"Well, the only other thing I have is maybe out the Rear or Rear Glen," Maggie said. "And maybe something like Columba's Road—is there anything like that around here?"

"Well, yes, there's a couple of places like that. Out the Rear, as they say, or the Rear Road. Anything off the main road is considered outback, or the Rear. Nearer the water is considered the front. The Rear of Christmas Island runs into the Rear Glen Road, or some people call it the Highland Road, or even the Rabbit Road, but that's just an old joke, you know."

"What does that mean, the Rabbit Road?" I asked.

"Oh, years ago, they were building all these roads and they built this particular road but the people said only the rabbits would be on it, so the name stuck," she said with a gurgling laugh.

"That's funny," I said.

"So the Rear Iona Road runs very close to the St. Columba Mountain Road, that could be it. Well then again, it's really off the Barra Glen Road, but they connect through another road. What's the name of that road? Oh, I know, it's the Fraser Road that connects them, I think. Yes, I think that's it, and they may just call that the Columba Road now. Things change, you know, and does any of this sound familiar?" she asked.

"Oh, yes, it's a help, for sure," said Maggie.

"So, there's not many out there in any of these places," the lady said. "What would you be wanting with these ladies if you did find them? I wouldn't want to cause them any trouble, if you know what I mean."

"Oh, no, we're just looking for some information," Maggie said. "I think they may have known my great-grandmother and some other relatives. We're just following up on an old story that my grandmother used to tell."

"Oh, well, that seems reasonable enough. So, your great-granny, eh? Well, these sisters must be quite old if you're in your twenties, so add three generations: forty, sixty, eighty, 100, so subtract that generation."

The mental math bounced around briefly.

"They'd have to be in their eighties or perhaps ninety. Does that sound right?" the lady asked.

"Probably, if you say so, but, yes, I think they're quite old," said Maggie.

A kind of bewildered look came over Maggie's face as if she had just been stumped by a math professor. This lady, cook, waitress, if you will, in fifteen seconds had figured out how old these ladies were from guessing her age and multiplying by four generations and subtracting one. It was rather strange, but seemed to work. Well, I was pretty sure she was right, but how was I to know?

She kept sort of humming or talking, I wasn't sure what she was saying. As I looked at her, the door blew in and a strong, cool breeze came with it, followed by a fine-looking man in his late fifties or early sixties.

"Good morning, Evelyn, how's everything today?" he asked.

"Just fine. How are you, Donald?"

"Just like the horse's back, thanks for asking."

"Donald, perhaps you know who these people are looking for," Evelyn said.

"Who's that now?" he sharply asked.

"They're looking for a couple of older ladies," Evelyn said.

"So am I," he flirted back.

"Donald," she said.

We all smiled.

"How old? But just to let you know I'd like at least one of them to have a lot of money."

"Donald!"

"Well, we think they're sisters in their eighties or so, and they might live out the Rear," Evelyn said.

"Which Rear?" he briskly asked.

"They don't know," Evelyn gently said as she leaned toward us. "Donald's from here and stayed here all his life so he knows just about everyone. I moved here from the city about twenty years ago, so I'm not as connected as he is."

"Did you say demented?" he said.

"I did not and you know it."

He winked and nodded his head toward us, but mostly toward Maggie.

"I was trying to say I don't have as many weeds growing around my roots as Donald does," Evelyn said.

She winked and smirked back, mostly toward me.

There was laughter for everyone.

"Will I get you tea, Donald?" she asked.

"That would be great. Thanks.

"Can I sit with you?" he asked.

"Well, of course," Maggie replied.

"Maybe we can figure out who these ladies are. Do you have any names?"

"Well, we have four to start with and we're pretty sure that two are right," said Maggie.

"Wait now, wait now, let's back it up a bit, back it up. Do *you* have names? For instance, my name is Donald MacRae. Now let's start with the lady."

He gracefully sent his hand across the table toward her.

"And you are?"

"Oh, of course, I'm sorry, I'm Maggie MacKinnon."

"Well, I'm pleased to make your acquaintance."

"And me, as well," she responded with a grin from ear to ear.

"And are you Mr. MacKinnon?" He offered me his hand.

"No, no, I'm Patrick MacLean."

"Oh, I see," he said as he rubbed his hand on his furrowed brow. "So you're not married or anything like that?"

"No, no," I said.

"You're still playing in the minors, are you? You haven't turned pro or anything?"

"I'm sorry, what do you mean?" I asked.

I heard Evelyn from the kitchen.

"Donald, Donald, just try to help them out."

"Oh, yes. So it's Maggie and Patrick. I've always loved that name."

He looked at me and said, "Maggie, of course."

We heard Evelyn bark from the kitchen.

"Donald!"

"I'm just entertaining myself, Evelyn."

"Now, I believe you were about to share a few names of these ladies you're looking for?"

"Well, we have the last name, which is MacNeil," said Maggie.

"Shocking," he said with a little twitch.

"And the options are: Margaret, Isobel, Sally, and Sadie."

"Well, those were the names of my ex-wives," he said with a straight face. "You know it was a real shame when my last one died, and I miss her so very much. She died ironing the clothes, you know got caught right up in the cord and choked. I couldn't even get a day off work to bury her properly."

"Donald, Donald, Donald," Evelyn said as she returned with his tea. "Stop that talk." She looked at us and said, "You can only believe about half of what he says."

"Evie, I'm a little bit hurt."

"I'll hurt you," she said.

"So then, they're in their eighties, they live in the Rear, they're sisters, and they're MacNeils, is that pretty much it?"

My God, the tea smelled amazing, I thought.

"Anything to eat, Donald?" Evelyn asked.

"No thanks, Evie. Just the tea for now, I have to watch my hips, you know," he said, winking toward Maggie again.

She winked back at him and said, "I don't know what you are talking about."

He smiled back and winked again.

"So how'd you do that?" Maggie asked.

"Do what?" he said.

"Not you," said Maggie. "Well, yes, you, as well, but before you came in, Evelyn figured out how old these ladies were and you just kind of figured it out, as well."

Donald looked seriously toward Maggie and said, "How old are you, around twenty-five?"

"That's about right."

"Same age as me." He winked again and nodded his tilted head.

"Donald, leave this couple alone," Evie said.

Geez, it was a good thing she was here. I tapped Maggie's foot under the table and mouthed the word "couple," and winked.

Donald spoke up again and said, "I'm not aging as well as you are, am I?"

"Well, I'm starting to think that Evelyn knows you pretty well. But you don't look a day over thirty to me," Maggie gently said, shaking her head and raising her eyebrows.

"I like her, Evie, I tell you, I like her. She reminds me of my second wife," he said, as he shook a little bit and chuckled.

"Now what's this math thing you're talking about?" Evelyn asked.

"Well, you guessed my age and then you knew these ladies were eighty or ninety years old," Maggie said.

"Oh well, if you're twenty-five and you had a child there would be twenty-five years to every generation, so you said your great-grandmother, correct?"

"Correct."

"Well, then that means three more generations would be about 100 years," Evelyn said.

"Yes, correct again."

"Well, now, especially in the old days, girls had families by the time they were twenty. In fact, if you didn't, you'd be labelled a spinster or there was something wrong with you. For that you can take off five or ten years per generation, so an estimate would put these ladies at around eighty or ninety years of age. It's just rough math, but it works in most cases."

"Close enough for the girl I go with, well, at least that girl I used to go with before my first wife. Do you remember her, Evelyn?" Donald asked.

"No, I don't, I'm not that old," she said, kind of sternly.

Donald grunted and asked, "So, did you say they lived together or not?"

"Well, I don't really know. Mam said they used to live together, but that was quite a few years ago now."

"Mam, you say. I called my grandmother that. It seems you and I have a lot in common, don't you know?" he said.

"Well, no, I don't," she said.

He looked at me and gave me one of those slow, heavy winks and shook his head.

"OK, I'll take sisters for $200. Just joking, do you watch that show? There are some smart people out there, I tell you. I'll take living together in the Glen for another $200 and MacNeil sisters between eighty and ninety for $600. That's $1,000, folks."

I was starting to think he just liked the sound of his voice—mind you, it was pretty funny if you were into *Jeopardy*.

"I'm sorry, I got a bit carried away, but is that pretty much it?"

"Yes," said Maggie.

"OK, you said Margaret or Isobel. And what were the other two names?"

"Sally and Sadie."

"Well, I can think of Margaret MacNeil from out the Glen Road, but she lived with her brother Johnny, so I don't think that's her. I can't think of an Isobel with a sister. There's an Isobel and Jimmy up the Point Road here, so that can't be them.

"Oh, now, there's Sadie and Mungie out in Rear Iona. I'll bet that's them!"

He clicked his thumb and pointed his finger toward the table.

"They're sisters around that age and for sure Sadie is there, and, well, Mungie, I'm pretty sure that's not her real name. It could easily be Margaret.

"Years ago it was a very popular name so that's probably some sort of a nickname. I think it is Margaret and they're pretty much the last of the Rory Gs. That was their father's family name and I think their mother was a MacKinnon, just like yourself," he said pointing at Maggie.

"We could be related," Maggie said.

"I think she was a MacKinnon from Barra Glen," he said, nodding his head.

"She was one of the Johnakinns."

"The what?"

"The Johnakinns. You see, it's just an abbreviation or a nickname for John MacKinnons.

"Oh my, they were great singers and they must have had a thousand songs and sweet, sweet, Gaelic. Oh, that's another tale. Perhaps if we had more time."

He winked again like a docile lamb and Maggie smiled. I couldn't believe what was happening right in front of me as he glanced toward me and shook his head. Maggie found that very amusing.

"Mungie and Sadie, you say. Do you think they would mind some strangers showing up at their doorstep?" she asked.

"In these parts, strangers are only friends you haven't met yet. I bet they'd love to have your company for a little while.

"You know, or maybe you don't, but when you get as old as they are you appreciate people a lot more than when you're young. They don't have a lot of close family around here anymore so they enjoy any company they get."

"That's kind of sad," said Maggie.

"It's not so bad, you know. Their sister and her husband are nearby and some of their nieces drop by. They have neighbours and friends that keep a close eye on them and they can still get out to church, of course. I suppose you go regularly, do you?"

"Ah, well, no, not really, not as much as I should," said Maggie.

"Well, you better try to bluff your way through that if you're looking for information from those ladies. You know for them it's one of the most important parts of their lives and they'd go to church every day of the week if they could get there."

"Well, why don't they move?" I asked.

Heads turned, eyeballs blew open.

"What? They've lived…oh never mind. They may someday, but I doubt it. They'll be going from the Rear to the church, to the grave, to eternal salvation, in that order.

"*Ach co-dhiù*, just go and see them. I'm sure you'll want to go back before you leave. Oh, just remember this, they've found their way and you're still looking for yours."

"Well, that's very good advice for anyone. How do we get there?" Maggie asked.

"It's not far from here. Do you think you can find your way or would you like me to guide you along?"

"Oh, I think we'll be OK if you could tell us how to get there," I said.

"OK, so you go across the bridge and take a right, you should see the church. It's the big brick building with the steeple on the right. I think the doors are open, so stopping in wouldn't hurt."

I didn't know if he was serious or not.

"It's about a mile from there, which would be 1.6 kilometres, if you've been raised on that food. You'll see a dirt road to the left and there is water everywhere at this point so you can go straight across a little sandbar to Washabuck or turn left there to go to Iona Rear."

"So, right off the bridge and left one mile later. Got it so far."

"That's it. For God's sake, don't go right or you'll land in the lake," he said, with a laugh.

"Now from there it's less than a mile or pretty close to it, let's just say one kilometre from the turnoff and it's the next road on the left. Now, they're the first house on the left—well, they're the *only* house on the left. Oh no, you have the Rory Paul's after that and then there's Dodie's, or R J's, but look for the first place on the left."

"So right, left, left, left, how far on that road?" I asked.

"About half a mile and, yes, you got it once you cross the bridge. You'll be in the woods, you know, so it's hard to get your bearings when you're surrounded by trees. It's a different story when you can see some water.

"This is all kind of funny, you know, they used to call Dodie's mother Mam. She was a dear, sweet woman and tough as nails. She walked that road more than most people drove it."

"Well, I think I have it. But we should write it down, just in case." I looked toward Maggie.

"Let me ask you this: do you think you could point to the northerly direction if I asked you?"

Both Maggie and I threw our hands in different directions.

"Never mind, just stop and ask for help if you need it. There are a lot of good people around here that will help you out, so don't be afraid to ask. In fact, take the number of the shop here and call it if you find yourself lost or anything like that, but turning left at the pavement should bring you back here. Just don't end up in the mountains, it can be bad news up there."

"So can we just drop by, would you say, and what's in the mountains that would be of concern?" Maggie asked.

"Oh they're not really mountains. It's just the end of the Highlands and sort of where the two worlds meet, the old-timers used to say. They're mostly just old stories, but you should stay clear."

"What's out there?" I asked.

"Oh, never mind all that. Those two ladies have their version of what that's all about so you can ask them. And, yes, I think you can drop by anytime. If it was later in the day I'd say give them a ring first. They're likely going to church tonight but you have lots of time before then."

"Well, thanks a lot, but I think we should carry on with our journey," I said. "You've been very helpful."

"Of course, no problem. Come back again. Here's the number to the café, just in case," Evelyn said.

We paid our bill and when we opened the door we were pretty near pulled out of the café. The wind and the lake were creating quite a little roar, as if to say *you stayed long enough, it's time to move on.* We saw a different side of her as the waves pitched her beauty to the shoreline.

It not only grabbed my attention, it demanded I take notice of her. It wasn't at all that I hadn't before, but now I was feeling totally impressed by it and Maggie said, "I feel so good here, as if I am from here or something. You know, we never talked about it that much when I was growing up, so maybe I am, and just don't know it."

"Gee, I hope we're not related."

"Very funny, but it's like I've been running from something, but not here. I'm not running at all."

"They say that everybody's running from something and when you get older you have more miles behind you and more things you wish you hadn't done."

"Well, that's not much to look forward to," she said.

"I didn't mean it like that. It's just that my mother was always regretting something in her life. I don't know if it had to do with moving or something she did as a kid, but she was never comfortable with herself. I'm just saying, everybody has a little baggage.

"I'm sure your life will be different and you'll of course have a fine man to go through life with."

"Well, sure, I get that, but I like to think the best is yet to come and I'm throwing the junk behind me."

"I like the sound of that better," I said.

As we walked toward the car, the sun slipped behind a dark cloud and, with a gust of wind, it was a lot colder than when we arrived.

"That food sure hit the spot and the information was great," she said.

"For sure, and the company, how about that?"

"Well, they seem like very nice people, especially Donald, that's for sure. He was a lot of…oh, you meant you. You're OK, I guess, you can drive me around for a while longer," she said, winking with a sly smile.

I sighed.

"Seriously, I'm having a great time and I'm very grateful to you for taking me here on this adventure. You know I've been wanting to do this for a long time and it just feels right to be here with you."

"I guess the time was right. How about a picture before we leave?" I asked.

We joked about asking someone to take it but there was no one there but us. We took a number of selfies and I took several of Maggie and her beauty seemed to quiet the lake and tame the scenery. Now, that was saying something. I couldn't believe I was there with her and now we were in a picture together.

I flashed back to when I was fourteen, holding hands with this girl I thought I was in love with. She was two years older than me and, now that I thought about it, she was just being kind. I don't think she knew I was over the top for her and how it made me feel.

This, this was way different. This could be, oh, shake your head, it was barely a date. But alas, I was wrong. We were on our second date and maybe even dating. I was way ahead of where I thought I'd be. Let there be no panic!

"Are you all right?" she asked.

"Yes, yes, never better."

"OK, are you ready to go?"

"Yes, I am." And we pulled away slowly, not wanting to let that moment go.

"What's waiting for us ahead?"

She pointed and said, "Our future awaits." And we headed for the Barra Strait.

The Girls of Rear Iona

Waltz

Paul K MacNeil

CHAPTER 3
The Barra Strait

As we headed down the hill toward the bridge, I asked Patrick to slow down so I could savour the moment. My mind was racing as I hadn't felt this close to Mam in forever. I thought of her crossing to the other side of this strait in some sort of boat that couldn't have been anything near as safe as we were.

I wondered what it was like before the bridges were here, before the cars, and way back before the trains. I wondered how safe it had been to travel across and if people had died there. I wondered if life was better before either bridge was here or if it was better with a boat running back and forth, which would of course slow everything down. Then again, what could be slower than the train? Walking, I guess. The whole time I couldn't believe it was so simple to cross this thing of beauty.

The highway bridge looked like a child compared to the old railway bridge that ran beside it. That one must've been built around 100 years before and certainly needed some love. I felt like I was on a ship as we crossed the half-mile span, being transported from one world into my great mystery, which was whatever was on the other side.

I didn't say anything but a million thoughts and images poured over my mind. It was overwhelming to think I was where I was and so close to meeting my connection to Mam. I hoped these two sisters were the ones and had feelings that could never be taken away from me.

Patrick slowed to a crawl about halfway across as we treasured the last few moments and turned toward the church. It was quite a structure, with its rustic brick and towering steeple. It was similar to what you'd see in old European buildings that leaked history, culture, and tradition. It looked old and was probably built around the same time as the railway bridge.

Patrick asked me if I wanted to stop in and, as much as I wanted to meet Mungie and Sadie, I felt it was a wise diversion. We pulled up to the front doors, got out, and Patrick said, "Do you think it's open?"

"Well, Donnie said it should be." I smiled.

"Donnie, really?"

I looked around and saw the two bridges running side by side with a large L-shaped wharf to their left. We had passed a service station and store and in the distance I saw a post office and a school. There was an old-looking grave-yard right beside the church where hundreds of gravestones stood, protecting the reposed souls. The hillside was scattered with well-kept homes, yards, and trees.

I pulled on the door. It eased toward me and I questioned why I was there. I was trembling as I thought about Mam and walked through the door, the foyer, and a second set of swinging wooden doors. The ceilings were as high as the hills that surrounded us and the windows were tall, new, and the… what the heck was that? It just didn't fit in the place.

There was some odd-looking painting of God, I guess, on the wall behind the altar and I was sure I could've painted something that respected the place a lot more. It must have been someone's idea of bringing modern art to the folks in the country, but it didn't belong in this building. The place was empty and felt very large but there was something about it that made me feel the opposite.

I felt great comfort in the quietness of the place as I walked around freely and looked at the large paintings on the walls. I made my way to the front of the church and looked back to see Patrick walking timidly and analyzing the paintings, so I said, "What a place. Are you coming, or are you one of those guys that sit in the back?"

"I'm coming, I was just enjoying it at a little slower pace."

When Patrick reached me he had a nervous look about him and I asked if he was all right. He said he was, he'd forgotten about the stations of the cross and all the time he spent with his parents, especially during Lent. He was quite impressed with the paintings and he shared some of his childhood memories with me.

We moved down the other side, returned to the back of the church and headed up the twisted stairs. I hadn't noticed the tartan drapes that hung from the large cedar pillars until I looked out over the main floor. There was a very different feel and look about the place from there and I said, "What a place for a wedding, don't you agree?"

"Well, yes, it would be, but, heck, I don't even know your middle name."

"Maybe I don't have one, but just picture this place full of family and friends, everyone nervous and not sure if the bride will show up. Just think of that."

"On that note, maybe we should go," he said.

"Yeah, maybe we should before you get scared."

We walked across the loft and down the other staircase, and he said he wanted to say a little prayer for his parents so I joined him.

He pulled the kneeler down from its sleeping position and blessed himself as he knelt. I sat back and said the prayers I remembered from childhood in my mind. We only went to church at Christmas and Easter and if I needed to get a sacrament, but we always did the beads. Mam loved to say the rosary and would usually pray them a few times a day. I liked doing them with her and thought of the old set of beads hanging by my bed that she'd given me before she died.

I could see her as plain as day and wondered where she sat, where Fiona sat, and if I was in their seat. It was a little bit spooky so I closed my eyes and held onto her memory.

Patrick sat back and I asked him if he wanted to sit in the silence for a few minutes. He looked content and smiled when I reached for his hand and held it. I was very much at peace sitting there with him and wondered what he was thinking about.

I sensed he had a deeper history of religion than I did from his quietness and respect for the place. I'd find out more about that at a later time, perhaps on another date. We sat there for quite a while and, jeez, I might have fallen asleep.

He was still holding my hand, and was he asleep, as well? I didn't move and closed my eyes and started to think about my mother. Why was I thinking of my mother when I was sitting here with him? For some strange reason I felt as though she was near me and I started to smile.

I opened my eyes when Patrick squeezed my hand and said, "Are you ready to move along there, happiness?"

"I am, did you have a nice sleep?" I asked.

"Oh, I wasn't sleeping, I was just resting my eyes and doing a lot of thinking. I could see you were wrapped up in something heavy, so I tried not to bother you."

"You *were* sleeping. In fact, I may have drifted off myself."

"Oh, really, you needed a little nap, did you? My parents used to nap all the time—well, mostly in the middle of the day. How about yours?"

I felt bad that I hadn't told him and knew it would come up sooner or later, like so many times before, and I said, "Well, here's the thing, I didn't really know my parents. My grandmother raised me and she pretty much slept whenever she wanted to. I'd hear her up in the middle of the night, baking or starting breakfast, or working on whatever she had on the go. She always had a project and was never sitting idle for very long unless she needed a nap."

It was a bit awkward as we got up to leave and I didn't know if I should say something else. I didn't want him to feel bad and when we were back outside, he said, "Look, I'm sorry about your parents. I didn't know. Do you want to talk about it?"

"No, no, it's no big deal," I said and opened the door to the car. "How would you know? We're just getting to know each other and there's nothing that can be done about it anyway. I feel bad for not telling you, but let's just leave it alone and if we need to, we'll talk about it."

Patrick got behind the wheel and we headed out the loop around the parking lot toward the Rear.

Helen's Hymn

March

Paul K. MacNeil

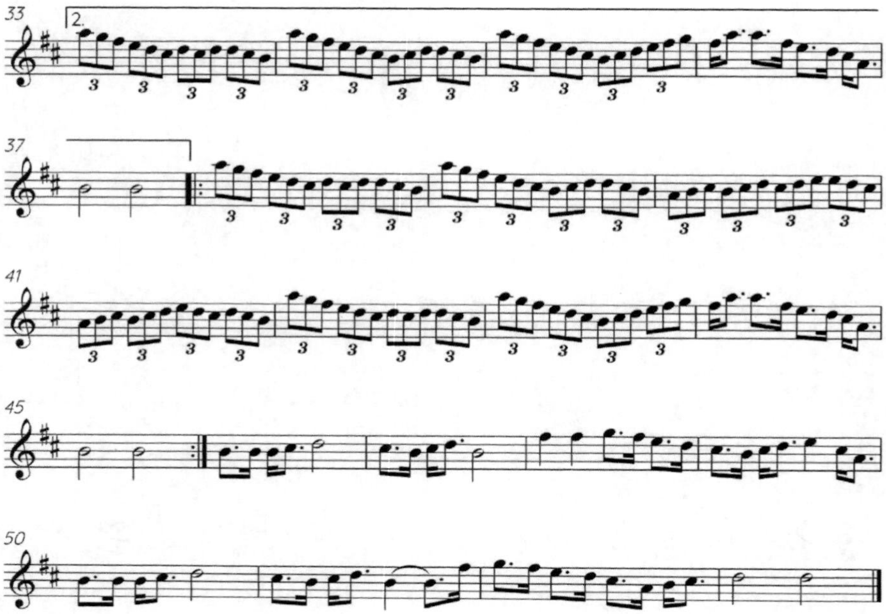
33
2.
37
41
45
50

CHAPTER 4
Rear Iona

I was glad to be driving again and confirmed with Maggie that we go a mile, take a left, and another mile, and a left, and then the first house on the left.

"Yes, that's it, I wrote it down. Right, left, left, left," she said.

The road was very twisty as it followed the body of a large pond that buffered the big lake from the road and shoreline, separated only by a sandbar. There were many escarpments, plastered cliffs, and a small island in the middle of the pond while the big lake was always in sight.

The sun, which was back out again, had set the lake on fire and turned it into an entity we hadn't seen in a while. When we came to our turn, I understood exactly what Donald meant. If we turned right, we'd be in the lake, for sure.

We turned toward the Rear and I thought about telling Maggie my thoughts from church—how my mother pretended to sleep while the boring preacher preached—but decided against it. I'd pulled one foot out of my mouth and if I replaced it with the other, I still needed one to drive.

There was a noticeable difference when we turned onto the dirt road as it narrowed and there were trees everywhere. It was a lot darker, except for a few openings that looked like old farms or homesteads. We were back into the trees again and, not long after, there was another road marked "Rear Iona."

This road got smaller again and it was a bit washed out in places. Quite passable, but narrow, and rough, and then, as we came around a fairly sharp turn we met a little wine-coloured car in the middle of the road. Well, we were both in the middle of the road, as we slipped past each other I saw an older-looking couple waving at us.

"It shouldn't be too far," she said. "I don't think I've ever been in a place like this before."

"Nor I. That must be their driveway there."

It was narrower still as we drove up the little hill. The trees were very close to the car and when we reached the crest, an old farmhouse stood comfortably in front of us with a light smoke twisting freely from the chimney. Looking across a little hollow, I saw an old hay rake and a barn that needed… well, it needed everything.

The barn had seen better days but the house looked lovely. There was no car in the yard as we pulled right up to the front door.

"Maybe they're not home," I said.

"No, I think I saw the curtain move and I just saw a lady's head. There's someone in there, I'm sure."

"I feel a little weird going into a complete stranger's home, don't you?" I asked.

"Not really. You can wait in the car if you want, but I'm going in. I've been looking forward to this for so long, I can't even remember. Besides, you didn't know Donald or Evelyn until thirty minutes ago, and they were nice people."

"You liked Donald, didn't you?" I asked as I smiled at her.

"Evelyn liked you, didn't she?" she replied.

She had me again.

"OK, I'm just saying."

We opened the doors and she was smirking again.

"What now?" I asked.

"You let me do the talking and everything will be OK. If I tell you to go wait in the car, you just go, OK?"

"Ha, ha, very funny."

As we walked to the door, I saw a very large pile of wood and the smell of it burning filled the air. The smell was like the one in stores at Christmastime, only softer and more natural, which seemed tailored for the place. As we reached the step I saw the inner door open and Maggie said *hello* as if she'd known this lady all her life.

The lady responded the same. She was tall and wrinkled looking with very bony features, grey hair, and a big white smile. She must have been a very powerful woman in her day; in fact, she was still very strong looking. She may have split that pile of wood herself, but you could tell the years were starting to show.

"I'm Maggie and this is Patrick and we're looking for Margaret and Sadie. Are we at the right house?"

"Oh, yes, you've found us, what did we do?" she asked in a high-pitched, crackling voice.

She must have had fifty teeth. I'd never seen the like.

"Oh, nothing, nothing at all," Maggie said. "We were hoping to talk to you and ask you a few questions, if you have some time."

"Oh, yes, I think I have some time left."

She pushed open the outer door and said, "You should come in, it's cold out there. You know, the wind picked up quite a bit since this morning."

We entered the house and she asked for our coats. She shook a little as she hung them off to the side and I heard a woman's voice calling from another room.

"Who is it, Mungie?"

"Come on in and never mind your shoes. The floor is cold in this old house. Come on into the kitchen, it's warmer in there. You're not with the government, are you?" She turned to block another doorway. "You know things haven't been the same since the Liberals got in."

"No, no, we're not with the government," Maggie said.

"Oh, well, keep on in then."

"Who is it, Mungie?" we heard again.

"I'm sorry, your names are Maggie and what was your name?"

"My name is Patrick," I replied.

We walked through a small dining room as we made our way toward the kitchen. I heard a groovy combination of bagpipes, guitar, and piano coming softly from a small blaster on the counter.

"Well then, Maggie and Patrick, this is my sister, Sadie."

Sadie was quite a bit smaller and meeker looking than Mungie and shared a lot of the same features, although she wasn't nearly as strong looking.

"Nice to meet you," we said.

"Yes, well, have a seat here by the stove. It will warm you up," Sadie said.

The kitchen reminded me of my parents' house with its old cupboards, shelves, and large porcelain sink. A picture of Christ hung above the table by the window and a wood stove that was cranking out the heat. A lovely old pendulum clock ticked its rhythmic time in the corner—somewhat hypno-tizing—and the sweet smell of baking and burning wood topped it all off.

"So, where is it you're coming from?" Mungie asked.

"Well, we were just in at the church," Maggie replied quickly and smartly. "But before that, we drove from the city."

"And are you from there?" Mungie asked.

"No, not really, we both just sort of settled there for school and work."

"Oh, I see, and so what brings you here?"

"Well, it's my great-grandmother and grandmother that came from around here and we were hoping you'd be able to help us find out who I am, I guess."

"Who was she?" Mungie asked.

"Well, I didn't know her, but her name was Mary MacNeil," Maggie said. "Mary Flora or Mary Fiona, I believe. By any chance, would you remember that name?"

"Well, I can't think of it offhand. Do you think she was she from out here in the Rear? Because we'd know her if she was from out here."

"Well, I'm not really sure. I don't really know much about her. It was my grandmother that told me about her. She called her Fiona from Iona, so it must have been from around this area somewhere."

"Fiona, eh? That's not a very common name around here, not like Mary. There are probably 100 Marys from around here that we knew ourselves. You know, we always think of that song 'The Four Marys' when we hear that name."

"Oh, John Allen did a great job of that," Sadie said.

"Do you know that song?"

"No, sorry, I don't, I don't think I do," Maggie said.

Who was that? It wasn't a name I knew and questioned if I should. I almost asked, but decided to let Maggie do the talking.

"So, you think this was your great-grandmother, is this right?" Mungie asked.

"Yes, that's correct."

"So then what was your grandmother's name?" Mungie asked.

"Oh, I called her Mam, but her real name was Nora MacKinnon. She married a Campbell and moved away for a number of years before coming home. I think her full name was Nora Liza MacKinnon before she married."

"I wonder if it was Liza *Mhór*. Did she go by Liza?" Mungie asked in a determined manner.

"Yes, I'm pretty sure she did," said Maggie.

"Who is it, Mungie?" asked Sadie.

"Well, I'm not sure, but I think she would be one of the *Peadair Custies*, or she could have been one of the Big Neil's. I can remember a couple of Lizas from that area."

"Oh, from out in Highland Hill," said Sadie.

"Well yes, or the rear of MacKinnon's Harbour and St. Columba Mountain area," Mungie said.

"They had a name for it, now. Some people called it the *Cùil* or the *Cù*, but it wasn't really the *Cùil*, and then others called it the *Cheeag* on the Camp Road or something like that. I think myself the people there considered it Highland Hill.

"Of course, they called the area near the main road 'the interval,' but up on the mountain, there was quite a settlement. You know, you're going back 200 years, and there's no one there now, you know. I don't know if the road is there now."

"Now if it's Liza *Mhór*, she lived in St Columba for a few years, as well."

"What's a Peddddaa Custeries?" Maggie asked.

"Oh that's the family name, it's Gaelic and it means Peter Christy in English."

"I don't suppose you have any Gaelic, do you, dear?"

"No, no, sorry, I don't," Maggie said.

"And you?" she asked, looking at me.

"No, I'm sorry, I don't either."

"Well, that's too bad. I guess your education is not yet complete," Mungie said, smiling.

"And you said Liza Vor, what's that?" Maggie asked.

"*Mór* or *Mhór* is Gaelic for big, so that would make her Liza Big, but in Gaelic, it's Big Liza. Do you remember her, was she a tall woman?" Mungie asked.

"Yes, yes, she was. I was pretty young and everyone was tall. But, yes, I remember her to be very tall and strong."

"Well, it might just be her. I can remember seeing her, when I was young, you know, she was older than me, but I remember how tall she was and a very pretty woman. I can see a resemblance to you, dear. It sounds like she has passed on, is that correct?"

"Yes, yes, it is. She died about ten or twelve years ago."

"Oh, I'm so sorry, dear."

"May the Lord have mercy on her soul," Sadie said.

"Oh, thank you both. She was in her eighties when she passed and she had been very healthy right till the end. I guess I was around thirteen when she died, so I was lucky to have had her as long as I did."

"She was very kind and full of fun, you know. She used to play ball with us when I was younger. She could hit the ball like anyone else and was always joking around with us. I wish I'd been older so I could've known her better."

"Oh, don't be wishing for the years to pass, you'll be old like us before you know it," Mungie said. "There's a reason we only get to spend so much time together in this world, you know."

"Well, I'm not sure I do. Why do you think that is?" Maggie asked.

"Oh, I believe we are here to see the world through our own eyes and experience it through our mind with the ones we love. I can't see it for myself if I'm always with someone and need to listen to what they see and think.

"Now, if you believe in life after death you will spend eternity with our Lord and Redeemer and the people we love. That's what I think. What do you think?"

"Well, I haven't really thought about it, but that's part of why we're here," Maggie said.

"Really, now, do you have some sort of message to share with me from the Lord?"

"No, no, nothing like that," Maggie said.

"Oh, well, that's a relief. Now at my age, you start to get a little curious about the whole thing."

She continued, "You know I heard this little story the other day. This man had a friend in the hospital, you see, so he went to see him, to see how he was feeling and make a visit and they both happened to be fiddle players, as well.

"So the two were having this nice visit and I guess the man in the hospital was not very upbeat about his condition, perhaps a bit depressed. So the healthy man said, 'You know, I had this dream last night.'

"'Oh, what was that?' the sick man said.

"'Well, I have good news and bad news.'

"'How's that now?' the sick man said.

"'I dreamt that I died and went on to heaven and when I got there it was the most glorious place I'd ever seen.'

"'Really, in what way?' the sick man asked.

"'Well, the sun was shining and there was this beautiful lake with a warm breeze. I could hear sweet, sweet music playing from this lovely-looking hall. So I walked toward it and there were flowers in bloom, birds singing, and beautiful voices that sounded like a symphony in the background.'

"'Oh, shut up,' the sick man said.

"'No, no, I heard children laughing and playing and dancers' shoes striking the floor. You know that cracking sound, like a team of horses in perfect time.'

"'Yes, yes, go on,' the sick man said.

"'Well, I opened the door and Winston was playing, Dan R. was there, and Estwood was on the guitar. Marie was on the piano, and, oh, they were clicking the knitting needles on the side like the old days and, oh my God, did it ever sound good.'

"'Yes, yes,' he said. 'Go on.'

"'You see now, all the great players and friends were there and the best of the best of the dancers were there, as well, so I was just amazed. Nobody spoke but everyone was nodding their heads and smiling at me and just having a great time.'

"'Could you get a drink there?' the sick man asked.

"'Not that I could see.'

"'Well, that's too bad,' he said.

"'Anyway, I walked around the place to see who was there and as I made my way around I saw the list.'

"'What list?' he asked.

"'Well, the list as to who was playing next.'

"'Yeah, yeah,' he said. 'It sounds great, go on.'

"'So here's the bad news.'

"'What's that?' the sick man asked.

"'You're playing Thursday night…'"

Everyone laughed and then the laughter was interrupted by a ding from a timer for the oven.

"Oh, my," Sadie said. "I forgot all about them. Mungie, will you make the tea?"

"You'll have a cup of tea, won't you?" Sadie asked.

"Oh, we just had some," Maggie said.

"So did we."

"Don't go to any trouble," Maggie said.

"Oh, it's no trouble."

She opened the door to what looked like a pantry of sorts and a very old, fat dog waddled slowly toward us.

"Don't you be a bother now, Betsey," she said as she tumbled toward us and wagged her tail.

It was like a SWAT team in action as Mungie headed to the woodstove with a teapot in hand. She swished some water into the teapot from the steaming kettle on the stove and then dumped it down the sink. She did it all again and in went a handful of tea bags and what looked like a gallon of water. The whole time she was laughing and prodding the dog and Sadie.

Sadie went to the oven and pulled out a tray of what looked like dark cake muffins or something I don't think I'd ever seen before. I wasn't that hungry, but the smell alone told me I was having one, at least one.

Then there were plates, teacups, sugar, milk, butter, knives, and short-bread from another old tin and I knew we needed to find a reason to come back. The dog got a cookie and limped toward the other room and, presto, like a magic act, it was all on the table.

"Come have a seat at the table," Sadie said.

It was all so normal and natural for them, like a New York musical. Fluid in motion and rehearsed to perfection. You can't beat live theatre.

"Where do you sit?" Maggie asked politely.

"We sit on the chairs," said Sadie, with a wry smirk.

"Sit anywhere at all, right there and there," Mungie said, snarling a bit toward Sadie.

She poured the tea like a seasoned bartender. Not a drop spilled and the cups were as even as a commercial on TV.

"There's milk and sugar, if you like," Mungie said.

"Milk is fine for me, but I have to ask, what do you call these beautiful cakes?"

They laughed.

"They're not cakes, they're molasses biscuits," Sadie said.

"I've never seen anything like them. Do they taste as good as they smell?"

"Most times, yes," said Sadie.

It looked so good I felt bad cutting it. She split like a boat cutting through water as the steam and fragrance rose toward me. It was just glorious.

I didn't know what to do next but I noticed Maggie watching the whole thing. I wasn't sure if she was following my lead or just waiting for my reaction. It didn't matter to me and I felt as though I could speak freely, so I did.

"Do you put butter on them or just eat them the way they are?" I asked.

Sadie said, "I put butter on everything. It's not as good as the homemade butter from the old days, but I'm after getting used to it."

The hot knife slid through the hard butter like a needle through a cloth and it dissolved on the steaming biscuit. Molasses, eh, we never really had much of it growing up, but it smelled like it was worth the wait. God, it was like cheesecake or pudding in my mouth and with raisins as soft and moist as the grapes they came from.

"Holy Mother," I said aloud. "These are out of this world!"

"Well, I'm glad you like them. You can take some with you when you go," Sadie said.

"Any chance I could have the recipe?" I asked.

"Yes, of course. I can write it out for you."

"Well, I could just take a picture of it if you already have it written out," I said.

"Oh, no, I don't, I'm sorry, it's all up here," she said, pointing to her head.

I was amazed by the whole thing and Maggie was smiling the whole time. Mungie asked if everyone's tea was OK and if we needed anything else.

We were just about perfect and it struck me that I'd never had tea like this before. It tasted like hot syrup sliding down my throat that warmed my inner core.

They both seemed pleased and encouraged us to eat some more as Mungie topped up our tea. After Maggie thanked them and said they didn't need to do any of this, Mungie brought it all back on track again.

"So, if it is Liza *Mhór* and her mother, Fiona—wait now, you said Mary was her name."

"Well, yes. It was either Mary Flora or Mary Fiona. Mam always said Fiona from Iona, so I'm not sure about that."

"Well, you know, I think Liza's mother's name was Mary. Do you remember, Sadie?'"

"No, I don't really remember her at all. You're quite a bit older than me, Mungie."

"I am not. Five years and that's it," she said rather sharply.

"Yes, but I think she was gone by the time I remember those things," Sadie said.

"You know what, I'll call Malcolm on the hill and if anyone knows, he'll know. He's from out there and only went away for a few years and came back. You know, they used to have a post office out there a long time ago, just like us."

"Really, a post office? And I'm sorry, but where is *out there*?" I asked.

"Oh, he's in Highland Hill, which is where Liza *Mhór* came from and, yes, they had branch offices in all the little communities long ago. We had one here, you know, and they would just be in people's houses of course or in a store if there was one. It would be a great place to visit and see people."

"It sounds like it was a busy little place at one time," I said.

"Oh, yes, they used to say they had a mill on the hill and a boil on the still. There was lots of business going on and people coming and going. It was Seumas Mhuracidh and his mother that ran the office, but Malcolm lived right next door," Mungie said.

"He's getting kind of old, Mungie. He may not remember as much as you think," Sadie said.

"He's younger than me," Mungie said.

"I know," Sadie said, laughing. "He's kind of old." She giggled some more. It was kind of funny.

"I'll just give him a call and see if he remembers," Mungie said.

The phone hung on the wall and there was a list of names on a piece of white poster board that she slid her finger down and slowed. "There it is there." And she spoke out the number as she dialled it.

"Hello. Hello. *Ciamar a tha sibh?*"

Their whole conversation was in Gaelic and it was sweet and fluid as a country stream bubbling its way from one phrase to the next. I could make out *Màiri* and Liza *Mhór* and the rest was a blur of words and phrases I couldn't understand. The language flowed like a Shakespearean sonnet and it was during those few short minutes I realized how beautiful it really was.

Mungie laughed and looked at us several times and turned away a few times and laughed some more.

"OK, I'll tell them, *Móran Taing*," and she hung up the phone.

"Sounds like he knew who they were," said Sadie.

"Yes, he did, and he can remember her as clear as the morning sky. We are pretty much right: Liza *Mhór* was one of the Big Neils and related to Peadair Custie. Now, her mother's name was Mary Flora and her mother's name was Fiona. But Mary Flora was often called Mary Fiona because Mary Flora's husband died right after they were married."

"So, I guess Mary Flora took her mother's name so people would know who she was. She was known as Mary Fiona. Now, Liza *Mhór* married Malcolm Campbell and they lived in St. Columba Mountain before they moved away."

Maggie's eyes cut right through me. I was like, *what?*

"So really it's my great-great-grandmother that was Fiona from Iona?"

"Yes, dear, I think that's right," Mungie said.

"And her daughter, my great-grandmother, was Mary Flora, but they called her Mary Fiona."

"Yes, I'm pretty sure that's it," said Mungie.

"And my grandmother, Mam, was Nora Liza, who you call Liza *Mhór.*"

"That's it, Maggie, that's it."

My head was spinning and my eyes were crossed.

"Well, that's just amazing. That's such a huge help to me, to us."

"So, now you haven't really told us the whole story about why you are looking for all this information, and you did say you had some sort of message from God, didn't you?"

"Well, no, I didn't mean for it to sound like that. I just made reference to wishing I was older when Mam was alive. You were asking me about what I thought and I said, that's sort of why I'm here."

"Yes, I'm sorry, you're right and I didn't mean to put words in your mouth, but there is something else to this that you're after, isn't there?"

I could hardly keep up, these people were brilliant, and I wondered if I should go wait in the car.

"More tea?" Sadie asked.

"Yes, if you have it," I said.

"None for me," said Maggie.

"Well, now, it may sound a little crazy, but Mam told me before she died that it was just a miracle that we were here."

"Well it is," said Mungie.

"No, I mean that we were born at all. I'll just say it, I guess. Do you believe in miracle babies?"

"I believe we're all a part of God's miracle, but that's just me. What do you mean when you say that?" Mungie asked.

"Well, that sometimes babies are conceived out of pure magic," Maggie said.

"Well, we believe that Jesus Christ our saviour was conceived this way. That's the belief of nearly all Christians around the world," Mungie said.

"Well, yes, I know that, but do you believe that it could happen to me or to you or your neighbour? Not just because it's part of the story of the Bible but because it might have happened to someone you know or love?"

It felt like the temperature changed in the room. It went kind of quiet and got a little weird. Sadie poured the tea and said, "That's not that uncommon, you know. There are lots of people that get married and can't have children for whatever reason and then they, well, they may adopt a child and the next thing you know they have conceived a child. Is that what you're talking about?"

"Yes, that's it and things like that. Or they get a blessing or something and they have ten kids or somehow they conceive a baby only to have it die at birth. There are all sorts of these things that I'm wondering about and I'm wondering about myself.

"Mam told my mother about both of you and I can remember her telling me things about it, as well. I couldn't remember your names but she said you were very spiritual and might know something about this sort of thing.

"And then you just mentioned Mary Flora and her husband dying right after they were married. So I know I'm getting a little excited here, but how could they have a child so quick? I think Liza *Mhór* was a miracle baby and that I wouldn't be here if it wasn't for that miracle."

Mungie seemed absorbed in thought as if she had a way of solving the whole conundrum. I had nothing to add to this conversation and thought about going to the car again. More tea would be good and were five biscuits too many to eat? I was eating like I was going to the chair.

"Well, yes, it's very possible," said Sadie. "Now let me tell you this little story that we heard from Father Rankin. You know, Mungie, when the couple came to see him because they were having trouble making a family?"

"I think they were MacInnises, but it doesn't matter because they were trying for a few years to have a child and not having any luck at all. So Father Rankin gave them both a blessing and told the lady to tie this certain scarf around her neck and don't you know the next thing she was 'trom,' as they say."

"What's that?" asked Maggie.

"Oh, sorry. She was heavy, heavy with child and you know everything was just great. So now they didn't see Father Rankin for a number of years and the next time he saw them they had seven children. So now when he saw this, he said, 'It's time to take the scarf off.'"

There was laughter again until Sadie told us of another young couple that had tried for ten years to have children. They were Campbells and when they got pregnant he was dead before the child was born.

"Yes, I think you're right," said Mungie. "One of John Murdoch's crew."

"So, Maggie, these types of things happen more than we know. I don't think it odd at all," said Sadie.

"Well, OK, but what brought me to you was that Mam said you had a relative or something that this happened to, and I don't mean to pry, but was there someone in your family that has a story like this or my own?"

It got quiet again.

"Well, yes, there is," said Sadie.

"Can you tell me?" Maggie asked.

"Well, yes, I can. Her name was Margaret and they called her Mugsie, but I think I should tell you about this first. You see we had a good share of tragedy ourselves here long ago."

"What was that?" Maggie asked.

"Well, now, back when we were just little girls we had two sisters that passed away very young, God rest their souls. Now by that I mean one of them only lived for a day, Christmas Day, and the other survived for eighteen days."

"Oh, I'm so sorry," Maggie said.

"Yes, well thank you, but those things happened quite a bit years ago when there were no doctors or any kind of medicine. Mary Liza and Mary Catherine were their names, Mary 1 and Mary 2.

"But anyway, what I'll tell you now is that sometimes special things happen to you because you had such a tough time or just because you have faith that something better will happen.

"You see, Mugsie was a distant relation and she had powers, you know. She could see things no one else could, you know, second sight and stuff like that. Do you know what that is?" Sadie asked.

"I don't know much about it, but I've heard of it," said Maggie.

"Well, it's like seeing something before it happens, you know, like a forerunner. You would know something or you would be getting a sign that something was going to happen before it happened. Most of these things would involve someone dying, but sometimes good things would happen, as well. But you usually only hear of the bad things."

"It's like a premonition or a ghost story and stuff like that," Maggie said.

"Yes, that's it. You know, the older ones were always trying to scare us when we were little and it usually worked."

"So now you see Mugsie could see the little people as well, you know."

"So now what does that mean?" Maggie asked.

"Oh, well, people call them fairies, but they prefer to be called little people."

"Oh, yes, of course, we had a little discussion about them on the way here today," Maggie said.

"Well, you see, they were the ones that warned her about the earthquake years ago."

"I don't know what you mean," said Maggie.

"Well, it must be close to 100 years ago that it happened, at least. Now, I don't remember it, but Mungie might," she said with a chuckle.

Mungie just frowned at her and Sadie said, "Of course you don't," and proceeded with Mugsie's tale.

"She was always talking to the little people and they told her of the loud noises they were hearing in the ground. They warned her that something terrible was going to happen and for her to tell people to stay out of their barns. If they saw their animals balking or lowing and neighing, they'd need to be very careful. Any strange behaviour from the animals would be a sure sign to get outside."

Sadie told us she went around and told the whole countryside that something bad was going to happen. "Now, some people laughed at her but most took her very seriously and it all came true. There was an earthquake and she didn't know how many barns fell down but nearly every animal around there was saved and no one was hurt.

"It was just amazing, people used to say. Because in those days, there was always somebody in the barns."

"So what does Mugsie have to do with you, or how is she connected to you? I don't quite understand that part," Maggie said.

Mungie jumped in and said, "Well, you see, she moved away, and again, she was a bit older than me, and found herself living over Baddeck way. So then the next thing we heard she found herself to be *trom*."

"*Trom*? Oh, yes, you said that she was pregnant."

"Heavy, dear, heavy with child."

"Oh, I see."

"Well, you know, dear, there were all sorts of stories that go along with that and any one of them could be true. Now, most people, at that time, believe she got a little too close to an old, old type of settlement like a fairy hill, but we have no way of ever knowing."

"Oh, don't say fairy hill," said Sadie.

"Well, yes, OK, a knoll of little people. Apparently, they prefer to be called little people. Anyway, the fairies took her to someplace the Norse people had travelled to years ago. This is where some magic may have happened. Have you ever heard of this?" Mungie asked.

"Well, yes and no. Mam told me the old tale of Boronia, but I can't really say I know that much about it. I'm not sure I even have that right, but I've heard of it for sure."

"Oh, you have some knowledge anyway. You know they have no real proof that it ever existed, but the old folks always believed in it. But that's another tale to work on.

"You know there are lots of books out there if you want to look up some of their histories. It's very interesting, just like our own.

"But all that aside, back in those days, having a child without a father was frowned upon and you wouldn't end a life like they do today. You know they'd often move away or go stay with a relative that lived someplace else."

Sadie jumped in: "Usually in a different time zone, you know that's what they used to say, send her to a different time zone!"

"There was lots of that when the girls would move to the Boston States, as they say, and have their little love child there, the poor things. You know what the Boston States are, don't you?" Mungie asked.

"Well, I think so, I was never there, but I know a bit about the place. I'm not sure, but I think Liza *Mhór* lived there for a short while."

"Yes, yes, that's it. Anyway, you know what I'm saying," said Mungie.

"Yes, yes, I do."

"So, anyway, Mugsie had her child, a beautiful little girl, and she was raised right here."

"Oh, my, where is she now?" Maggie asked.

Mungie told us she was married, had a large family, and lived about a half hour away. They were very proud of her and since neither of them ever married, they helped raise her children just like their own. They kept in touch with the young people that way and they were so proud of them all. She started to tell us all of their names and Sadie stopped her and said she needed to slow down. It was a bit of a long story but I found it interesting even though I didn't know who anybody was.

Sadie asked if we wanted more tea and it was like she was reading my mind. I gladly accepted and they insisted I have another biscuit while they were still hot. Sadie said they wouldn't get any better than they are now so I started on another.

"So what was the baby's name?" Maggie asked.

"Her name was Louise, but we often called her, 'LOU I Love You.'"

The two of them sang it together as if they had said it a thousand times before.

"And did she, I'm sorry *does* she have any special sort of powers, like Mugsie?" Maggie asked.

"No, no, I don't think she has any sort of gift like her mother, but she has many gifts in her own way. Just not the same kind, as far as we know," said Mungie.

"And so how did she come to live here?"

"Well, it's another long story, but we had heard she was living in Baddeck—you know, we heard, you know, and Sadie was here with Mama and Papa and she was taking care of them, you know. And, well, you see, Sadie was the baby, and as we told you earlier, we had a couple of sisters that died very young, one of them only lived a day and the other for a couple of weeks."

"Eighteen days, God rest their souls," Sadie said.

"Yes, I guess that's right, eighteen days. So, you know, Sadie never left here, you know."

"Well, I went to Toronto that time to see Alec," Sadie scorned.

"Yes, yes, I know, but you lived here all your life. What is it you say? You had one address all your life! Not many people can say that these days."

"I suppose not. In fact, it's probably pretty rare," Maggie said.

"You know, Sadie always wanted a little brother or sister, so they made contact with them and it was all arranged. You see, Mugsie wasn't really able to look after her, and Baby Lou came to live here as our sister. Just like that, you see."

"Well, what did people say, if you don't mind my asking?"

"Oh, no, it's OK. It was no secret—you know, we all have our own little secrets. You see, you can't really worry about what people say or think because most everyone we knew thought it was just a great gift to all of us, you see. We had a new child in our lives and Lou had a loving, stable family to grow into."

"So, I guess she *was* a miracle after what we'd all gone through—you know, losing a couple of sisters. As I mentioned before, I think every child is a blessing and a miracle, if you will. This child had no ill intentions coming into this world, so why should anyone toward her? They're here to be loved, taken care of, and to help foster, to grow. Where would we be without children?"

"We'd all be old like you," Sadie said with a little chuckle.

"Well, yes, I can see that now. I never thought about it, but of course you're right. And so what of Mugsie, what became of her?"

"Well, you know she kind of floated along the way. The last we heard she had gone to the north of Scotland and then we heard she was in Scandinavia, but we don't know if that's correct."

"So, I guess that's what brought me to you, as Mam would say. It was a connection to Lou and Liza *Mhór*."

"Well, it may very well be and perhaps there is a connection to Mary Flora and the way that you and Liza *Mhór* came into this world.

"Well, you know now there were lots of tales of the Vikings connected to Scotland and our island, years ago. Of course, you see, they were part of the stories that came over from the old country. There was a long history of Viking raids and bad relations 2,000 years ago that our people lived through. You see, these waters are all connected and touch both continents. The waters of Iona touch the channel between Baddeck and Washabuck, the Sound of Sleat, and Loch Alsh, and places like that in Scotland. It touches both shores, as they say."

"Well, does that have anything to do with…what did Donald say? Oh, yes, the Highlands. He was telling us to stay away from there in a friendly sort of way."

"Oh, yes, yes, the Highlands. Yes, well, they do. You know that's the area we're talking about right there. Oh, and who is this Donald that you mentioned?" Mungie asked.

"Oh, he was a man we met at the café by the bridge. He was very helpful. We were there before we stopped at the church and then we came here."

"And does he have a last name?" asked Mungie.

"Yes, it was MacRae, I believe."

"Donald MacRae, you say. I wonder, was it Donald Willie?" asked Mungie.

"Well, I don't know," Maggie said.

"Was he kind of a charming fellow and not too hard looking?"

"Well, I guess," Maggie said.

"Oh, Maggie had herself in some sort of spell. I think she found him charming," I said as she gave me a look.

"Oh, I think it must have been Donald Willie. He's got a silver tongue, they say, and he can twist a tale pretty good when he wants to," Mungie said.

"Well, as I said before, he was very helpful to us and he got us out here to meet you beautiful ladies. Now, you fine ladies have been very helpful and it's just been amazing, but I think we've taken up too much of your time already. Thank you so much for everything."

"Oh, we were glad for the visit and there is no rush to leave."

But just as we were getting up, Betsey got up from behind the stove, jumped onto the daybed and started to bark gently while looking out the window.

"*Bi Modhail*," or something like that in Gaelic. "Shush there, Betsey," Sadie said.

I saw a car coming up the driveway. Holy shit, it was like the Mafia or some big gangster car. It was a very large, wide car, a green and white Chevy, I thought. Sadie said it must be Joseph coming to take them to church. He usually came by for tea and sometimes he'd come back for supper. They were going to the store for a few things before mass and Maggie said we needed to leave.

"He's our chauffeur, you see. That's what people say."

"Oh, that's sweet," said Maggie.

"Yes, well, you should meet him. You know, he worked in the city all his life and then moved back here when he retired some years ago. And he's a MacKinnon, like yourself."

"Well, we're MacKinnons, too. Our mother was his father's sister, so we're first cousins. We might all be related," Sadie said.

"I think we better save that connection for another time. I know less about my father's side than my mother's," Maggie said.

I heard the door open and Betsey waddled off in that direction. He asked Betsey how she was doing, if she'd been baking, and if her sisters were home. He was having a big old chat with Betsey and Mungie called to him and told him we were down by the stove.

"Yes, I'm coming, hello," he said.

When he entered the room I noticed how tall and thin he was and that he had a fairly large nose. His grey hair was slicked back and he had a meek and gaunty look about him. They introduced us as being from the city and he stepped toward us and stretched out his arm, which seemed as long as his legs.

"Nice to meet you, dear," he said.

"Likewise," I said.

"And you, as well, miss," he said. "The pleasure is all mine, dear."

"Mine, as well, and I'm sorry but we were just about to leave," Maggie said.

"Ach, don't rush off on my account, dear," he said.

"Yes, yes, there's no rush," said Sadie. "Have a seat there, Joe, and I'll get you some tea."

"OK, thanks. You know, you're lucky you stopped by here today," he said.

"Why is that?" I asked.

"Well, I came in here last week and the kettle was hanging right here on the arm of the rocking chair and it was boiling away. Just as if it was on the top of the stove."

"Well, you didn't seem to mind at the time," Sadie said.

"No, I suppose I didn't. So you live in the city, do you?" Joe asked.

"Yes, we do. We both live and work there now," I said. "The ladies told us you spent a lot of time there over the years."

"Yes, yes, dear, I did. I worked at the mill most of my life and lived down around Ferry Street most of my time there. There was a boarding house and that's where I spent many, many years. I would come back up here when I wasn't working or some weekends but I never owned a house in the city."

"I had an apartment—or a flat, as we called it—but I never really needed the space. I didn't really care for all the room and now here I'm living in a big house by myself and I don't know how that happened. Not like this house," he said.

"Did you know they moved it from over near my place, on that mountain?" He pointed past where the cars were parked. "From across the pond to here and they used to climb the mountain both ways to go to school in Barra Glen."

"Well, no, I didn't know that, but it's very interesting. Now I really think we should be going," Maggie said, as she gave me the eye.

"I wonder if we could keep in touch with you somehow," Maggie asked.

"Oh, of course. I'll write down our number and I'll give you Malcolm's, as well. He's very knowledgeable about the history of Highland Hill, you know," Mungie said.

"Oh, I think she'd like Donald's number, as well, if you have it," I said, smirking all the way.

"Oh, you never mind about Donald," Sadie said.

"You best just run into him like a fly, as they say," said Mungie.

Sadie had been writing away for minutes now and Mungie was peering at her list on the wall, looking for Malcolm's number. They were pretty much done at the same time, like teamwork, and Mungie handed Maggie a piece of paper.

"Thank you again for all your help," Maggie said.

"It was our pleasure, dear," Mungie said. "Please come back again."

"We will, for sure," said Maggie.

Sadie handed me a piece of paper at the same time.

"What's this?" I asked.

"Well, you wanted the recipe for the biscuits, so here it is."

"Oh, my, take some with you," Mungie said.

"Oh, no, we couldn't," Maggie said.

"I'll take some," I said. "They were just over the top."

Maggie gave me the eye again.

Mungie put six in a bag and said, "Come back again and we'll give you a dozen."

Sadie winked at me and said, "My number is there on the recipe in case you need any help."

She gave Maggie a little look and her face changed to a wide, glowing smile.

"Oh, you two, thanks again and nice to meet you, Joe," Maggie said.

"The same, dear," he replied.

They showed us to the door and we were out. It was cooler now and the smell of the wood fire in the air was intoxicating. You could see the pond that Joe had mentioned, tucked below the mountain off in the distance. It was mostly wooded, but you could see some cleared areas that must have been another old farm. It was much like this one but maybe deserted years earlier.

"It sure is peaceful out here," Maggie hummed.

I felt kind of surrounded as if we were at the bottom of an anthill. We were enclosed by the road, pond, fields, and the wooded mountains and all I could hear were birds singing and, oh, that smell. I felt a little sting on my leg, like a wasp's sting but much gentler. I saw nothing and I gave my leg a little rub and it was gone. I thought I felt another on my back but it also retreated.

"Yes, it's quite divine," I said.

"Divine? Well, that's not a word you hear every day."

"Oh, it's an old word my mother used to say quite often. I like it."

"So do I," said Maggie.

"Anyway, where to next?"

"I don't know. You're driving."

"Well, let's see if we can get out of here first."

I backed up around a huge maple tree and got turned around. The whole time I was thinking I'd be coming back. I just didn't know when.

We headed down the driveway and I saw the pond clearly and wondered how they moved the house from there to here all those years ago. We were back on the dirt road, which had seemed so narrow when I turned onto it earlier. It now seemed wide compared to the driveway and the encampment we were in. As we drove away, Maggie opened her purse and started looking for something.

"Is there something that you need?" I asked.

"I need to take some notes while this is fresh in my mind. I need to try and keep it all straight."

"Well, I have a pen right here," I said, reaching down beside the door. "And I think there is a notepad in the pouch in the backseat."

She reached back and grabbed it and, by that time, we arrived at the first dirt road, which looked wider again than the one we were on. It appeared so much bigger than when we first drove on it, and I said to Maggie, "Would you like to see where this road takes us?"

"Sure. Do you think you can find our way back?"

"Yes, I think so. And, besides, what's better than an adventure on top of an adventure?"

'Càit A Bheil Nora Liza?

Jig

Paul K. MacNeil

CHAPTER 5
Cash's Mill

I turned left at the end of the Rear Iona Road and Maggie was writing and talking to herself, trying to keep all her information straight. This road seemed like a highway compared to when we first turned onto it. We carried on beside a little brook and when we started to climb it, it became very twisty again. I could see why they called it the Highlands and I could see higher mountains farther off to the right.

I wondered if that was the north or west because I didn't know and I thought about Donald for a few minutes. There was no sign of the lake we'd been driving beside all day. It was pretty much trees, sky, and the road, which at times became very dark with the strapping canopy.

During those moments, it felt quite eerie and then things opened up to the odd driveway and what must have been old farms that had been left to die by themselves. We passed a number of driveways that stretched farther into the forest, if you could have imagined, that didn't look well-travelled.

It was Joe that said they went to school around here, so there must have been a post office as well and I wondered if there was a store. Wouldn't it be something if you could just slide back in time and see what it was like, that long ago?

We passed a dirt road intersection and I saw the sign that said Fraser Road, so I said to Maggie, "I think that was the road to the Highlands we just passed. Do you want to go there or should we keep going?"

"Keep going, let's save that adventure for another time."

"Another time? Seems as though this is becoming a very serious relationship all in one day. Two dates and planning a third already. Wait, now, we went to church and met some distant relatives. Oh, yes, you also kissed me in the car, and my head is still spinning from that, by the way. You sure do move quickly," I said in an obnoxious, confident sort of way.

Where the hell did that come from? I thought to myself.

"Well, I'll have to see if you can keep up," she said as she softly smiled and raised her shoulders.

"You know you passed most of the tests so far and you did very well back at the house. If you can get us out of here and back home, you may have a future." She tapped my hand.

"You do have a good job, don't you?"

"Well, it's steady and, yes, it's good. You just control yourself over there and don't rush me. Didn't you ever hear that you can scare men off by moving too quick?"

"Yes I've heard that, but don't really give it much creed."

"Creed, eh? That's an old word, as well."

"OK, divine, keep driving," she said in a raised tone.

I asked her if she had all her notes and thoughts written down and if there was anything I could help her out with. She ran most of it by me and it seemed to make sense. We seemed to be heading downhill for a change and then we saw a sign for Highland Hill and I slowed down.

"Do you want to go up?" I asked.

"They said not to go right on the dirt road."

"I know, but this is where Malcolm lives, so let's just go a little piece. See the sign there? It says no exit and I'll turn around anytime you want me to."

She was OK with that and we started up.

And it was up, and crooked, but it settled into a plateau for a little while and then it went up again. The road was a combination of the two we'd been on. It was wide and open at the start but became very narrow as we moved along and then it opened up again. Off in the distance to the west, I thought, was a lovely-looking house and barn. On the right side, which had to be east, was, what was that? Was it a sawmill? A gate crossed the road directly in front of us when we reached the sawmill and the driveway to their house.

"This must be it," I said.

"Look at the mailbox, M, J MacNeil. M for Malcolm and J for his wife, I guess."

"It must be it. It's the only place up here," Maggie said.

There was no sign of anybody, but there was a car in the driveway and smoke coming from the chimney.

"So, this is not so scary," Maggie said.

"Well, do you want to get out and go for a walk in the woods?"

"No, I'm good. Maybe we'll do that the next time we come back. So going back over my notes, I think this is where I came from. I think this is where Liza *Mhór* and *Peadair Custie* lived. I really think we are close and I need to get out for just a few minutes."

"Sure thing. Just let me get turned around and off the road."

"Are you expecting a lot of traffic?" she jokingly asked. "I'm not sure we met a car since we came out here."

There was a large area to turn around by the mill so I backed in there. Maggie jumped out and touched the ground with both hands and brought it to her face.

"This just has to be it. I feel so different here, even compared to what it felt like at Mungie and Sadie's. It's just different."

It was different, for sure, as the scent of fresh-cut spruce and sawdust filled the air. The mill was surrounded by slabs, logs, lumber, and a smell you could sell. It was quite a little operation considering we were in the middle of nowhere. There were hay fields, apple trees—a lot of apple trees—and, a long way off, I saw the lake.

I suppose we looked a bit intrusive, just parked and standing at the end of their driveway beside his business. When I looked up toward their house I saw a man walking toward us so I said to Maggie, "I think you are going to meet the man on the hill."

"What do you mean?"

"Well, someone is heading our way."

The driveway was long and flat and he was moving at a pretty good clip, approaching quickly. He looked like a tall man from a distance with quite an able frame. A black-and-white dog was racing ahead of him firing warning shots in our direction.

Maggie said, "Can I trust you to do the talking?"

"What do you mean?"

"Well, do you want to break the ice, you know, man to man?"

"Oh, sure, don't worry. I'll look after you."

"Oh, spare me. Don't I feel safe now?"

He was pretty much upon us and I stepped toward him and said hello. He was indeed a large man who must have been very rugged in his day. Tall and wide with jet black hair.

"Hello to you both," he said, with a deep, strong voice that had a melodic ring to it.

"Are you here to look at the mill? Joan said someone called earlier today when I was out. Said they were dropping by to look at her. I'm afraid I don't really have time to show you everything right now. We're heading out to church pretty soon, but we won't be that long and I have all day tomorrow, if you like."

"No, no, that wasn't me that called, although I am interested to see it now that I'm here. It looks like a beauty. Did you set it up yourself?"

"Yes, yes, I did. I had a bit of help here and there, but we got her going and she runs pretty darn good. She cuts like a hot knife through butter when the blade is sharp.

"But sadly now I need to sell her. I get lots of phone calls and these people will say they're coming by to look at her but most don't show up at all."

"Well, I'm sorry about that. I'm Patrick and this is Maggie and we just kind of happened along to your property. Now, are you Malcolm MacNeil?"

"Yes, yes, I am, and it seems you have me at a bit of a disadvantage."

"Well, it's so nice to meet you and I hope you don't mind," Maggie said.

"Don't mind what?"

"Oh, us just dropping by. I, I mean we, we were just at Mungie and Sadie's place and I think she phoned you. You are Malcolm on the hill, that's who she said she was talking to."

"Yes, yes, that's me. They call me Max or Maxie, as well. A lot of people know me as Maxie Dan Angus from the men before me, but I'll go by Malcolm for today if you like. And you were asking about Liza *Mhór* and Mary Fiona."

"Well, yes, I was. It seems that they are my people, like my great-grandmother and grandmother. It's just so great to make the connection, you see. We didn't plan on coming here. We were just carrying on from our visit with the ladies and we saw the sign for Highland Hill and here we are."

"So you don't want to buy the mill either?" he asked.

"No, no, I don't. I don't think so, anyway. It's just so, so we don't want to keep you, but this is where they lived, is it, you know, Liza *Mhór*. Is it here?"

She sounded a little frantic, I thought.

"I just feel close to it. Am I here?"

"Well, yes, of course you are here. But they lived about a mile or two from here. Farther up the hill and to the west."

"And which way is west?" I asked.

"Well, you see the sun over there? Well, it's setting in the west," and he pointed in the direction I thought.

I forgot to look at the sun.

"Right."

"I knew your people very well a long time ago when I was a boy. You'd have to go up to Big Neil's and then it's further west to where *Peadair Custie* lived but they were pretty close."

"Can you drive there?" Maggie asked.

"In a car? No, no, I wouldn't, but you could get through on a 4x4, I'd suppose. Or you could get through there on a bike—you know, a quad or four-wheeler. Lots of folks go through there on a bike. It's a nice trail like that.

"They have these gates here that are locked, you know. The roads are supposed to be fire roads and we hope they never need them. But now, you can get permission if you ask and they'll unlock them. Now the bikes can just drive around them."

"So, I could go there? Do you know where their place was and is there anything left there?" Maggie asked.

"No, no, there's nothing there, but I could find the property, for sure. There's no house or anything like that. You can still see the root cellar from

Big Neil's there, that's pretty easy to find. He was the last one up there and held out to the end. Now I could probably find where *Peadair Custie's* house was, but it's a long time since I was there. It's pretty well all after growing in, you know."

"Do you think you could show us?" Maggie asked.

"Oh, I could take you there sometime, but not today."

"Oh, no, I understand. We don't want to hold you up. But perhaps we could line up a time and come back. Would you mind that?"

"No, no. I've got lots of free time in the run of a day. I just don't know how many days I have left. I'm glad to help, you know. It'd do me good to go back up there and remember it all again."

"OK. Mungie gave me your number. She didn't think you would mind. I'll call you and set something up that will work for all of us."

He asked us a few questions about where we worked and lived. He seemed quite interested in learning about our lives in the city and if we'd ever been in his part of the world before. I asked him how much he wanted for his mill and he said, "Well, I was looking for a certain price but if the right fellow came along the price could go up."

He laughed and turned away.

There was a rumble in his voice as he looked back at us. He called to his dog, who had been frantically digging in the sawdust pile.

"Come on, Sawdust, let's go. Come on, Dusty. *Thugainn ma-ta.*"

"Come back any time," he said, as he waved his hand and headed toward his house.

We just stood there in awe and Maggie was beaming. The look on her face said it all, as if her circle of life had been completed. I was sort of numb as she walked toward me and gave me the warmest hug. She held me tight and pressed her creamy cheek against my own and in my ear she said, "Thank you so much for the day. It's been more than I ever could have imagined."

She held me tight and I felt her all around me. Oh my God, I held her back and she felt so good against me. She kissed me several times on the cheek and our lips almost touched and she whispered, "We should go."

I didn't want to move but there was nothing I could do.

We got back in the car and said nothing as we slowly coasted down the hill. When she looked back at Maxie and Dusty, they had just arrived at their front door. She waved, knowing he couldn't see her but I think it made her feel good anyway.

I wasn't sure what to do. I thought about making a joke about breaking the ice but decided I should just let her have a moment or two. I said nothing and then she asked, "Now who does he remind you of?"

"Well, you know, I felt like I'd seen him before or something."

She shook her head slowly and it all went very silent, and it just came out of me again.

"Well, you know that's three dates in one day. It's quite a pace we're on and we're right around the bases, I'd say."

"Not all the way," she said. "Getting from third to home is the hardest base."

"Jesus, I got it! Third date, I take you to see a guy selling a sawmill and it's Johnny Cash. It's Johnny Cash."

"What?"

"It's Johnny Cash. That's who he reminds me of, Johnny Cash.

"You must have heard of Johnny Cash," I chirped smartly.

"You know, 'Big River,' *Walk the Line*. He's a country singer."

"Yes, I know who Johnny Cash is," she blurted in an unimpressed tone.

"Do you like his music?"

"I guess so. I don't know all that much of it, really. He did that stuff in the prisons, didn't he?"

"Oh my God, he's been around forever. He did 'Folsom Prison Blues,' 'Ring of Fire,' that's one of my favourites. He did 'The Cremation of Sam McGee.' Well, that last one is a poem by Robert Service, but the others he wrote himself. He must have fifty albums."

"Robert Service, eh? You do continue to surprise."

"Yeah, yeah, I know I'm awesome. It's OK. His hits go on and on."

"Who, Robert Service or Johnny Cash?"

"Well, both, really. But I was thinking of Johnny Cash. Here's a little-known fact: he was actually Scottish, or at least his father was. Cash is a Scottish name and I think his father was born in Scotland. Maybe his mother, as well. You don't mind if I go on a little bit, do you?"

"No, by all means. It's riveting, really," she said sarcastically.

"Well, you see, as they say around here, he was born J. R. Cash, but after his time in the air force, he took on Johnny as a name. And the R is for river, which was his mother's maiden name. Now some people say it was for Ray, his fathers' middle name, but most say it was for river. So what do you think of that? Jeez, he might be related to Liza *Mhór*."

"Well, I don't know, it's sort of, uh, I don't know what that is."

"I know, useless information. I'm kind of full of that at times. But you know, he was just like him. Tall, jet-black hair, weathered face, and a big deep, rumbling voice."

"OK, OK, you've got something there, but let's just call him Malcolm on the hill like the others."

"Well, we don't need to tell him, it can be our little secret. But I can tell you this. If you told me I reminded you of Johnny Cash, I'd be feeling pretty darn good about myself."

"Oh, I thought you were more of the Elvis type," she teased with a smile.

"And are you sure Cash is a Scottish name and not some name he made up, like a stage name? You know, it's pretty ironic that we're in this so far and we meet a guy that reminds you of Johnny Cash and now he's Scottish. It's kind of a stretch, don't you think?"

"Well, I'm good with it."

We were at the bottom of the hill and I said, "We go left, right?"

"Right," she said.

"We go right. Are you messing with me? Remember we turned right to come up here."

"OK, we'll go right," I said.

"Remember, they said not to go right or we'd end up in the Highlands, but we turned right to come up here to Highland Hill."

"You are so right. So we just keep going until we get to the pavement and then we turn left, right?" I questioned.

"Aagh, yes, left at the pavement. It's a good thing I was paying attention," she said.

It wasn't very far when we reached the end of the road and turned left. We were back on the highway and I felt as though I had just passed through some mysterious world. Like it could all seal over when it got dark or for ten years or something. It was like a land for fairies or little people, as they say and really tall, large people who were very smart. It wasn't at all what I was expecting when I left this morning, which seemed like a week ago.

As we headed down the road, the big lake was back in sight and taking up most of the scenery. The lake, the road, and the sky. Everything was so much more open now and it seemed as though we were in a completely different space or place than where we had been two minutes earlier. Maggie was busy writing down more notes so I didn't disturb her.

I was rather curious if she was feeling the same way I was. I also wondered what she wanted to do or if we were heading home now. The day was moving on and the sun was getting low in the sky, but there was still plenty of daylight left in this late spring day.

I noticed a road to the right that said Beach Road, and I thought about going down to check it out but decided against it and kept on driving. The thought of sitting on the beach and opening the bottle of wine was very appealing to me, but I decided to keep going. I assumed we couldn't be that far from the church, the bridge, and the café where all this seemed to start from.

I didn't think that we had driven very far on the dirt road but then again I felt like we'd been in a time warp and could be hours away. It was only a few more minutes when we came around a sharp turn, marked Hector's Pt., and saw both ends of the lake married together. This glorious strait of water looked to be about two miles long and a third of that distance wide. We saw the bridges in the distance, the spire of the church, and I said to Maggie, "Does this look familiar to you?"

She looked up for the first time in a while and said, "Yes, it does. It's quite beautiful here, isn't it?

"Oh, yes, it's divine," I said, as she rolled her eyes and smiled.

This time she looked different to me. It might be me, or the light, but she just looked really happy. It was probably the light and I said to her, "You know, I saw a road back there that said Beach Road but I decided we should keep going."

"It's a little cold for swimming, don't you think?"

"Ah-ha, yes, I know but I have a bottle of wine in the back. If you'd like to stop and have a little glass, it might top the day off."

"Well, I think I'd like a large glass, but I also wouldn't mind stopping and using the washroom. Do you think we could stop at the café and see if they are still open? If not, I guess I could do a nature pee."

"Oh, a nature pee. I seeeee, you are one classy date and I have definitely underdressed for it."

She smirked a bit and said, "What can I say? You do what you have to these days."

I slowed down coming toward the bridge and I could see a few cars already at the church. I saw Joe's big green and white gangster car turning around and pulling out from the little store.

"Look there, Maggie, there's Joe's car leaving the store heading to the church."

"That's so cute," she said.

We started slowly across the bridge.

"Goodbye, this place, and can you hurry up, I really need to pee," Maggie chirped.

"What's that, slow down?"

"Get moving before I leave a stain."

"OK, I'll kick it down a notch."

"Is this as fast as this will go?" she asked.

"I can go slower, and why didn't you tell me you were in such a state?"

"Well, I wasn't until I saw the water again."

We turned off the main road and arrived at the café. There was a car there and a light on inside as Maggie ran for the door. It reminded me of the old joke my father used to say but I decided to save it.

I watched Maggie pull on the door and when it opened, she didn't look back—she may have forgotten about me altogether. Oh, well, it was fun while it lasted. I turned the car around and questioned if I should go in and use it myself while I had the chance. *Ach*, I was all right.

"Oh, sorry, we're closed," I heard, entering the café.

"Oh, hello, Evelyn, I was here earlier. I just wanted to use the bathroom, if that's OK."

"Of course, go right ahead. Take your time."

Holy shit, I thought I wasn't going to make it. Just when I sat down and got it going, my phone rang; it was Patrick. What was he doing?

"Yes, did you miss me that much, so soon?"

"Well, yes, and no. I was just wondering if you heard about the black-smith's dog?"

"What?"

"The blacksmith's dog," he said.

"What, the blacksmith's dog? What are you talking about?"

"He made a bolt for the door," Patrick said, laughing like crazy as he repeated, "He made a bolt for the door, goodbye."

I didn't get it and he was gone. Can't a gal take a leak in peace? Bolt for the door? Bolt for the door? What does that even mean? I washed my hands and walked toward the counter to thank Evelyn again.

"Oh, no problem. How did you get along out in the Rear? Did you find the ladies and was it the right place?" she asked.

"Oh, my, yes, it was and we had a great visit. They were very helpful and just a delight to be around."

"Well, that's great. Now Donald was talking about you all day, every time he came in. He'll be in here three or four times a day when he can. You know he has lots of information from around these parts if you ever need help with anything."

"Well, you know I'd take his number if you have it and I might give him a call if we keep after this thing."

"Well, I have it right here. He left it here in case you came back."

She turned back into the kitchen and returned with it in her hand.

"You have to keep an eye on Donald. He's been single all his life and he has no shortage of words, you know. He's really harmless in case you were concerned and, really, I found it kind of cute the way he fixed up on you."

"Oh, I noticed. Patrick has been giving me the gears about him since we left here. He thinks I have an admirer and won't let me forget it."

"Was Patrick uneasy about him?"

"No, no, I don't think so. He didn't say that much. In fact, he was just having a little fun with me, that's all."

"Well, he seems like a fine young man. How long have you been together?"

I paused, not really knowing what to say. Today seemed like forever but I hardly knew him, so I couldn't really answer honestly.

"Well, you know, not that long, but we've been on quite a few dates, so maybe it's longer than I thought."

"Well, you seem like a lovely couple. I hope you are happy together. It's not easy to find that someone you are meant to be with."

"Yes, well, we'll see how it goes, I guess. You know, I was wondering if I could get your number, as well. You know, in case I can't get a hold of Donald or if he happens to be here."

"Sure, sure," she said as she wrote her number on the back of an order paper and handed it to me. I told her we were on our way back to the city but would certainly return in the summer.

She was just about to leave for the day and encouraged me to stop in on our next trip.

When I walked out of the café I saw Patrick in the car on his phone. He looked toward me and smiled. He looked different, far more handsome and rugged than I thought earlier. Maybe I didn't notice so much before but he had a peaceful strength about him. With his thick brown hair and sturdy chin, he was easy enough to look at and he seemed happy or somehow different. Was it the light, and where did all the birds come from?

All of a sudden that was all I could hear and then I got a little sting in my hip. I looked for a fly or something and gave it a little rub and it was gone.

My phone dinged again and I realized I had a pile of messages. I hadn't looked at it all day or at least since I was here.

There was one there now from Patrick, so I stood in front of the car, nodded at him, and read it.

> *I know our last date ended very suddenly.*
> *I was wondering if you would like to have a glass of wine and*
> *watch the sun drift into the water.*

I smiled at him and walked to the door.

"Of course I would. Do you have glasses, as well?"

"Well, I do have a couple of cheap paper glasses."

"Yes, well, let's do it and what's the joke about the dog? I don't get it."

"You know, a blacksmith makes nails and hinges and bolts and that also means running for the door. Oh, by the way, did you make it on time?"

"Yes, yes, I did, and I get the joke now, as well. Good one!"

The Barra Glen Road

Slow Jig   Paul K. MacNeil

CHAPTER 6
Beach Wine

When I pulled out the paper glasses, Maggie said, "They look a little rough, maybe I'll just run in and grab a couple of take-out cups. Unless you want to go in and see Evelyn?"

"No, that's OK. So will we just stay here?"

"It's fine with me. There's a picnic bench and a shelter over there that we could sit at."

I grabbed the wine and headed for the shelter, which wasn't far from the car, and Maggie went inside to get a couple of fancier glasses. It was a lovely evening and it might have been as warm as it was all day. It cooled down quickly when the sun dipped behind the clouds as Maggie returned with the very best of beach wine glasses.

"I hope you like red."

"Oh, I'll drink both."

"Well, I didn't even notice this when I grabbed it this morning, but this is a California wine, called McManis. Isn't that ironic? Another one of those Scottish connections. Have you had it before?"

"No, I don't think I have, at least not to my knowledge. Mind you, I'm not really any kind of a wine connoisseur, if you know what I mean."

"Nor am I."

"You know if it comes in a glass or a bottle, I usually like it. I don't consider myself a big drinker but it's nice to relax to," she said.

"It's a twist-off, so some people would say it's no good, but I don't think they're here right now."

I poured a generous amount into both glasses and she said, "May I make a toast?"

"Well, of course."

She raised her glass.

"To one of the best days and dates I've ever had."

"I'll drink to that." I touched her glass and took a drink.

She had a drink as well and leaned toward me and kissed me on the lips.

"I really did have a great day and I have you to thank," she said.

"Well, I can't take all the credit, it kind of all worked out. I'd say we did it together." I raised my glass and said, "Here's to us."

She touched my glass.

"To us."

I leaned in toward her and kissed her gently on the lips and told her how much I enjoyed the day, as well.

"It would have been nothing without you," I said.

"Ah, you're just saying that because it's true."

I laughed and my mind was racing like it was when I woke up this morning and I decided to go for it. I put my glass down on the table and reached for hers.

"Stop me if I'm out of line."

I leaned toward her and reached to embrace her. Our lips converged and she reached around me as we deeply kissed. Our tongues were dancing as she held me tight. My hands moved over her shoulders and back while I felt her doing the same as she pulled my neck and head toward hers.

I guess I made the right move, I thought to myself. I couldn't believe the feeling I was having right now and wished it could last forever, but it didn't. We slowed down together and sort of backed off. It seemed so right as if we were on the exact same page.

We let each other go and she winked at me and smiled. I couldn't help but smile and I touched her kitten-soft face with the palm of my hand.

"Well, that felt pretty nice," I said.

"It was OK. Ah, I was just joking. It was really nice."

"I think the wine tastes better off your lips."

"Well, I'm not sure about that, but I've enjoyed it so far."

She backed away, picked up her glass, and turned toward the shore. I started to follow her as she looked back at me and said, "I wonder what it was like 500 years ago or even 2,000 years ago when Boronia and the Vikings were here. Can you imagine if they were right here at this spot?"

"Well, that would be something, wouldn't it?"

"Well, I wonder what it would have been like with no houses, bridges, docks, or the church? What do you think the people saw or were thinking when they first sailed through here on their big old wooden boats? Did you even think about that?" she asked.

"Well, yes and no. I did think about the bridge not being here when we crossed it earlier, but not all the rest."

"Well, I wouldn't have thought about it either, but it's the same as what I thought about before, well, the same only different. I've thought of New York or San Francisco or Montreal or any of those big harbours in the world. You know, what it would have been like to be the first people there. I think it would have been pretty special and so different. I don't know. I don't know. I just think it would be so humbling to discover a place for the first time."

"Well, it would be pretty special, for sure. But today was special, it was just a little different." I raised my glass and said, "Here's to them, to the explorers of the world."

"To the explorers," she said.

We both took a healthy drink and it touched something as she seemed a little distant. I said nothing and, thankfully, a large fish snapped in the lake just ahead of us.

"WOW." And again.

"Did you see that?" I asked.

"Yeah, pretty slick."

"I wonder what it was."

"I'm pretty sure it was a fish," she sassed, smiling again.

"Yes, I know that. I was wondering what kind of fish it might be."

The lake cracked, again and again. It was very loud and clear.

"I'd say it's feeding time for the bigger fish." She finished her drink and turned toward me.

"Are we staying for more?" she asked.

"Yes, of course," I said and took her glass and walked back toward the table, quite content.

I heard the birds again and the loons were singing on the lake from a distance. It was pretty darn sweet.

I topped up both glasses and put a little extra in hers since I was driving and I didn't want to concern her with that. I returned to her as we watched the sun crash into the lake.

"I guess it's pretty well done. It seemed to drop off so quickly at the end."

I agreed, handed her glass to her and wanted to hold her again, but it felt like something had changed. She held out her free hand and reached for mine.

"Let's just walk up the shore for a few minutes, hand in hand, as they say."

It felt pretty nice but I had to ask. "Did I say something before? You seem a little distant."

"No, no, it wasn't you. I just kind of caught myself. I was thinking of the sailing ships and the great unknown, kind of like today and my life a little bit. I don't want to rush anything, and I don't want to confuse you in any way."

"Well, there's no rush on my part. It's all been perfect, as far as I'm concerned. I'm no expert on relationships, but sometimes it just happens at its own pace. Life just happens as long as you let it."

"Yes, I know. I just got caught up in the moment for a minute and I felt a bit awkward. I'm having a tremendous day and I'm really glad to be here with you right now. I get ahead of myself sometimes and then I start to second-guess things."

"Hey, I think it's normal. You should have been a blood cell in my brain this morning. I was in a lather. I had no idea what would happen and I wasn't even sure if you would respond. But here we are after having a great day and if this is all it is, that's OK, too. You know some people never have a day like today, so let's just enjoy the rest of it and see where it goes. I'm not in any rush for anything."

"I'm sure it has something to do with the day, as well. It seems like a week went by, there were so many good moments," she said.

"Yes, it feels like we've been together forever and it's been so very good for me and you, I think."

"Where did the wine come from, by the way?" she asked.

We took another drink and I told her a bit more about my dither-some start to the day. The one thing I felt good about was taking the wine and mentioned we had bread, biscuits, and cake in the car.

"Well, I like all of those things, but I don't need anything to eat right now. You were planning a little picnic all along, weren't you?" she said with a sly little grin and a wink.

"Good Lord, no, I wasn't planning anything. I was just thinking you can't go wrong with a bottle of wine and some sort of bread—you know, in case we got stranded somewhere."

"Well, that's not a bad plan at all and I am enjoying the wine."

The sun was long gone and the pinkness of the sky was blending into the plain grey look it takes before the darkness sets in. We turned back toward the shelter and we saw Evelyn leaving the café in her car. She tooted and drove away.

"Oh, my, I forgot to give you this."

"What is it?"

"I don't know. Evelyn gave it to me earlier when she was closing up. All she talked about was you when I was in there and she wanted to make sure I gave you this."

"You're playing games," I said.

She handed me a piece of paper that looked like it was from an order slip.

"There's nothing on it."

"What is it?" Maggie asked.

"Yeah, like you don't know."

It was folded backward on the plain backside, and when I opened it up, I saw that it said, "Call me anytime!" Happy face! Evelyn and her number.

Maggie let go of my hand and started running, laughing, and taunting me.

"Paddy's got a girlfriend, Paddy's got a girlfriend."

She headed down the bench, turned, and jested.

"Are you sorry you kissed me?"

She kept laughing and running, all the while saying *girlfriend, girlfriend*.

I wasn't quite as jovial or impressed but I chased after her anyway. She was a quick one, that's for sure.

We reached the shelter and I asked her, "How did you get that?"

"Whatever are you talking about?"

"You know," I replied.

"I told you, you have an admirer."

"You didn't answer me."

All the while I was stunned by the beauty in her face, full of the devil and twice as much fun.

"You didn't answer me," she said. "Are you sorry you kissed me?"

"In a word? No. No, I'm not."

"Well, that's good, I figured I should try and scoop you up before she did. I saw the way she was looking at you through the window."

"And you? Are you sorry you kissed me? You know, in a word?"

"In a word? Humm, no, no, I'm not. Not one bit."

I leaned toward her and kissed her again.

"More wine?" I asked.

"Well, sure, why not?"

I topped up her glass but the bottle was starting to show its age and I asked, "Do you think we should head back on the road?"

"Are you going to have some more?" she asked.

"I still have a little bit so I think you should finish it since I'm driving. I'll have more the next time."

"Oh, there'll be a next time, will there?"

"Well, I hope so. We could spend the night someplace and drink a couple of bottles."

"That sounds like fun. So here's to another date," she said, and our glasses touched.

I finished my glass and, as much as I wanted to stay, the evening was settling in and cooling off, as well.

"You're ready to go, aren't you?" she said.

"Well, yes and no. I'd like to stay all night but I only brought one bottle of wine and it's pretty well gone."

"Well, why don't you finish it?"

"No, you take it with you and finish it en route. I'll drive and you enjoy the wine for me."

She grabbed the bottle and headed toward the car and, over her shoulder, I heard her say goodbye to the place. I followed behind her and when she reached the car she turned toward me and said, "It may be the wine talking, but could you come here for a second?"

She put her glass and the lonely bottle on the roof of the car and reached out for me. I couldn't respond quickly enough as we embraced and kissed each other. Our bodies were tight together and she felt like a breathing blanket against me. Her lips and mouth were like fresh watermelon in the summer. I was in no rush to release her but she pulled back ahead of me and touched my face with her hand.

"I think you better get in and drive before this goes any further," she said with a skeptical smile.

"I was just about to round third base."

"Oh, you think so, eh? Well, the coach just put her hands up and held the runner. Did you see that?"

I smiled, laughed, and said, "I guess I'll need Donald to drive for me now."

Maggie grabbed her things off the roof and jumped in the car. She settled in then reached in her pocket and pulled out another piece of paper.

"Well, here's his number, if you need to call him for a little help," she said with a sly look about her.

"You gotta be kidding me. Donald, you have his number? How did you get that?"

"My friend Evelyn gave it to me."

"Oh, did she?"

"I think she's trying to break us up. You know, get Donald after me and then she could slip right in and scoop you up on the rebound. It's a classic girl power move."

"Oh, is it? Break us up? What made her think we were, you know, together? Did you say something?"

I coyly looked at her as I started to pull away.

"Well, I didn't tell her any different when she asked. I hope that's OK?"

I just looked at her and couldn't believe what was happening.

"It's more than OK."

"You know, I haven't looked at my phone all day and I haven't missed it one bit but I do have a pile of messages here. Do you mind if I get back to a few people?"

"No, not one bit. I checked mine while you were with Evie and I wrote back to Doug; the rest can wait. He's been worried sick about me all day."

"Wait now! Evie!"

"Yes, Evie, my friend from the café."

"Oh, I seeee, and which one is Doug?

"He was around last night, but I don't know if you met him. I was hanging with him most of the night. The tall guy with a thin, dark beard."

"Oh, yeah. Sounds familiar and I couldn't really keep the names straight."

"Well, you remembered mine and that's the main thing, but he's an old friend, probably my best friend."

"Ah, that's nice."

"Yeah, he was at my place this morning when I picked you up. I told him I had something on but he didn't believe me. He came over anyway but I wasn't there, I was with you."

"What did you tell him?" she asked.

"Did I tell him I was with you? Oh, Jesus, no. I couldn't really say anything because I wasn't sure what was going to happen. Now tomorrow I'll have a huge story for him," I said, laughing.

"Oh, really."

"Well, I'll have to tell him something, won't I?"

"Well, I don't really know the man, so I can't say one way or the other."

"And I suppose you told everyone you had a big date and excursion on, did you?"

"No, no, I didn't say much at all. Just that I was busy. I think they thought I was working."

"Yeah, well, I usually hang with Doug on Sundays, so I'll have to have some sort of controlled story. I don't want him getting too worked up about this so I'll have to ease into it. How about you? Is there any big news or APBs out on you?"

"No, not really, just my friend Jenna wrote me a few times and wants to know what's going on."

"Well you do your thing and if you could give me an idea of what you'll be telling your people, then I'd be able to share the same story with my people. Know what I mean?"

"I'm pretty sure we can come up with a safe story for both of us. Don't you worry your pretty little head," she said.

"I won't leave you standing on the side of the road by yourself. Now, if you don't mind, can I respond to a few people here before we get home?"

She tapped my hand and sipped her wine and started to reply to her messages.

"Oh, shit, I may have to work tomorrow at the clinic. Other than that, everything was pretty cool."

"Would you like to listen to some music?" I asked.

"That's fine with me," she said.

Maybe Johnny Cash would be on and I wished I had a CD. Then I found Vinyl Tap on the CBC and that seemed to hit the spot. It was generally quiet, which I enjoyed, with Randy Bachman laying down the cool stories between songs. I sort of wished Danny Finkleman was still on the air with Finkleman's 45s.

Maggie laughed every now and then and, after a while, she said, "Are you sure you don't mind if I finish this bottle?"

"Of course, there's hardly enough for one glass."

"Would you like a drink?" she asked.

"Well, I would, but I would prefer for you to enjoy it for me."

"That's so kind. Are you sure?"

"Yes, I am."

"I'm almost done here, are you doing OK?" she asked.

"Oh, yes, I'm fine."

Ten minutes or so passed and she put her phone back in her bag and said, "That's it, the rest can wait. These phones are great things, but man, oh, man, they drive me crazy, as well."

"Oh, yes, I know what you mean."

"I didn't miss mine all day and now I feel like I'm tied to it."

"Yeah, well, it will be something different in ten or twenty years' time. Look at television and the way it changed everything and radio before that."

"Yeah, Mam always said getting the power in their home was huge. Today, we just take it for granted—unless of course, it goes out, and then the crying starts. Wars and medicine were the other things she always talked about."

"She sounds like she was very wise."

"Yes, I think she was. *Everything changes*, she used to say. Everything changes but we can't always see it. And everything changes whether we like it or not. That was another of her favourites."

"Well, here's something that's changing. The city lights are starting to take over our sightlines. What's next?"

"Well, I was thinking you could drive me home. Would that be OK?"

"Well, yeah, whatever you like. It's not that late—it's just dark."

"OK, how 'bout you take me home and we pop into Loweries for a drink? One drink and that way we can figure out what we are going to tell people. But only if you want to?"

"I'd love to have another drink. Do they have their own brew there, like a microbrewery?" I asked.

"Yes, I'm pretty sure, and Loweries is right by my place. But I'll have to go after that. My friend Clair, from down the hall, is in need of a friend and wants to have a drink with me. She's just getting over a bad relationship and I should really go see her."

"Oh, sure, sure, would you rather just go see her?"

"No, I'd like to spend a little more time with you, in case I never see you again. You know, I might be scaring you off and you could be just putting up a front and then you'll disappear. Some men do that, you know."

"Well, I might be, so maybe we should have two drinks."

"Tell you what, let's have one drink now and we'll have another one real soon."

"It's a date," I said, with a grin and a wink.

We passed the bar and I parked not far from where I'd picked her up that morning. We walked back toward the bar, which didn't look very big from the outside—kind of a small local set-up. There was music on and a half dozen couples at tables. There was another table with a number of girls at it, and three guys, on stools at the bar, watching a game on TV.

"I got this," she said.

"Hey there, Jimmy," she said to the bartender.

"Hi, Maggie, what can I get for you?"

"I'll have a red wine and my friend here will try a Jew's Harp."

"You got it. I'll bring it over."

"Let's sit over here in the corner," she said.

The boys at the bar took a pretty healthy look at her as we walked by.

"Evening, boys," she said on the way by.

They struggled with hello or any kind of response. I thought they might be in a state of shock or about to throw up a little bit as we reached the corner and I asked, "Do you know those guys?"

"No, not really. One of them lives around the corner and I see him here pretty regularly, whether I'm in here or walking by. He seems like a nice guy. And Jimmy's here all the time. He's awesome. He's the main bartender and part owner."

"So do you come here often?" I asked with a grin.

"Well, that's an old one."

Jimmy came by with the drinks and put them on the table.

"We're just having the one," Maggie said.

She handed him a twenty, he made some change, and she gave him a tip.

"How was the day, Jimmy?"

"Ah, pretty good. We had a real busy afternoon and it's just after slowing down. Most of the crowd headed farther downtown. How about you?"

"I had a great day. We were out for a big adventure in the country."

"Ah, that's great. I'll get some details another time. I'm the only one on tonight. Thanks again."

"Cheers," she said, looking at me and raising her glass. "Have you had that before?"

"I'm not sure—what is it? Is this called alcohol?"

"Ha, ha, cute. It's a Jew's Harp."

"No, I haven't, but look at that, one more sort of coincidence for the day. Too much. Oh, it's quite nice. Smooth, but has a little zing of hoppiness. I like it!"

"Yeah, I like it myself. Thanks again for the day."

"Well, thank you, as well. We had quite a day, didn't we?" I said.

"Yeah, we sure did. It was like a workout with all the stuff going on and we didn't even have a meal."

"But we ate all day. I guess it was a lot of bread, but it kept us going and I'm not one bit hungry, are you?"

"No, no, I'm not, but I was wondering if you would like to go out for a meal sometime."

"Well, of course I would, but are you sure? You don't need to think you have to," I said and then paused.

"Have to what?" she asked.

"I don't know."

I was pretty much stuck for words, like the guys at the bar were five minutes earlier, and felt another shoe go in my mouth.

"Well, do you think I just go around kissing every guy I meet at a bar?" she scorned.

"No, no, no, it's not that. I just want you to be sure. You said yourself you were a bit worried, so I'm leaving that door open for you."

"Well, who can be sure after one day together? And that was before you got me drunk with your fancy wine. Now I want to see you again. OK?"

"OK, OK, it's great with me. I'd love to have supper with you, soon. I'm smiling, can you tell?"

"Yes, it looks that way all right."

I tipped my pint toward her and said, "To our first real meal together."

This toasting thing seemed to be normal now.

"So when?" I asked.

"Oh, geez, I don't know. How 'bout we get our story straight for our friends first?"

"Agreed. What if we just say we're friends for now? New friends and we went on a drive today to see if we could find out where your Mam came from. I could say I thought I had relatives from around there as well, so we decided to go together. Most of it's true. But we could fatten the lie a little bit if we need to."

"Fatten the lie?"

"Yeah, you know, thicken the soup, make it more believable."

"OK, I get it. I guess we could just tell people what sort of happened but leave out the wine and kissing for now. Then we came here for a drink tonight and really had a great time. We're just going to take it slow and we're not sure when we'll see each other again."

"Well, we're both busy," I said.

"Busy at what and, ah, how did we meet?" she asked.

"I don't know. Work, I guess and, well, the way I remember it, you came onto me at the bar on Friday night and I couldn't resist. How do you remember it?" I asked with a smile.

"Well, it wasn't quite like that, but we did meet at the bar. Let's just say through some mutual friends. And work. OK, what exactly do you do? We didn't really talk about it all day and I do feel a bit bad about that right now."

I told her not to worry since there had been no shortage of conversation all day. I told her about the engineering firm and a few of the bigger projects I was involved with. I explained some of the invention-type things that were very much in the early stages. I asked her about her own job, which, from what I could remember, was in a lab. I assumed it was at the hospital and she said, "I do work at the hospital and that's my main gig, but I also work at a private clinic. That's where I met Barkley, my old boyfriend. And Zoe, the girl you admire, works there, as well. I think they belong together and I'm pretty sure I'm getting out of there fairly soon. I don't want to say much more about that at this time. It's another story for another time."

"No problem, maybe over supper. Barkley, really? That's his name?"

"Yes, I thought it was cute when I first met him."

"Oh, it's cute, all right. It's cute for a dog," I said, laughing.

"That's funny. So you're an engineer. I guess that's a pretty good job."

"It's good when we're busy and a little tricky when things slow down. It's hopping right now so I guess with my two jobs and your two jobs we are pretty busy.

"This beer is delicious, by the way." I took another drink.

We figured the story was true enough and fit pretty well together. It felt like we were on a speed date and I was starting to feel tired. We were pretty sure we had it covered and we'd just tell people we were friends for now. There was no need to overthink it and we trusted ourselves to let it happen. I needed to ask, so I did.

"Do I need to know anything else about Barkey? Or will we save that for another time?"

"Well, I don't mind telling the whole story, but I'd prefer to have that conversation another time, if that's OK."

"Oh that's fine, for sure. We don't even have to talk about him—I just thought I'd ask. I guess I would like to know that there's nothing still brewing there."

"Well, it's over as far as I'm concerned. I don't know and couldn't care less what he thinks. How's that?"

"Well, let's leave it at that."

"We should save something to talk about over supper," she said.

"Oh, yes, let's go there, another date, right. We're pretty much going steady already."

"It's been one day," she said.

"Yes, but I've been thinking about this, and the way I see it, we've had multiple dates."

"Like?"

"1. When we were driving to the café you kissed me and said you enjoyed our first date.

"2. We had lunch at the café and you said that was a second date.

"3. We went to church and held hands and then we slept together—remember that?"

"What? That's a stretch."

"4. We went out to Mungie and Sadie's and they thought we were a couple.

"5. We went and saw Johnny Cash and his mill, remember that?

"6. We had wine on the beach and you kissed me—often. That was my favourite, by the way.

"7. Here we are now, and seven is, of course, that lucky number."

"Oh, yes, it is. But some of that. Oh…"

"Remember the colours in the rainbow, seven notes in the scale."

"OK, OK, you were paying attention. Full marks."

I drained my drink and noticed her wine was looking pretty thin at the bottom of her glass. I tipped my glass toward her and told her I thought seven was a great number, and it was my favourite after today.

"Lucky number seven," she said. "I better go."

"Can I walk you to your door?"

"Yes, of course. It's just two minutes away."

"Thanks, Jimmy," she said walking past the bar.

"OK, Maggie, see you soon."

We were only on the street for a short time and she said, "This is me here."
I reached out to hug her and she did the same.

"I'll call you," I said.

She leaned back slightly, kissed me lightly, and said, "You better or I'll
have to track you down." She was smiling all the way.

I smiled back and as I turned toward my car I felt a little sting on my
ankle. *What a day, did that really happen?* The street was bright and the cars
went by, but all I could see was her smiling on the shore. What a sight. And I
heard pigeons cooing…Really, more birds.

Tha Mise Ag Iarraidh Pòg

Jig

Paul K. MacNeil

CHAPTER 7
Back to the Grind

When I got home, I sat down and responded to the messages that had piled up throughout the day. I'd turned my ringer off earlier in the morning when I picked Maggie up and I didn't really give it much thought all day. I had no need or interest in talking to anyone else but her and I realized I had it pretty bad. Which was good.

I had a couple of work questions from Mike that he eventually figured out on his own. He said he was working because he had nothing else to do and I knew what that felt like. Then there was Doug, my friend Douglas, who'd sent me five texts and called two times. He said he was going out and he wanted me to call him, so I did.

"Hey, buddy, what's happening?" he asked.

"Not much, I just got home."

You could tell he was at a bar or a party because there was loud music playing in the background, which sounded like a live band.

"Are you coming out? All the guys are here at Tony's and the band is great."

"Tony's, eh? What's it like?"

"Full house, full house, if you know what I mean. Full house."

"No, I don't think so. I had a long day and I'm just going to watch a game on the tube and crash."

"Ah, come on. The night is but a pup. Come on out!"

"No, no, I can't, I'm pretty well gassed. Let's just hook up tomorrow and shoot some pool in the afternoon or whenever you get going. Send me a text or call me—it's up to you."

"Are you sure, 'cause I think it's going to be a hot night on the ol' town tonight. I've just got a feeling, you know?"

"Yeah, yeah, I know, and I'm good. Besides, I've been on your hot nights before and they end with a donair and a Coke at the corner and then a search for a cab ride home. Let's chat tomorrow—and have fun tonight."

I grabbed a beer from the fridge, heated up some leftover lasagna and turned on the game. The hot lasagna and cold beer tasted great and I went back for a second piece. The hot food hit the spot as I stretched out on the couch to watch the game and fall asleep. I woke up at three a.m. and went to bed.

I had no trouble falling back to sleep and slept clear through until ten. That was like two nights in a row that I hardly moved or heard a noise. I wondered how Maggie was and then I thought about Doug. At that moment, I realized Maggie had just bumped him down a notch—sorry about that, friend.

I wanted to write her right away, but also knew I needed to give her some room. I wasn't in the frenzy I was yesterday but was very curious about what was going on in her head. What was she thinking?

I gave some thought to bothering Doug. It would be kind of funny if he'd picked someone up last night. I could torture him like he tortured me yesterday by insisting on coming over and I'd make him squirm. I saved that for later, and if it was a dud of a night, which it probably was, he'd be calling me anytime.

I headed for the coffee pot and started the process to get a little jolt going in my day. As soon as it started to make a little noise and smell, I thought: *I should have made tea.* I had tea bags, I just never thought of it in time. I made some toast and cheese and read the news to find out what was going on in the world.

I didn't catch any news on the radio or read anything yesterday and it didn't matter. But then again, it wasn't like my normal day, that's for sure. I read for a while and realized I hadn't missed a thing. It was pretty much the same old stuff, and I guess that's good because it's usually the bad stuff that comes flying hard and fast, trying to grab the headlines. I enjoyed my coffee, caught up on the scores, and hit the drops to enjoy my thoughts.

I enjoyed my shower and, for a change, the water was hot right from the start. When I finished I opened the window and let a little steam out and heard the birds singing again. They were just cranking it out and if I closed the window I still heard them faintly. I opened it again and the concert was back on.

It reminded me of when I was young at my parents' house. My mother would spoil the birds with her mix of homemade suet balls and mixed seeds in her feeders. Late in the spring when they'd returned from their winter vacation, they would start. If you were up early in the morning before the noise of the day took over, you'd witness their splendour.

In no time at all it went from zero to amazing; it was a wonder any of us could sleep. When we were little, she said it was the birds that woke the rooster. It was a beauty of a day so I opened a few more windows and poured another cup of coffee and just listened to them go.

As time went by I wondered why I hadn't heard from anyone. *They must have all gone to church this morning*, I joked to myself.

It wasn't so bad really. I was alone but I knew I wasn't alone. Friendship was only a moment or a call away, so I decided to dust off the pencil and pad and draw for a little while until this fantasy ended.

With the birds singing love songs in my ears, my hand started moving across the page with her face the only thing in my mind. I had her picture on my phone from yesterday but I didn't need it. Her image was seized inside my head as my fingers released her beauty to the paper below.

I sketched her face in a few minutes. She was so easy to draw with the wavy hair, high cheekbones, a few freckles, and the smile that made her light blue eyes sparkle. Oh my God, one ear was much larger than the other. How come I didn't notice that yesterday?

Wait now, I drew that, it must be me! I fixed it. I could shadow it a bit more but it looked pretty good in its simplest form. She didn't strike me as overly complicated yesterday so I just left it kind of neat.

I decided to draw another one from the side since that was what I saw most of the day, sitting beside me in the car. Slightly tilted toward me, that was it. That look she had when she was telling me about the Vikings and the Scottish lady. She just had a look about her that was really driven, excited, and lusty, really. Perhaps driven is best.

It was like I saw her in that light as well when I thought she just looked great. Oh, hell, she looked great in any light and I don't think she much cared, it was all so natural. She was just so humble about everything and seemed carefree. She was as easy to draw as she was to be around. I wanted to draw another but I needed to stop or she'd think I was obsessed with her if she ever saw my sketch pad. I wouldn't be in any hurry to show her my book although I was feeling pretty good about these sketches.

I decided to draw the two old ladies instead. It wouldn't be as easy, mind you, but I could remember them pretty clearly. Mungie had that strong jawline and high cheekbones. She was much more serious than Sadie so I put a hint of a smile on her. I wanted to get her teeth in there because they just jumped out at me when I first saw her. She was pretty for a woman with so many wrinkles and short, greyish hair. And, oh, yes, the glasses.

Now Sadie was a bit tidier looking with a rounder face and a very kind and humble look about her. I didn't remember her with so many wrinkles but she had the same short hair and glasses. She must have been very attractive when she was younger. I was pretty sure they both had a chain and a crucifix hanging from it. That wasn't too bad for just going from my memory.

The whole time I was drawing I was regretting not taking pictures of them. It would've been nice to have and I knew I had to take a couple the next time.

I poured another cup of coffee as the birds continued to sing and was feeling relaxed. Every now and then I heard a mix of music that seemed to be completely in tune with them. Was it the cars going by or someone in the area? It wasn't something I was used to hearing.

As relaxing as this was, I started thinking of her again and was tempted to text her and wondered why she hadn't texted me. It had been a long time since I enjoyed drawing that much, so I scratched out the man with the mill.

I could've been funny and drawn a picture from a CD, but this guy Malcolm had a different look. It's hard to portray a person's height with just a headshot, but I tried. Jet black hair, strong chin, a narrow set of eyes with wisdom and peace all around him. He had a little twist in his nose and a few wrinkles, but he couldn't be as old as the two other girls.

You know some people have so many features and others are like a loaf of plain white bread. They look good and taste OK, but they just don't add a lot to the meal of life. He had some history, for sure, that guy.

If I was lucky enough to go again I knew I needed to take pictures. Then again, now that I'd been there I could go on my own if I wanted to, but it wouldn't be the same. I could take a hundred people, one at a time, and it wouldn't be the same. I felt like I was finished but how was I going to show her these and not the ones of her and the rest of my work? I suspected she'd want to flip through all of them—or some of them, anyway. I was a bit flustered and decided I'd redo these on a six-page sketch pad and give her the whole thing.

I'd redo one of Maggie so it wouldn't seem too strange and of course the other three. Who else did we meet? There was Joe and Betsey and, wait now, we met Donald and Eveline, as well. So I had to decide. Oh, I had it and it was going to be fun.

I started by re-doing the four sketches I'd done and they turned out pretty well. Then I sketched one from the Barra Strait from long ago and then the fun began.

Donald sprang to life just like the others and I added a few little features. There was a wart here and a wart there. Oh, there now, his right ear was a lot larger than his left and, oh my goodness, there sure was a lot of hair growing in there, just like his nose. I didn't want to make it too crooked and ruin it. There was just a little twist but many, many hairs. Was it one eyebrow or two? I always found one eyebrow looked a little creepy. One it was!

Oh my, oh my, Donald, you sure were losing your hair fast. You hardly had any and you really should get a cut and tidy up what you had left. Ah, geez, Donnie boy, the cold sore on your lip looked really terrible; it was too bad we didn't catch you on a better day.

Well, I found that very funny—I cracked myself up sometimes. Oh, there was just one more thing, your teeth looked very crooked. A bigger smile and, one missing tooth would be enough. There now, Donald Willie, you sure were a slick dude—and that was exactly the way I remembered you.

I considered giving him a little scar but the more I thought about it, he would look a little tough and we couldn't have that. I could always add more, but sometimes less is more, so I left it at that. As my Uncle Buddy used to say, "Who was more fun than people?"

I hoped she'd laugh about Donald. I was sure she'd have something to say about him not looking like that, but it was funny. I sketched them all in the six-pager and I thought about drawing her and Donald together in the end. Or I could have drawn Eveline as a raging beauty as if I thought she was so pretty. I kind of liked that idea better. She would have to…no, I think her and Donald together. She could be the raging beauty and Donald could be the cartoon character. I could do that in the big book and show her sometime down the line.

So I'd say that looked pretty good, with Maggie on the first page. Then Mungie, Sadie, Malcolm, the Barra Strait, and then poor old Donald. That was pretty darn good.

Now, holy shit, the time, ach, why did I care about the time? And at that moment, the phone rang.

It was Dougie.

"What's going on, are you moving?"

"Yup, I've been on the go for a while."

"OK, I'm coming over."

"OK, but I'm not home," I said as I laughed to myself.

"What, where are you?"

I waited a few minutes.

"I'm home, I'm just kidding. Do you want to go knock some balls around?"

"Not sure, I'll be there in twenty minutes or less."

"Oh, how long did you wait for me yesterday?" I asked.

"Very funny, not that long."

"Ha, ha, is there anybody with you now?" I asked.

"No."

"Oh, A hot night, eh!"

"Yeah, well, it cooled off pretty quick after I was talking to you. I'm going to grab a shower and I'll be right there after that."

"OK, see you in a bit."

He was going to be here in twenty minutes and he was just getting in the shower now. That sounded more like thirty or forty minutes to me. It would take him ten minutes to walk here—unless of course, he caught the bus or a cab. I guess it could be twenty minutes if it all fell into place for him, which it usually did. At least it gave me time to finish this.

I spent a bit more time at it and figured it was good enough for today, knowing I could always come back to it later. I hadn't enjoyed drawing that much in a long time and I wondered if I should show Doug. No, not unless…no, no, no, not yet. He didn't even ask, so he had no idea what I was doing. I needed to put it all away and perhaps I'd show him in a few weeks. Maybe it was my little secret.

I grabbed my laptop and decided to search up some history of the Norse and Nordic countries, along with Highlands and islands of Scotland, Ireland, and bits about England. I didn't find very much about the Norwegian people, but there were plenty of sites about Scotland and the history of emigration. The time passed very quickly and Dougie was at my door.

"Hey, there, come on in. Did you cab it?"

"No, no, I saw the bus up the street when I came out my door, so I made a run for it. I planned on walking but it was right there and I thought there was no point passing up my good fortune. Slick as a snot on a rooster's lip."

We talked for a while about the weather and compared it to the day before and Doug talked about a market he saw on his way to my flat. We decided that we'd make that our first stop of the day and I sensed it was going to start and he asked, "What were you doing all morning?"

"I was just looking up some history stuff for work."

"For work? What do you mean?"

"Oh, I was just looking for some old stylings for a project we were working on. It's more architectural stuff and decorative ideas with a bit of history that they're looking for."

"I see, what kind of history?" he asked.

I needed to be very careful not to spill all the beans and I tried to act casual.

"I was just looking at the Nordic countries."

"Did you know Finland was captured by Germany in the Second World War?" he said.

"No, I didn't."

"Well it was complicated but the Finns were back and forth, with and against the British."

"Well, that's not really what I was looking for. It was more like Scotland or Ireland or something like that. Some sort of Celtic design that's not the usual kind of scrolls and knots."

I was making it up as I went along and I knew I'd be like that all day.

"So what did you find?" he asked.

"Well, I'm kind of interested in the boats and sails or oars. I'm not really sure."

"What about the rigging or rope?" he asked.

"Sure, maybe, but that's kind of like knots."

"Yeah, I guess," Doug said. "What about those heads they had on the boats. I'm pretty sure they had figures on the bows of their vessels, whatever they were called. I've seen lots of that on the old British buildings. You know, you've seen it before, images that look like trolls or monsters or gargoyles or something like that."

"Yeah, that's all good but what do you know about their navigation and how they got around years ago? Was it the stars and certain landmarks?"

Doug knew quite a bit about this stuff and I hadn't thought about it until then. I brought him into the loop without him even knowing.

"You know, I covered some of this back in school when I took that nautical course. I never thought I'd ever use it but I've got stuff on this at home. I'll dig it out and see if there's anything interesting. I do remember some kind of tool that they used, like a sunstone or crystal reflective device. In fact, I saw somewhere that they'd found an old one in a shipwreck somewhere recently."

"Well, that's interesting, a navigation tool found in a shipwreck," I said with a chuckle.

"Well, ships get wrecked today and the technology is a lot better."

"True that. Anyway if there's pictures of something it would be really helpful. I'm not sure about crystals, but I don't know anything about it so let's see what you find out."

"Yeah, yeah, I'll get you something for sure. So are we going to navigate our way out of here or what?"

"Yeah, I'm ready to go."

It was during that conversation that I remembered this guy at work that was pretty dialled in to the whole history thing. He was an older guy I didn't know that well but I often heard him talking around the office about his trips to the country. I was sure he'd be able to help Maggie and me on this new adventure we were on.

We walked toward the market and I felt like I'd dodged it pretty well so far. I might even have some information for Maggie on our next date. I realized I was gonna have to play this game all day and perhaps for a few weeks. I needed to be fairly vague and distant about his night to keep him from pinning me on my own.

The market was very nice with quite a few vendors, some great food, and some artsy stuff. I was sure Maggie would like this sort of thing, perhaps I'd take her sometime. I asked one of the vendors how it all started and it was just getting organized. They were planning on having it all summer when the weather was nice. Dougie called me over to look at one of the vendors who was doing sketches for people.

"You could be doing this," said Doug.

"Do you think?"

And I thought of what I did this morning just from my memory.

"Oh for sure, you know you can."

"Yeah, I might be able to, but would you pay for it?" I asked.

"Well we're friends. Of course I'd pay for it. What are friends for?"

The guy was pretty good and I liked his stand and set-up. It looked like something he would have made himself.

"You should talk to him," Doug said.

"No, not now, he's busy and has a bit of a lineup. He doesn't need me asking him a bunch of questions. I'll just grab his card and give him a call to see if he plans on being here every week. At twenty dollars a sketch, I'd say he does pretty well in the run of a day."

I could have made a hundred dollars this morning itself.

"Well, I've seen enough. Do you want to go and shoot some balls or do you have other plans?" I asked.

"No, I'm ready to go."

We headed down the street to The Bank Shot and grabbed our usual table down the back by the window. There were these two British guys working the punching machines that were acting like complete knobs. They were extremely annoying and looked like a father and son team. The older man was very large and could make the bells ring on the machine, but what an ass. The lad, who was smaller and I would guess younger than me, was not near as powerful as his father.

I said quietly to Doug, "Oxygen thieves."

"Yeah, those knuckle draggers give apes a bad name."

"Let's just shoot some balls and ignore them," I said.

I couldn't help myself and had to ask. "How was the night? Do you have any stories or did anything exciting happen?"

"Well, the band was great and we had these girls up dancing and then they just blew us off around eleven. We stayed to the end and went down to the Seahorse after that but it was pretty dead. We had a drink and, you were right, donair, Coke, cab ride home. It was still a lot of fun and a couple of those girls from Friday night were there."

"The girls that were in the corner."

"Yeah, I was chatting with one of them on Friday and she was out last night, as well. Heather is her name."

"Ah, Heather," I said.

"Yes, Heather. She's really nice and just works around the corner from where I live."

"OK, nice, anything else?"

"Well we had a couple of dances and I got a number," he said, smiling. "I didn't push it, but I think she likes me a bit."

"Nice, you got something going on. When are you seeing her?"

"I don't know. We just said we'd get together some time. She had to leave early last night 'cause she was working today."

"Oh, I see. You know her work schedule now—this is moving very quickly, don't you think?"

"Oh yeah, real quick."

"I'm just kidding."

Now if I could just quiz him all day, he wouldn't have time to ask me a question. Better offence than defence.

"So, she left before you were trying to hook up with those other girls, or how did that work?"

"No, no, she came in just before they left and I didn't see her right away. That was a while after I was talking to you and it was pretty busy. I saw her looking at me so I waved and it kind of went from there, you know."

Oh, yeah, I knew.

"Yeah, yeah, I know. Go on."

"So I just went up and asked her to dance. She was a lot of fun and has a really nice look about her, kind of pretty."

"Oh, yeah, she was pretty for sure. I remember her," I said. "She's kind of tall with long brown hair. That's Heather, right?"

"Yes, that's her."

"Heather, that's kind of a Scotchie name, isn't it? What's her last name?"

"I don't know and I'm not sure I asked. She was with that group we were all dancing with on Friday night."

"Yeah, yeah, I was there."

"You were dancing and chatting up that pretty one with the black hair on Friday night."

"Yeah, we seemed to hit it off pretty good. Her name is Maggie."

I needed to change the subject pretty quickly.

"Do you remember that other odd duck that was there on Friday? She looked like she belonged with those two bozos in the corner," I said, looking toward our British boxers.

"Yeah, what was her name?"

"I think it was Zoe. She needed everyone to know who she was."

"Yeah, she was around last night and she's got those goofy rings going through her eye and her nose, and the nice purple hairdo, as well. She must know one of them because she was lingering around their table when we were dancing. I wasn't talking to her, but do you know her?" he asked.

"Oh jeez, no, I just remember her, and she seemed a bit odd. It could have just been her hair and her look but she just seemed to be trying too hard or something on Friday night. I don't get that whole look. It's like: *Look at me. I'm weird. Wanna talk?* I just don't get it."

"No, man, me neither. But to each their own."

"I guess. So are you going to call Heather this week?"

"Yeah, I think so. There's more to life than shooting pool with you on a Sunday afternoon."

"Oh, I see, you're dumping me for her."

"You'll find someone, don't worry."

He didn't have a clue.

"So where were you yesterday?" he asked.

"Me?"

"Yeah, you."

"Oh, I ended up going for a drive in the country."

"Really, all day?" he asked.

"Well, the day kind of slipped by, you know. It's been forever since I was up there and I enjoyed the break from the city."

Here it comes, I thought.

"Who were you with?" he asked.

"Me?"

"Yeah, who were you with?"

"What makes you think I was with somebody?"

Oh, shit. I told him.

"Well, you told me three's an odd number. Remember?"

"Oh, yeah, well."

I was pedalling about as fast as I could.

"Well, I couldn't really tell you everything yesterday because I wasn't sure what was going on but here it is. I went to the country with an old friend."

"Oh, anyone I know?" he asked.

"No, I don't think so. My old friend James Lee was in town. We went to university together a few years back and he's working for an engineering firm that's looking into cleaning up an old mine site."

"What has that got to do with you?" he asked.

"Well, he's trying to recruit me to do some work for them on the project."

"Really?"

"Yeah."

"Really!"

"Yeah, is that so hard to believe?"

"No, it's not hard to believe. I'm just not sure I believe you because you have that look."

"What look?"

"You know, that I'm-not-sure-I-can-believe-you look."

"Gee, Doug, I wouldn't lie to you. You're my friend."

"Yeah, yeah, yeah, I heard that before."

I was kind of smiling and knew I was getting through this and said, "Look, I can't say much more about this, you know. I haven't seen James in years and they're just trying to sort out a bid on this thing, so maybe nothing happens and maybe something does."

"But what if it does?" he asked.

Oh, he believed me. I'd tell him the truth eventually, but for now, why would I ruin a perfectly good lie? It just needed to be fattened up a little bit.

"Well, if it does, I'd work part-time as a contractor. I can't see my company bidding on this job and I'd be free to do my own thing.

"James's company works right across the country so I could just keep working for them. He said there are lots of opportunities if I was interested in moving on with them."

"So was he putting pressure on you?" he asked.

"No, no, no pressure. I told him I'd help them with this bid and go from there. It's still a long shot, but who knows? And speaking of a long shot, long bank with the seven."

Bam, it went straight in. Was that a premonition or what?

"Nice shot," he said.

"Thanks. Back to Heather. Does she have any friends?"

"Well, I don't really know. I don't know if she has any friends that are available."

"Ach, you just sort yourself out first. I'm just sniffing around and I'm not really serious."

We finished the game and played a few more as we enjoyed a couple of pints and some food. We'd been there a few hours and, on our way out, Doug said, "I might give Heather a call and see if she wants to catch a movie. She may be too tired from working but I'll give it a shot anyway."

"Do you want me to go with you?"

"Ah, no, three's an odd number, remember."

"Oh, yeah. I think I'll go home and do some work."

"Work, really?"

"Well, I've kind of got a *nòisean* to do some sketching."

"Really, have you been drawing lately?"

"No, not much, but I have some images in my head that I want to get out and after watching that guy today I think today is as good a day as any. Plus, I need to do something for the rest of the day."

So we headed off together and split to go our separate ways.

When I got home I spent some time touching up the sketches from the morning and decided to do the other ones I'd thought of earlier. I guess it was like anything else, if you're at it all the time it can be mundane and boring. Because I hadn't sketched in so long, it was very enjoyable again.

I still hadn't heard from Maggie so I thought she must have gone to work. I remembered her mentioning that on the way home last night as I fondly remembered the day before.

I returned to my shoreline sketch as it may have looked 1,000 years ago. There were no bridges, docks, tables, roads, tracks, houses, not even a church. I wasn't sure it looked any better back then than it did yesterday as I'd sketched a lot of trees, water, birds, and beaches. Beautiful beaches on both sides of the Barra Strait.

It looked pretty good, so I took a picture of it and sent it to Maggie with a note.

> How was your day?
> Do you recognize this place?
> It makes me feel good!

I wondered for a few minutes if it was too much but it was gone now anyway. She texted me back about an hour later.

> Did you draw that?
> It's beautiful!
> I had a busy day and I'm still at it.
> That made me smile.
> Talk soon.

I could visualize her before I looked at my sketch and then the picture on my phone. I wanted to send it to her but I thought better and left it caged in my device. I'd send it later in the week if things were looking good and I went to bed kind of early. I sent her a text to say good night with a happy face.

Monday morning struck with the usual thud. The sky was grey, the streets were wet, and the wind was showing everyone who was boss. Even the birds were having trouble getting excited for the new week and, just like them, I enjoyed my job but all I could think about was the amazing weekend I'd had.

I thought about Maggie and our adventure and the projects in my head. I thought of my sketches and the nice fat lie I told Dougie. I thought of the forest and the Highlands and the old farms. I thought of the little pond they moved the house across. I thought of the spirits of the lake and I wondered if there was something else I should be doing or some other place I should be. And I thought about Maggie, and I thought about Maggie, and, thankfully, on Wednesday night, she texted me.

> *Hey, you. How is your week going?*
> *Mine has been crazy.*
> *Some friends and I are going for drinks after work on Friday.*
> *We are going to Ginger's, for a change.*
> *Do you want to meet us there?*

I replied.

> *Yes, I do, for sure.*
> *How many friends?*
> *I don't want to get in the way.*

Maggie responded.

> *Well, it's not a date, but it could be if you play your cards right!*

I replied,

> *What time and should I bring friends?*

Maggie responded.

> *Probably around six. And, yes, bring some friends.*
> *It would look sad for you to be there all by yourself.*

I replied,

> *OK. Six it is and I'll drag a couple of guys along.*
> *You know we don't normally go drinking on Friday night but we'll make an exception.*
> *How many girls, do you think?*

Maggie responded,

> *Not sure, probably three or four.*
> *See you then.*

I was dying to ask her how to play it out with her friends or if what we talked about was still the play. Oh, shit, why wouldn't I ask.

> *One more thing.*
> *Do your friends know about our trip to the country?*

Maggie replied,

> *No, they don't.*
> *Let's just go and have some fun.*

I replied,

> *Got it.*
> *Good by me.*
> *I've not said a word.*
> *I look forward to seeing you!*

> *Me too.*

I knew she liked me, I said to myself.

I spent most of Thursday doing all sorts of research on the Nordic explorers and the Highland Scot immigration and I asked Jackie at work if he had some time on Friday to chat. I don't think he really knew who I was but he said he'd find some time, maybe around lunch.

I woke up early after another great sleep and decided to walk to work in the warm Friday air. I did that when I planned on staying downtown for a few drinks after work. The birds, like me, were going full tilt, singing their praises as I thought about talking to Jackie, but more so knowing I'd be seeing Maggie.

The morning took forever to pass before I caught up with Jackie in the lunchroom. Jackie was a big man in his forties with curly brown hair and huge hands. He wore glasses that matched his gentle smile and hearty laugh. His lilted voice reminded me of Donald and he seemed to be toying with me, leading me along, or maybe he was just trying to figure me out.

"So where's all this interest coming from?" he asked.

I didn't want to give away the farm right away, so I said, "I've always been kind of interested in it and then I met someone who's wanted to know more about it for years."

"Oh, *someone*, eh? Anyone I know?"

"I don't think you'd know her, her name is Maggie MacKinnon. She is a lab tech and has a connection to the Iona area."

"Oh, is that right?"

"Yes, her grandmother came from there."

"Oh, is that right? So maybe I know her people. Do you know who they are?"

"Well, I don't really know. I know they were MacKinnons and maybe MacKenzies and there was a Liza *Mhór* who married a Campbell, I think. She also talked about Fiona from Iona but that may have been a nickname."

It wasn't that I didn't want to tell him anything, I just wasn't sure I had it straight myself.

"I'm planning on meeting her at Ginger's after work today. A few guys from here are going to go for a drink or two if you'd like to join us."

I never thought he'd consider going. He was older than us and I knew he had children so he probably wasn't much for going to bars.

"Ginger's, I've been there and it's nice of you to invite me, but I'm not sure I can. What time are you going?"

"Well, we were planning on going straight from work. Probably leave here around five. It's not far from here and I think Maggie will be there around five-thirty or six, whenever she finishes work."

"I'll think about it. I'll have to see how things are on the home front. I'm not sure what the plan is at home but I might be able to go for a couple of pints. I don't get off the main road very often these days so a little dirt road spin might be fun."

"I suppose your family keeps you pretty busy away from here," I said.

"Oh, yes, for sure, but they're getting big and aren't near the work they were when they were really small. You'll see for yourself someday."

"Well I hope so. I'd like to have a family someday, but there's no rush."

He was feeling more comfortable with me and he started filling me in with more information than I could possibly retain. Some of this stuff I had read online last night but he went into great detail about a bunch of stuff that happened in Scotland. Wars they had with the British that led to a lot of families moving not just here but to all sorts of places in Canada.

He knew when the first pioneers settled in Iona, Grand Narrows, and the Washabuck peninsula. He went into great detail about being related to them and having grown up there. How different it was and the way so many people moved away just in his time.

He talked about the Highlands and some of the stories he heard growing up. How that area out back was so populated 100 years ago and how they were the first areas to empty out. It was now the front area around the lake that was being drained by the same plague. You'd think he was reading from a book but he wasn't; it was just falling out of him.

I was feeling quite a bit more comfortable and told him we were at the church in Iona, the café, and out to see Mungie and Sadie and Joe in the Rear. He knew them all and spoke of them in a way that sounded so respectful.

He kept on going and more and more of it sounded familiar to me. I really was picking up a lot of it but at one point I had to stop him and said, "Maggie would love to talk to you—if not today, another time. She will find all this so interesting and it's her that's trying to figure out her family roots but I have to ask you this, as well.

"Do you know anything about the Vikings being here long before the Scottish people came here? Maggie was also talking about a Scottish woman who was brought here by the Vikings way back when and she was supposed to have special powers. I think her name was Boronia."

"Well, I don't know much about that but I've heard some stories about her. And, yes, there were the Old Norse sagas that pretty much prove they were here long before what we know as the European arrival. That was more than 1,000 years ago, maybe even 2,000 or longer. A long time before Columbus crossed the Atlantic, that's for sure."

"Yeah, yeah, that's the other thing I was wondering about."

"Well, I do know there was a small town or encampment in Newfoundland around that time and there is proof that they wintered there and many people believe that they were here in Cape Breton, as well. Which would only make sense to me. If they could travel all the way across the Atlantic Ocean, albeit hopping from one island to the next, why wouldn't they keep going? It only makes sense that they would."

"The more I learn about it the more sense it makes to me," I said. "Now the story Maggie had was that Boronia led some Norse sea captain here to Cape Breton. She was supposed to have special powers and they came here to solve his fertility issue and make peace between their nations."

"This Maggie sounds pretty smart to me. I don't know if anyone knows for sure if all this is true, but I've heard all this before. But the old fables say she saved her people—our people, really—and, yes, she sailed with the Vikings and these powers were from the little people or fairies."

"Is it true you shouldn't call them fairies?" I asked.

"Well, yes, I think that's true. There are many types and they're not all like Peter Pan or Tinkerbell. Although they say they exist, these are more like small people of many different shapes and sizes. But surely we don't need to cover that right now," he said.

"No, I guess not."

"I believe she saved her people. The people from the Highlands and islands of Scotland whose descendants ended up settling here, and who we came from. Many believed she brought the Vikings right up to the end of the Washabuck River and something happened there.

"I also believe in some strange way that's why our people settled in that area and survived in peace."

"Do you believe that?" I asked.

"Yes, I do, and I know that people also say that old Laughlin MacLean had some kind of connection to them all and that's why he lived so long."

"What do you mean, lived so long?"

"Oh, he lived to be 114 and was spry and healthy right up to the end."

"That is very old," I said.

"Well, yes, it is and back in the 1700–1800s, people were lucky to make it to fifty. So there's something a little out of the ordinary there because you don't live to be that old these days without medicine or doctors. With all they went through you'd need some sort of special power to survive that long. That has always puzzled me."

I couldn't remember if we'd asked Mungie or Sadie if they were familiar with the story of Boronia. Then again, we were trying to find out Maggie's history, so it didn't have so much to do with all that. We could always talk about that next time if we needed to.

"Listen, Jack, thanks a lot. This is all great stuff."

"No problem. Glad to help, if I did."

"Oh, you did for sure and think about after work—I think you'd like Maggie."

"If not today another time," he said.

"I'm sure we'll go again if today doesn't work out."

"I'd love to go, but if I don't, I want you to find out who she is and who her relatives are. I might be able to answer a few questions for her."

"OK, I'll see what she says, and can I get your cell number?"

He spit out a number and I texted him to make the connection.

> *Hey, Jackie, it's Patrick.*

> *Got it,* he replied.

Well, if the morning took a long time to go by, the afternoon was worse. It was like waiting for the last day of school when you were a wee lad. It was painful and my head was nowhere near work. I thought about leaving a couple of times to just go for a beer and get out of the office.

I thought about not going with everyone from work and just meeting Maggie by herself and then I realized she had asked me to join her, so I couldn't do that. The four hours seemed like four days but it finally passed and I was off to Ginger's. Two of my work friends were thirsty like me and Dougie was meeting us there around six.

Then Jackie wrote:

> *I've got time for a beer.*
> *Are you still going?*

I replied,

> *Yes, we were just about to leave.*
> *I'll wait for you out front.*

Jackie replied,

> *See you shortly.*

Marching Orders

Strathspey

Paul K. MacNeil

CHAPTER 8
Ginger's

I was standing on the sidewalk with my work buddies, Joey and Mike and Jesus—the next thing this honking big black Chevy king cab truck swung around the corner and pulled up right beside us. It was Jackie.

"Jump in, boys, I'll give you a lift."

I was shocked as I jumped in the front with the guys in the back. The truck was spotless and beautiful and there was no sign of car seats.

"I wasn't sure if you were coming," I said.

"Well, I wasn't either but I have an hour or so before the warden starts looking for me," he said with a smile. "I used to go to Ginger's years ago so I told Donna about your invite and she said I should go for it. The kids go pretty hard all week but Friday is usually kind of quiet. Two of them are staying with friends tonight so there's just one at home. Donna's working on some summer work plans with her so they don't really need me around."

"Ah, this is great. Maggie will be thrilled."

The boys in the back chimed in together: "Who's Maggie?"

Everyone looked at me and I knew I had to try and play it cool here.

"Maggie's people come from the same place that Jackie comes from. Up the country, as they say. You guys might remember her from last weekend at Rosie's. She's a nice-looking girl, kind of tall with black wavy hair."

"You were talking to her for quite a while," Joey said.

"Yeah, that's her."

I needed to fatten this thing up and stay beneath the radar.

"Yeah I've seen her around a few times and we just hit it off a bit the other night. She's really nice and her people come from up that way so she's trying to connect some of the dots. Jackie here is a bit of an expert so I asked him to meet her and help her out if he could."

"Well, I don't think of myself as much of an expert, but I might be able to help."

"Yeah, well, you know a hell of a lot more than those two so that makes you an expert."

"Well, we didn't know there was an entrance exam to Ginger's," Mike said.

We all laughed and Jackie asked the guys a few questions as it turned out he had worked with their fathers years ago when he first started. They were the older guys and he was the young pup.

They carried on making connections for a while and I sent Maggie a quick note:

> There's an older guy from work coming with us that I think
> you'll enjoy.
> He's from Iona and he has a pile of history.
> Can you come chat with us when you get to Ginger's?
> He can't stay all night.

Maggie responded right away:

> For sure.
> We're just leaving now.

I responded:

> We just got here.

Jackie parked the truck and we fell out and marched into Ginger's. A steady flow of people came in and filled the place up pretty quick. There was a ball game on the big screens with some easy kind of folk music playing as we grabbed a table near the back and off to the side.

I liked these types of places, with tall tables and stools. People could stand and talk to you and you could stay seated. It was very comfortable, not too fancy, and it seemed as though the place was from two different eras. The part down the back looked older, with hand-hewed beams on the ceiling and around the walls. The walls were covered with old paintings and artifacts. I'd say they made a nice effort with the new part where they copied some of the older features but it was just a little too shiny. Regardless, I was digging the place and it could only get better.

"What would you like, Jackie?" I asked.

"I'll have a Kitchen Party if they have it."

"I think they do," I said as I scanned the bar taps. "Will you guys have your usual?" I asked the boys.

There were smiles and nods all around. I stepped up to the bar and caught the barman and ordered our drinks.

He started pouring and took a copy of my credit card as I was sure we'd be staying for a while. I returned to the table, glasses were clinking, and we were all thankful the week was over and the best part of Friday was on its way.

Jackie said, "I used to come here years ago. It must be ten years since I was here and it was a pretty happening place back then. Of course, it was just the old part and it was a lot smaller."

"I didn't know there was an old part, it's always been like this since I've been coming here," Joey said.

"It's just over there on the other side of the bar, where it ends there. Can you see the change in the structure where the old beams are and the new-looking walls? And of course, none of this was here, where we're sitting. I tell you we used to be jammed in here like peanut butter in a jar."

"I see it now," Joey said.

"Well, they did a pretty good job of matching it up but you can see it if you look for it," Jackie said.

"When did they add the piece on?" I asked.

"Oh, jeez, I'm not sure, It must be five years ago at least and probably closer to ten. I know we came here when Mel moved away. Do any of you guys remember him?"

Nobody knew him.

"We used to call him Mel Tormé, the Velvet Fog. He was a good guy who was always singing; hence, the name. You know he was in a good mood all the time and very, very smart. He was one of those guys we really missed when he left. A guy we always went to when we were stuck on something and he'd always help you out. Except for this one guy, Sid. Yeah, Sid Robertson rubbed him the wrong way a second time and that was it for Sid. 'Don't even ask,' he'd say. Any of you guys remember Sid?"

None of us knew him either.

"Sid used to get the new guys to go ask Mel for help for him. But old Mel could smell them out pretty quick. He'd fire so many questions at them their heads would be spinning and they wouldn't have any answers. He'd say, 'Tell Sid to do his own work and if he can't handle it, tell him there are plenty of opportunities in the food and beverage industry.' That part used to crack me up.

"He'd say the same thing to the young guys if they were complaining, you know about having to do some task they felt was below them. You know there are plenty of opportunities in the food and beverage industry," he said, chuckling.

"The point is, guys, it's a whole lot easier to get work done when you work together. You need to do your own work and if people see you trying they'll help you out."

The boys were getting to know Jackie a lot better and I was doing my best to fill in some lines, act interested, and be cool. I was so unsure of how it would all play out or how to react when she got there. I was bouncing like a rubber ball on the inside as I watched the door, longing to see Maggie. It was like our first date, or worse, it might have been our tenth, but I was as nervous as a teenager on his first date and then she texted.

> We're not going to Ginger's.
> Sally wants to go to Jenny's Tavern instead…SORRY.

What?

> What about Jackie??

But, really, what about me?

She sent back a smiley face and I saw her and some friends coming around the corner and they entered Ginger's bar. She got me again.

She was there with four other girls and I watched her scan the bar. I assumed she was looking for me but I didn't want to jump out of my seat flailing my arms around. They headed to the other side of the bar to a vacant table and when she turned back to the room she saw me and kind of pointed, waved, and smiled as if to say hi and I got you again.

I texted her.

You are nasty!

I saw her smiling.

She sent back sad eyes and said she'd come over shortly once they were settled and had gotten a drink.

No rush, we're good, I replied.

I kept chatting with the boys and tried to act all normal as I checked on her steadily. It looked like she was doing the same to me but I couldn't be sure. The boys pounded back the first pint and Joey headed to the bar to reload. I figured that was as good a time as any to tell them that Maggie had entered the building and would be over in a few minutes.

"Who is Maggie?" Mike asked.

"She was the girl I was telling you about on the way over."

"Yeah, yeah, I know. She was looking for info that Jackie has but what I want to know is why doesn't she want info that I have, and who is she, really?"

"Oh, it's a long story."

"Well, I have all night," Mike said.

"You'll get to meet her," I said. "She's over there on the other side of the bar sitting with four other girls. You can see her, she's facing this way with the dark hair and the glowing eyes."

"Yeah, I see her," Jackie said.

"Where is she?" Mike asked.

Joey was back with drinks and he and Mike were like a couple of old hens.

"Where is she, where is she? I don't see her."

Their heads were spinning in all directions as if it was Groundhog Day in Pennsylvania.

"Oh, for Pete's sake."

Maggie saw them gawking and gave them a wave.

They waved back. Oh, God, I needed support.

She pushed her chair back and leaned into her table for a few seconds and her friends turned and looked toward us as she walked our way.

The boys turned around and said, "Jesus, Paddy boy, she's a beauty. What else are you keeping from us?"

"Yeah, I know. Try and control yourselves, for fuck's sake, and let Jackie do the talking. Don't be drooling all over her."

"Hey there, Maggie." I stood up and gave her a hug and a smile, but no kiss.

"Hello, Patrick."

"Here, take my seat. This is Jackie, Joey, and Mike. Don't pay any attention to these two." I pointed to Joey and Mike. "Guys, this is Maggie." Handshakes and smiles made their way around.

"Nice to meet you guys."

Oh, the sound of her voice was sweet music to my ears. I hadn't noticed her light brogue, which sounded a bit like Jackie's. And with that, support arrived, as he jumped right in.

"So, Paddy said you have a connection to the Iona area. Is there anything I can help you with?"

Maggie started with the connection with Mungie and Sadie and meeting them last weekend. I heard her move on to Liza *Mhòr* and then Joey started talking to me so I kind of drifted out of that conversation and slid into one with him and Mike. I figured the best thing for me to do was to keep them away from Maggie and Jackie for as long as possible so they could chat.

I was listening to them with one ear and talking to the boys with the other. It was a fairly difficult task but something needed to be done and a distraction would be great.

I heard them talking about the Highland Road, St Columba Church, the Glen Road, the Rear, Malcolm on the hill, Big Neil, and some other characters. *Peadair Custie* and *Pòl Thòmhais* and the beat went on. Jackie was right back in his element firing off names and places and I thought Maggie's head might spin off her shoulders but she was clearly enjoying his company.

Joey and Mike looked over and saw the pool table was free and decided to have a game, which was exactly what I needed. They asked me to play but I told them I'd play the winner.

I was sitting there thinking this couldn't be going any better than it was. I didn't know how long it would last but I was thankful for what I had. Jackie seemed to be slowing things down a bit while Maggie was once again taking notes and he gave me the eye.

"I heard you were up to Highland Hill and talked to Maxie," he said.

"Yes, I did. He was trying to sell me his mill."

"It's a nice mill," Jackie said.

"Yes, it looked that way."

Jackie looked at me with a twisted smirk while his massive hand scratched both sides of his face and chin. I could tell from the look in his eye he had something he wanted to say but he held it in. Maggie spoke up in a confirming sort of way.

"Yeah, so Big Neil's is up past Maxie's, he mentioned that, and there's an old road that goes back out to MacKinnon's Harbour one way, and where was the other place? Oh, you said Washabuck, right."

"Yes, it goes back to St. Columba Mountain and that can get you to Washabuck. I think that was the old camp road, but I'll have to double-check that. I don't know if you can travel on it now, but I'll ask.

"I still have a lot of connections around Iona. My parents are there and some cousins and their families. You know, they're on the four-wheelers all the time and they go out that way by my cousin's place in MacKinnon's Harbour. It's been a few years since I've gone with them through there. It's a great trip through Cain's Mountain into Washabuck and you'll come out near the falls."

"What do you mean, the falls?" said Maggie.

"Oh, the Washabuck Falls, waterfalls. It's a pretty cool spot and they're fairly impressive on a day after a big rain."

"How big are they?" Maggie asked.

"Oh, they must be sixty feet high, maybe more, and there is a large pool at the bottom."

"I bet they're something," she said.

"Well it's not Niagara or anything like that but for the middle of nowhere, they're pretty special. We used to swim there long ago, in the pool, that is. Pretty cold, as I remember."

"Are they hard to get to?" she asked.

"No, no, not at all. You can drive there in a car and just walk down the hill, maybe a three-minute walk from the road."

"I'd love to see them."

"Well, we should make that happen. I'll check with my cousins there in Iona and see if they can round up a few bikes and take you for a little small-town tour."

"Oh, my, I don't want you to go to any trouble."

"It's no trouble, I'll just ask and see what's on the go. The worst they can say is no, right? You know I'd love to get back out there myself and see it all again. It's been a few years since I was on a little run like that so you'd be doing it for me, really," he said, smiling. "You see, now you have to go, for me."

"Well, it sure sounds like a great way to spend the day," she said.

"Oh, it's a blast. We can take a few wobbly pops and a bite to eat and make the day of it. Some of the young guys like the hippie hay and that's OK with me, too. You just need to keep it all in check."

"Hippie hay, what's that?"

"You know, Mary Jane, a cup of tea, mental floss, *Smùid a mo rùin*," he said.

"OK, OK, hippie hay. Good one," she said with a nodding smirk.

"Yeah, it might work out and it might not. But right now you have just about nothing, would that be accurate?"

"Well, I wouldn't say that, but this is a huge upgrade, that's for sure."

"OK, great, but I have one condition before I ask anybody anything."

"What's that?"

"Patrick here has to come along, as well," he said, winking and smiling at me.

She almost spit out her beer and said, "If he *has to*, I guess. Are you sure? I'm not sure he wants to go."

"I'm right here," I said in a confused manner.

Jackie plowed on.

"I was telling Paddy here about Laughlin MacLean," he said, and he looked at me. "Did you tell her?" he asked.

"No, no, I haven't talked to her since we spoke earlier."

"Who is Laughlin MacLean?" Maggie asked.

"Well, I was telling Patrick about him earlier today. He was one of the pioneer settlers in the Washabuck area and he lived to be 114 years old. There's an old pioneer graveyard not that far from the falls and that's where he is buried."

"Wow, that's pretty old," Maggie said. "But I'm not seeing the connection here at all."

"Oh, well, now, this was around 200 years ago when he died, and Patrick had brought up the connection to the Vikings and their visits here over 1,000 years ago. Some people believe it was the Washabuck River the Vikings sailed up to and some magic powers had been received and left there, and that's why he lived so long. There's more than one tale of mystical and magical powers that happened in that area over the years."

"Well, we were kind of told to stay away from there on our little trip," Maggie said.

"Oh, it's not dangerous. They probably didn't want you to get lost. It's plenty safe, but I've always felt like there was something special and spiritual about that place."

"Well, now I really want to see it," she said.

"Yeah, you need to see it for yourself. You'll want to hear it, smell it, feel it, and I'm already curious what you'll think of it.

"I guess you heard of the fairy hills and the likes of that, have you?" he asked.

"Well, yes and no. Mam, that's what I called my grandmother, who is Liza *Mhór*, said she used to be able to see them. Now, I have no way of knowing if it's true, but then again, why would she make it up? And Sadie said we shouldn't call them fairies but little people. Even though I've never seen them myself, I believe in them."

"Me, too. I've never seen them either, but I believe they're out there and Sadie would know what to call them—so little people it is."

"Now there are many stories of them being all around that area and a number of magical things have happened around the falls. Young people have been lured away from their groups only to return safely some time later. There was a young lad just a few years ago that went missing."

"Oh, no," said Maggie.

"Oh, it ended OK. You see, this young guy, about thirteen or fourteen, was with some family and friends and the next thing he was gone. Right out of the blue, someone turned to say something and he was gone."

"What happened?" asked Maggie.

"Well, there was quite a panic and cell phones are pretty sketchy in that area. After the word got around, they found him a couple of hours later just walking on the road. Not on the road where they parked the car but one that was farther down the brook that flows from the falls."

"And what did he say happened to him?" she asked.

"He couldn't tell them what happened but he did say he was not hurt or scared. He just showed up on the road."

"Oh, my. They were really lucky."

"Yes, they were. Everyone involved was grateful, of course, but they felt like something mysterious had happened. And I know, I heard tell of a similar incident about ten years before that around the same time of year, as well. And there were other things over the years, just in my time alone, that you'd say were a bit out of the ordinary."

"And what time of year did these events happen?" she asked.

"Well, I know the last one was in the fall of the year—late fall, around the end of October. There was a hurricane and a lot of rain so the falls were just bursting. I liked to go myself after a big rain 'cause it made for a better experience, of course."

"I see, I get the part about the big rains, but is this the same place as the Highlands they were talking about?"

"Well, it would depend on who you ask. Some people say the Highlands are only in Inverness County, while others say just look at the maps and tell me what it looks like. It's pretty much the same piece of rock to me, so I say it is. Why do you ask?"

"Well, Donald said to stay away from there and I was just making sure it was the same general area. He did say not to go up there on our own."

"Who was that?" he asked. "Donald the dog?"

"Well I'm not sure about the nickname, but it was Donald Willie, at least that's what Mungie called him and she may have called him Donald Willie and his dog. We met him at the café there near the docks. He was a MacRae, I think. Do you remember, Patrick?" she asked.

"No, I can't remember, really. He didn't have much to say to me; he was far chattier with you, I'd say."

Jackie gave me a concerning look and asked, "Did this guy think he was pretty slick?"

"Well, Maggie, what did you think of Donald?" I asked.

She smiled and said, "He was very helpful and not the least bit shy at all. And, yes, he seemed to be very confident."

"Oh, that must be Donald the dog. They sometimes call him DD or Double D. Do you know if he is married?"

"No, he's not," Maggie said. "Evelyn told me that."

"Oh, then it must be Donald Willie, for sure. They did call him Donald Willie and his dog because he never married and he drove around with his dog all the time. Hence, the name, but then the dog died and it became more apparent that he was always flirting with women in the area, so it switched to Donald the dog."

We all laughed.

"That doesn't happen overnight," Jackie said. "That alone took twenty years, but he's a good man just the same, and knows the genealogy of the area very well."

"Well, you think you know someone," I said, jokingly.

Jackie looked puzzled and Maggie grinned. Mike called over and asked me if I wanted to play, but I didn't want to leave the table. Some of this was new information for me so I decided to stay. I told them to play again, and I'd play the winner for sure.

Mike cutely nodded, winked, and gave me the thumbs up. He didn't have to say anything but I had a pretty good idea of what he was thinking and I jumped back into our conversation.

"What else, Jackie? What else do you know about the fairies—or little people, I mean? Is there anything else that comes to mind?"

"Oh, well, there's lots to say about it, for sure, and, like I was telling you before, without making too much of it all, you'll need to go there and see it for yourselves. I've been there many, many times and I love it there, but I don't get any wild emotions when I go there. But you know there are people that do.

"There are so many stories of second sight and the like that some people have and others never experience. You know what second sight is, don't you?"

"Yes, Mam mentioned it to me, but Sadie told us a lot about it when we were there. And the more I've thought about it, I think Mam said she had them a few times over the years and her father had them, as well."

"What about you?" he asked.

"Well, I don't think I have," she said.

"What about you, Patrick—did anything like that ever happen to you?"

"No, no, not that I can recall."

"Well, you see, that's just the way it is so I'll try to find someone around there that has experienced it and you can talk to them. You know, there's an old guy that lives not far from the falls who could help, and he'd certainly know more about it than I do. You know people don't just make these things up. Now, they may enhance the story, but it all starts with something out of the ordinary."

"This is so exciting," Maggie said.

"Oh, my, some of this stuff will make you shiver," he said. "You know there was so much of this stuff years ago. It's a shame the way it's disappearing."

"Why is that?" she asked.

"Well, there's a couple of reasons, but mostly because people used to walk or be on a horse and wagon, they'd be travelling at night and of course back then there were no street lights. So it would be as dark as a crow's pocket and they'd hear noises and see things in their travels.

"The other side of this is that it would be entertainment. There were no televisions or radios and there was no power until the late 1940s, so that's how people passed the time. It was the original horror film with a cast of locals."

"I'm getting shivers just thinking about it," Maggie said.

"Well, I'm getting shivers, too, but it's because I have to go to the bathroom. The beer I drank is getting scared of the darkness and needs to see the light of day—excuse me for a few minutes."

Jackie went to the john and Maggie reached over and touched my hand and gave it a squeeze.

"Thank you so much."

"For what?"

"For lining this up with Jackie—he's awesome. He's just like the folks we met last weekend, so full of knowledge."

"Well, it's just another one of those things that worked out for us. I didn't really know him very well before today but I reached out to him and we talked at lunchtime. I couldn't believe all the stuff he knew, so I thought you should meet him and he was able to come for a drink. So here we are."

"Oh my God, he's a treat. Do you think he meant it about the small-town tour?"

"Oh, I think so. I don't think he would have said it if he didn't mean it."

"Well, I really want to go back there. Do you want to go back there again with me?" she asked, smiling.

"Well, Miss Maggie MacKinnon, are you asking me out on a date?" I said rather coyly.

"Well, yes, I suppose I am."

"Well, then, I suppose I would. In fact, I would love to go back and explore the Highlands with you."

"Oh, it sounds so romantic when you say it like that."

"And when will this date be taking place?" I asked.

"I don't really know. You see, I'm working on a few logistics right now so you'll have to give me a bit more time."

"Oh, you are, eh?"

The bike trip sounded like a blast and we talked about offering to rent them or something like that. I suggested we just leave it with him and see what happened over the weekend. I was pretty sure he'd sort something out like the fresh new round that was being poured by our tender.

"I'm really excited about it," she said.

"Well, I like it when you are excited. I don't know if it's me or that place, but I sure like what it does to you."

"It might be a bit of both, but it's probably the place."

Jackie dropped a beer in front of me and Maggie and one for himself and we offered our thanks. He headed back to the bar for two more and made for the pool table and gave them to Mike and Joey. He spent a few minutes at the pool table before returning to join us. Just then we heard a small calamity there and Joey yelled over.

"Come on, Pat, you're up!"

Mike was laying down a few curse words and shaking his head. It looked like he scratched on the eight and everyone hates losing like that. I didn't really want to trade tables, but I also thought I should let Jackie and Maggie have some time on their own. They seemed completely comfortable with each other and I wanted to give them some space.

I asked them if they minded and neither one seemed to care so I went to the table and racked them up. Now, I don't normally like to lose, but right then I didn't really care because I could always play later. I was chatting with Joey as Mike went back to the table with Jackie and Maggie. He didn't seem to be all that engaged and, thankfully, one of his buddies came in and they moved over to chat by the bar.

Joey and I were struggling with making shots and I couldn't wait for the game to be over. I kept my eye on the two at the table. They were chatting away, completely content and comfortable with each other.

One of Maggie's friends came over and sat with them for a few minutes and I saw Maggie say *ten minutes*. Joey wasn't very good at pool and I pretty much threw the game so he'd win. It seemed to take forever but mercifully it ended and I returned to join the other table.

Mike racked them up again and came over to our table and asked, "Are you having another drink?"

"Well, I am," I said.

"Jackie said no, another time. I have to get going as soon as I finish this one, which won't be long."

"It's at the panic line, Jackie," I said.

"No, thanks. That's it for me. Another time, Mike."

"How about you, Maggie, can I buy you a drink?" Mike asked.

"Well, sure you can, but I have to rejoin my friends very shortly."

"No worries."

He headed for the bar and by the time he returned, Jackie was on his feet saying his goodbyes and thank yous.

"It was really nice to meet you, Maggie," he said. "And I'm so glad I came out for a beer with you all. Thanks for asking me, Patrick."

Maggie stood up and gave him a hug and thanked him again for all his help.

"Well, I enjoyed myself very much, so I need to thank you for the company. I hope to see you again real soon."

He turned toward me and said, "That is a real fine woman, young man, I hope you know that."

"Yeah, she's awesome."

"So, I'll check on the bikes over the weekend and let you know next week. This was fun, but I got to run."

He waved to the guys at the pool table and headed out the door. "See you Monday."

"Well, he's a gem," Maggie said.

"Yeah, he's a pretty nice guy. I should have gotten to know him better at work but we haven't really been on any projects together. We see each other around the office and everyone speaks very highly of him."

"Well, he spoke highly of you when you weren't here."

"Oh, did he now? And just what did he say?"

"Oh, I'd say he was being very kind and honest. He said you had a very bright future and people enjoyed working with you. You were a real up-and-comer, I think is how he put it."

"Well, that's pretty nice of him. And how did all of this come up, my little detective friend?"

"Oh, it just sort of happened naturally enough. You know I can't really say much more about it."

"Why is that?" I asked.

"Well, I wouldn't want to betray his trust since we are becoming such good friends."

She was smiling again and I said, "I think you were snooping on me and trying to find out some inside information about my other life."

"Well, you'll never know. Anyway, how are you? Did you have a nice week?"

"Yes, I did, actually, but today was the best part. It's really nice to see you again."

"I bet it is," she said, smiling. "Just kidding, it's really nice to see you, as well."

"What about you?" I asked.

"All in all, it was really good. It was a bit of a grind to start but today is the best part for sure. You know, that was another huge help talking to Jackie. My head is still spinning a bit but he gave me a lot more to go on and cleared some things up."

"Yeah, I know what you mean. I'm pretty much the same, but it's not from Jackie."

"Did you have too much to drink?" she jokingly asked.

"No, it's not the drink. I feel like I have 500 questions for you and twenty-eight seconds to ask them."

"Oh, my, you have yourself tied in a little knot and you are struggling to get free."

"Well, I'm not trying to get free."

"Let me help since I have lots of questions myself. So how about I ask you one question with a follow-up and if that question is on your list then we both answer that question for now."

"For now," I said.

"OK, here's my question. Are you ready?"

"Yes."

"Are you glad to see me and, if so, why?" she asked.

"OK, that's on my list," I said.

"And the answer is?" she asked.

"I'm really glad to see you and I want to spend time with you," I said.

"That's a great answer. And my answer is, I am really glad to see you and want to spend as much time as I can with you this weekend."

"Well, that's a great answer, as well," I said.

She reached for my hand and held it gently and then gave it a little squeeze.

"OK, that makes me happy. But I need to get back to my friends over there. A few of them have to go home, as well, kind of like Jackie, and when they do, you and I can spend the rest of the evening together. How does that sound?"

"That sounds great and I can see your friends are looking for you over there, so you should go."

She got up to leave and said, "Hang on to that pool table so I can kick your butt later on. We'll see how happy you are to see me then."

"You're on,"

"Oh, you're on, eh—that's the best you got?"

"I'll think of something smarter later."

I watched her walk away and couldn't keep from staring at the shape of her. I thought her back might be better than her front and her front was pretty darn fine.

There was a chance I had been busted as I saw her friends sounding off to her a little bit and they were giving me a second look. They looked to be giving Maggie the gears and laughing while one of them turned her head around completely. I wondered if I should tip my glass to them or just act like it was nothing out of the ordinary. I gave them a little smile and turned away.

I thought I was about to have a little panic attack but I started feeling much better. Thank God it passed and then I felt another one coming. Dougie was at the door.

"Hey, buddy, how's it going?" I asked.

"Great. There's quite a crowd in, and it's early."

"Yeah, for sure. They've been coming in steadily since we got here."

"What time did you get here?"

"We got here around five-thirty. Jackie just left but Joey and Mike are playing pool with one of their buddies, I didn't catch his name."

"Nice, I need a beer. Who's Jackie?"

We walked toward the bar and I explained to him who he was and I wanted to spill my guts but I held it in.

Part of me was dying to tell Doug, Mike, Joey, and even their friend, who I didn't even know, the whole story. Well most of me was, but I needed to keep it as low key and cool as possible. You know, promise low and deliver high.

"Would I know this Jackie guy?"

"I don't think so, 'cause I didn't really know him that well, but he's a really great guy. He's mid-forties with a family at home and he had to leave because they had stuff on tonight. He's pretty smart and a really good guy to learn from. How was your day?" I asked.

"Oh, it was fine, but I was cracking to get here all afternoon."

"Yeah, I know what you mean, I was the same way. Do you want to have a game? We could partner up if you want."

"Yeah, sure, but you're sitting at a good table here. Do you want to give that up?"

"Oh, shit, I never thought of that."

I was pretty content to keep an eye on Maggie and her friends from there so I asked him to check in by the pool table. He went in and said hello and returned a few minutes later. There was nothing free but the guys told him they'd grab one if it opened up.

Time went by and we took turns guarding our seats and playing pool. After an hour or so, a few of Maggie's friends left and a small table became available near the pool table. I caught Maggie's eye and gave her a little point toward the pool room and she gave me a wave and we went in.

There weren't enough stools for all of us, but at least we had a table to huddle around and that was perfect. I was just as happy to stand and keep an eye on the other side of the bar anyway.

We started up a game of partners and, halfway through, Mike and Joey started talking about going to Tony's Bar. Their buddy was driving the plan because he wanted to hook up with some other friends.

I was dragging my feet on the whole idea with every intention of letting them leave right away. I was thinking this might work out pretty well for me. But what was Doug going to do? I realized I needed to let a little air out of the balloon.

"What do you want to do, Doug?" I asked.

"Hey, buddy, I'm happy here and I can slide down to another joint, no difference to me. What about you?"

"Well, I need to spend some time with that girl over there, so I'm not going anywhere."

"Which one, where?"

"Across the bar, pretty looking with a few freckles and long, dark hair sitting by the girl with the blondish hair, do you see her?"

"I see her but that's not happening," he said.

"Yeah, it is. I was talking to her earlier and we should be having a drink and maybe a game anytime now."

He started coughing and struggled to hold back his beer.

"So, listen, I'm not going to the other bar unless I'm following her later."

"You're not serious?"

"Oh, yes, I am. So you can hang with me but I may have to ditch you or, she has a friend with her that I know nothing about so you may be able to entertain yourselves. And that, my friend, might work out nicely for everyone."

"You're serious," he said, with a slow, shocked look on his face.

"Oh, very much, so listen up. I'm going to go see what she wants to do so take my shot if it comes up and take some notes and see how it's done."

I gave him a shot on the shoulder, winked, and walked away feeling like I owned the place. I don't think I'd ever done that in my life, but it felt great. I wanted to turn and see the look on his face but I wanted to see Maggie's more.

I saw her looking at me as I approached her table and she got up and gave me a big hug. Quite a different greeting than the one earlier but it was perfectly comfortable now.

"Hello there, handsome," she said, as she held me and leaned back.

"Patrick, this is Clair. Clair, this is Patrick."

There were handshakes and salutations both ways.

"Can you join us?" she asked.

"Well, just for a minute, for now," I said as I sat down. "We were just trying to figure out the next move, and I'm in a game right now, so, without being rude, do you want to join us for pool or can Doug and I join you here? I'm pretty sure the other three guys are heading to Tony's Bar."

"Well, I could do either. What about you, Clair?"

"I'm not very good at playing pool but I'll give it a try if you can put up with me."

"OK, give us a minute or two and we'll come over," Maggie said.

"OK, great. Nice to meet you, Clair."

"You, as well," she said with an alluring smile.

I headed back to the pool table and Dougie was looking at me taking air notes and when I got to him he jokingly applauded and said, "Very impressive, my friend. Very impressive."

"You liked that, did you?"

"Yes, yes, I did!"

Doug and I won the game and the other guys decided to head over to Tony's Bar and we told them we may catch up with them later on. Doug told me if the gathering with Clair and Maggie didn't work out for him, he'd head to Tony's on his own or go home.

When the guys left we started another game and, as I watched Doug shoot with my back to the rest of the bar, I felt a quick tight pinch on my ass cheek. I jumped and turned around quite startled and who was smiling like the cat that ate the canary but Miss Maggie, in full devilish mode.

"Come here often?" she asked.

"I'm going to from now on. You surprised me."

"Well, I can't take it back now."

"I don't want you to."

"It's your shot," Doug said.

"Hey, Maggie, this is my friend Doug. Where did Clair go?" I asked.

"We might have met last week," she said. "Clair is in the bathroom, she'll be right out, I think."

I checked out the table to see what shot I liked but I was really stalling trying to figure out who Clair was and how would I get rid of her and Doug later on. Jesus, that sounded like I was plotting some sort of crime. I was sure I'd heard Maggie mention her before, but which one was she? I hoped she was single so she and Dougie could hit it off and we'd live happily ever after. OK, that was a stretch, but I just hoped something easy happened.

I made a few shots as Clair joined them and introductions were made. Our game continued back and forth and Doug came out with the win, as usual. He was always better at this game than me, but I had the girl for now as we lined up a doubles game.

It was Maggie and Patrick vs. Clair and Doug. Clair said many times that she wasn't good to play but she'd definitely handled a stick before and Doug was doing a great job of helping and coaching.

One of the things I liked most about playing pool, and especially with a partner, is that you get to hang together and talk while the other team is shooting. Now if you just wanted to sink all the balls right away this would probably make you think about doing something very bizarre. But if you were standing beside a beautiful woman who just pinched your ass cheek and you were tripping over things to talk about, you would be feeling pretty good about life. Now bring on a few beers, Friday night in a cool bar, and you'd be like a rooster taking credit for the sunrise.

Dougie and Clair seemed to be hitting it off pretty well and Maggie and I were catching up on the past week. I got the low down on Clair and Maggie got the lowdown on Doug and I was wondering how long before Doug got the low down on me and Maggie. I had this feeling that Clair already knew about me just by the way she was giving us space. Maggie told me that Clair was the girl that lived next door to her and who she went to see after our trip last weekend. Maggie had told Clair about the great day she had with me and Clair was excited for her.

So, as all of that was going on. Doug was looking for whatever information I could get from Maggie about Clair and, you see, as they say in the country, Maggie was looking for whatever information I could give her about Doug for Clair. There sure was a lot of stuff going on around this table but by the end of it everyone was pretty well filled in on everyone. I still didn't think Doug had the full info package on Maggie and me although he tried on several occasions to pry it out of me.

The night was upon us and we'd all had quite a few beverages, so we decided to trade in the sticks and sit for a while. The place had started to thin out a bit and some tables had opened up where the girls had been sitting, so we all moved back there.

A three-piece band had just started playing and they were pretty darn good, playing mostly older pop and country classics. I'd been wanting to ask Maggie to dance for ten minutes but something always seemed to jam me up. A conversation with Doug while the girls took a bathroom trip lasted long after they came back and then ordering up some more beer was a bit complicated, but then…

Dah, dah dot, dah dot, dah da dahhhhhh…Dah, dah dot, dah dot, day dah dahhhh…I looked at Maggie and said, "We have to dance to this one, come on, let's go for a rip."

"Do I know this?"

"Yes, you do, trust me. I know you'll love it." I reached for her hand and made a little hustle to the dance floor and by the time we get there we heard: "Love, is a burning thing, dah dot, dah dot, da dah dahhhh. And it makes a fiery ring, dah dot, dah dot, da dah dahhhh. Bound, by wild desire, dah dot, dah dot, da dah dahh. I fell into a ring of fire."

"Do you know it now?" I asked her.

She was moving and smiling from ear to ear and said, "It's Malcolm on the hill."

I grabbed her and squeezed her and we did a little two-step then back on our own and we were both smiling and singing whatever words we knew. It wasn't a big dance floor but half the bar was up there now kicking up their heels for this country classic.

When I looked back at our table there was no one there and then I spotted our friends having a blast dancing away like everyone else.

The place was just rocking and everyone was singing at the end of it and then they ripped in another classic, "American Woman" by The Guess Who. Ginger's was rocking and I was shaking all over watching her move on the floor. It brought me back to the week before and the morning of our big trip when all I could see and remember was her dancing. Stop yourself and enjoy it, I told myself again and again, and I did.

The song ended and they slipped in a hugger and I reached for her and she did the same.

"Are you good to stay up?" I asked.

"I've been waiting for this all night," she said and pulled me close. "I don't really want to talk, I just want to be held for a while."

We danced another slow song like that as we hardly spoke and it didn't matter. We were filling a need and controlling our desire. Our two friends were still on the floor but nowhere near as close to each other as we were. Still, they looked pretty chummy. Toward the end of the song I said, "What happens after this?"

"I guess we go back to our table and get a drink," Maggie said, giving me a little pinch just below my waist.

She pulled back a bit, smiled, and I leaned toward her and kissed her lightly on the lips. She didn't back away. The song ended and we broke apart and decided to return to our table for a drink. I held her hand and our friends stayed on the floor, which gave us a little time by ourselves.

"So, this is a blast," I said.

"Yeah, it's great. What are you doing tomorrow?"

"I was hoping to spend it with you, and what are you doing tomorrow?"

"Well, here's the thing. I have to work tomorrow until around two but I'm free after that, and I'd love to be with you."

"Well, that sounds great—not the part where you have to work, but I'm all yours whenever you get off."

"I wasn't sure what you were doing, or what we were, what we were doing," she said. "You know, they just texted me to work tonight after Jackie left, you know when I said I wanted to spend as much time as I could."

"Yeah, yeah, it's OK. Work is work."

"It was the clinic and they were jammed up, so I said yes, and I'm regretting it now."

"OK, so what about tonight? I assume you'll need to go home before too long and be rested for work," I said.

She smiled at me and rubbed her foot against my leg and said, "I'll need to be rested for tomorrow night, as well." Then she winked at me and pulled her foot away. She reached for my hand, held it softly, and said, "Stop me if I'm out of line here but how about if you have me over for supper tomorrow night and I'll make us breakfast on Sunday."

I smiled and said, "Keep talking. That's so not out of line."

"But I thought you were saving yourself for the right woman."

"Maybe you are the right woman."

"You are a lot of fun," she said, as she squeezed my hand again and took a drink.

I tipped my glass to her and smiled.

I could sense that our time alone was coming to an end and was feeling anxious but needed to know about tonight, so I asked her: "What about tonight?"

"You mean when we go to leave?"

"Yeah, what about Doug and Clair, what do you think is happening with them? And us, too. I assume you're going home."

"Yes, I'm going home with Clair. We'll just grab a cab; I can't see her staying out any later with Doug or anything like that. They just met, you know."

"Yeah, yeah, I was just checking and I can see them coming back to the table now."

They seemed to be pretty happy getting back to the table and thirsty like us and not long after that, the girls went to the bathroom.

"Holy shit, you've been holding out on me," Doug said.

"What do you mean, about what?"

"About what, well, let me think. OK, Maggie for one through eight, and Clair, she's awesome, by the way, for nine and ten. I've been watching you since you told me to start taking notes and well."

"Well, what?" I said.

I had him in a nice spot, which wasn't easy to do.

"Well what, well what, well, you've been working on this for a while and I'm just finding out. I thought we were friends."

"We are."

I was smiling and having a great time with this.

"We're best friends," I said.

"Well, this just doesn't happen like, like—I saw you on the dance floor and she's awesome as well, by the way, but when did all this happen?"

"What do you mean, look at you and Clair. That seems to be just sort of happening?"

"Yeah, it does. I like her and she's a doll but she's just getting out of some relationship so she's a little tender."

"OK, just go slow. Slow and steady wins the race, they say." And with that, the girls returned.

Maggie took the lead when everyone settled in and said they were staying for one more drink and some dancing but needed to leave after that. They lived in the opposite direction from us so they were going to grab a cab and we'd be left to our own devices, which probably meant a donair, Coke, and a cab.

We spent most of the time talking, laughing, and enjoying the music and every now and then I got a little foot touch and a wink from across the table. We both sensed that the minutes were almost done so Maggie and I went up for another slow song and Dougie and Clair did the same.

We were dancing real close and I said, "As much as I want this evening to continue, I'm looking forward even more to tomorrow."

"That's beautiful. That could be on a greeting card. Really, what a great outlook," she said.

"Well, it's because of you. Now what should I be preparing for supper tomorrow night?" I asked her.

"Oh, it's up to you, because I will eat pretty near anything."

"Well, that's easy but do you have a preference—you know, chicken, pork, seafood, beef?"

"OK, chicken or seafood, but I like it all."

"All right, potato, pasta, rice, or salad?"

"I love salads, every type, *and* all the rest."

"Ok, how about the vegetable, is there anything you don't like?"

"I like them all. Squash and parsnips are not something I'd order at a restaurant or buy at a grocery store, but I will eat them."

"Well, that should do it. I'll figure something out and I suppose you'd like something sweet, as well. Chocolate, maybe."

"Yes, and yes—who doesn't like chocolate?"

"I will bring the wine and lots of it, probably both colours. Can I bring anything else?"

"No that's plenty. I'll do the running around in the morning and get things prepped up or maybe you want to do it together."

"Well, that sounds nice, let's do it together."

"OK, it's going to be fun." And the song ended.

She pulled me tight and kissed me and I didn't back away. As we walked back to the table, I asked her, "Would you like me to pick you up after work or when you're ready to come over?"

"I'll see how the day goes and let you know. Is that OK?"

"Yes, for sure."

She turned toward me and said, "I have a lot of stuff to tell you, that I want to tell you and I hope you're OK with that. Some of it's tough and some of it is just normal but I want you to know some things that other people don't know."

I told her the more I knew about her the better, and we hugged and returned to our table.

I was walking behind her and I saw two images out of the corner of my eye. One was that girl Zoe on the other side of the bar and back farther in the corner was an older gentleman that was a dead ringer for…Who is that, who is that I asked myself?

I took a second look and Zoe was there but the older guy was gone. Who was that, or was I seeing things? It was Joe, the guy from Iona Rear. He was smoking a cigarette and having a beer and a lifter, which was rather strange, and I questioned how much I had to drink. Why was Zoe here unless she was spying, and Joe. What about Joe? I didn't think I should say a word to Maggie.

We finished our drinks and headed for the door and there was a cab waiting nearby. We walked the girls over to the cab and Maggie and I had a nice long kiss, and Clair and Douglas, surprisingly, had a shorter version and we all said good night.

"Well, that was fun," said Dougie. "Do you want to have a lifter around the corner and grab a cab after that?"

"Sure, why not?"

We popped around the corner and dropped in to have a shot. I didn't think I could drink any more beer tonight and I said to the bartender, "Give me two lifters and put a squirt of oil in one of them."

His eyes squeezed together and his ears jumped out like a dog hearing cheese slices opened at the fridge.

"What was that?" he asked.

"Rum and Coke, rum and water, just like the old-timers," I said.

I paid the man and Dougie and I took a seat at a nearby table.

"So, what's the story?" he asked.

We tipped our glasses together.

"I really like her and I can't stop thinking about her."

"I could tell by the way you walked over to her. You're playing at a new level and I'm happy for you."

He tipped his glass toward me again.

"Well, thanks, Doug, I don't want to get too worked up, but we're having supper tomorrow night at my place."

"Can I come?"

"No! Three's an odd number." And we both laughed.

We had another lifter and laughed our way all the way home in the cab. I crawled into bed and lay there like Christmas Eve thinking about tomorrow.

A Thousand and One Wishes

Waltz

Paul K. MacNeil

CHAPTER 9
Let It Blow

The first thought that entered my mind when I opened my eyes was I'd once again slept right through the night. Well, it was sort of like sleeping through since the first five hours felt like someone took an eraser to my mind. It might have had something to do with the last two lifters we had on the way home because when I woke at five I thought I'd been in a coma. But to quickly fall back into a deep sleep for another four hours was just as good as going right through the night.

Oh, my, the dreams I remembered were so vivid—but what did they mean? I saw my old friend standing over a whelping palace with a pile of pups on their hind legs like circus animals. Their faces and bodies looked like something I should be able to identify but I couldn't quite figure it out.

Then I was driving my car around a slippery, snow-covered parking lot only to go over a little bank and flip the car on its roof. I jumped out and flipped it back and kept on going.

I could remember another car buried in the road that had been uncovered because they were repaving. It was one of these old black cars or trucks from the forties.

Next, I was in Joe's big gangster car, holding the pretty blonde girl's hand. Her hand was so soft and she was so pretty. I woke up reaching for her and wanting to touch her face.

What did it all mean and would a professional help? I wondered: if these were the dreams I remembered, what in the world happened in all the others? I suspected I'd never know.

Regardless, it was time to move along with this day so I started the coffee. I then remembered the tea and, since this was going to be a nice cooking day, I decided to start with a fresh drink. It was a simple enough task and my plans from the night before returned.

There were so many options but the stuffed mushrooms and bacon-wrapped scallops with strawberry sauce would be a winner. I could put the rest of the strawberries out with some chocolate dip and whipped cream. And maybe a spinach salad since I had the spinach from the mushrooms and the strawberries, as well. The only thing I was missing was the main course. I was leaning toward chicken but I had some time to make that decision and, with all that, the tea was ready.

It didn't quite smell the same but then again nothing was the same as I dropped a bagel in the toaster. That should hold me until Maggie gets here—hopefully early in the afternoon—and then we could graze until later that evening and have the main course.

I thought back to last Saturday and the panic I was in, worrying about everything from cleaning the car to not knowing if she remembered my name. It was strange to think what a difference a week could make.

Oh, shit, cleaning the car was nothing, this place needed more than a lick and a promise, I could say that.

I needed to calm down and enjoy my tea and bagel, which had returned from the tanning salon in a much darker suit. I remembered my youth again, as I buttered the boiling biscuit.

We would open the lids on our old wood stove toasting our homemade bread on the end of the long forks. It had a taste and a smell you could sell, which I'd never seen on the market. My millionaire senses were tingling as I relaxed, read the news, and enjoyed my little feast.

The day looked kind of grey and the forecast called for a lot of rain with some heavy winds at night. Snuggling weather, I thought, and after a short time, the news didn't interest me that much and my mind revisited the night before and how perfect it had been. I enjoyed the tea and thought it turned out pretty good for city water as the thoughts from the night before forced their way upon me.

I thought of it all again and how lucky I was but mostly of what Maggie said: "Let's just have some fun." I was sure I wasn't the only one who over-thinks all sorts of things in the run of a day, week, or lifetime, but I guess I'd also said that you need to let stuff happen. And last night had just happened so sweetly.

That, of course, put the pressure squarely on today and I was going to make sure we had some fun, in a cleaner place than this. It didn't take me long as I generally kept it pretty tidy, which wasn't that hard to do when you lived alone. I thought about my old place and how lucky I was to find this flat ten months ago. My two roommates back then weren't much for keeping it clean or doing any cooking so when this came up it was really easy to make the change.

Without missing a beat, I thought of last weekend and Joe telling us he never owned a house but preferred the boarding house. It seemed to me that this size place was perfect for me and, perhaps without a family, I wouldn't need a house either. There was plenty of room here for me to enjoy it the way it was.

I had the place cleaned up and was ready to hit the drops when my phone buzzed. It was Dougie.

> *Hey, buddy are you moving?*
> *What a great night.*
> *Got any breat...Give me a shout.*

He was hungry and looking for food. He'd told me about his classmate when he was young who didn't have very much and he would always ask for "breat." I suppose he wanted to chat as well about his own electric night, so I poured another cup of tea, put my feet up, and gave him a call.

I talked to him for about ten minutes and he was hungry and wanted to come over but I told him I'd just cleaned the place and that wasn't happen-ing. I told him I was heading out to get some groceries and I'd pick him up in thirty minutes if he wanted to join me for part of the day. He sounded like a pregnant woman. Rambling, stammering, glowing, beaming, and I wondered for a second what I looked like myself.

I had opened the windows earlier when I was cleaning and the flat was quite cool from the morning air. So when I jumped in the shower it felt just like a sauna that warmed me to the core like a nice drink of scotch. I thought about the two feelings and decided to stay in the shower longer than I intended and, as they say, time enjoyed wasted, is not wasted time.

When I was ready to leave I sent Doug a text and I also touched base with my prettier date to see how she was.

> *Hey there, how's your day going?*
> *I really enjoyed last night.*
> *I'm just heading out for some groceries, let me know if there's*
> *something you want me to get.*
> *Any idea when you'll be done and the offer to pick you up is*
> *still there.*
> *Let me know.*

That should do it and I said goodbye to my little electric pigeon.

I headed out for Doug's with my list in my head and hand, just to make sure I didn't forget anything. I was fairly well-stocked if I did, but the fewer surprises the better.

Doug met me in front of his building and we headed to Sobeys for our little order. He was in a great mood and well he should've been after his unexpected score the night before. He had her number and she had his so we debated who would be the first to call and why. I told him to get right after it as they seemed to be running smoothly together. He nervously asked me if I knew anything more about her.

I told him I was pretty sure he knew her better than I did since I only met her yesterday. He seemed to be uncertain of what to do next and I told him again he should just call her and line up a date. I think he felt reassured after our conversation and said he'd go for it.

With that, we'd reached the store and agreed to meet back at the car when we were finished.

I couldn't help but think of Mungie and Sadie heading to town, as they'd said, and getting their little order before church. This was the same only different.

I grabbed the things I had thought of earlier and decided to get a shrimp ring, some apples, caramel sauce, and a nice loaf of bread. I picked up some chicken for the main course and a bottle of Thai sauce to go with the vegetables I had on hand. I figured we could graze on all the other things and have a stir fry for the main meal later on.

Maggie texted while I was shopping and said she'd be done around 1 p.m. She also had a ride home but would take me up on my offer once she was showered and ready to go, around two or two-thirty. She needed nothing from the store but suggested we stop for the wine together.

That was all good with me and then I remembered about dessert, which had slipped my mind. Well, I knew what I wanted but figured I should have a dish ready anyway. *Quick, fast, and easy* was racing through my head and strawberry shortcake sprang to mind. The local berries were available and so much better than what they ship from another planet most of the year. I was in the dairy section and grabbed the whipped cream and a lump of old Canadian cheese that was aged longer than I had been in the city.

I thought we could make Sadie's biscuits for the base of the dessert, which would be a lot of fun. I sure hoped they'd turn out. I grabbed a few other things I needed for my place and headed for the checkout. "We'll make do with what we have," I said and I heard my mother's voice in the back of my head.

Doug and I met at the car and started for home. I suggested again that he call Clair and see what was going on in her head. He said he would and thanked me for the drive and jokingly said he'd be over around six. I told him I had an opening for him on Monday as he wished me luck and I said the same.

I continued on my way and once I got everything in my flat I thought it through all over again and was pretty sure I had everything I needed. I was now just waiting for the clock to catch up to my mind but it would not deviate from its stoic pace. I pulled out the sketchpad I was giving to Maggie and touched up a few things that somehow looked different in my mind today compared to a week ago. I wrote a little note to her on the back of the front cover:

> "Hope you enjoy the memories.
> It was a great day.
> Patrick"

I did a few little things like cutting vegetables and washing fruit, and tried to busy myself and, finally, she texted to say she was home and ready in about thirty minutes. I gave myself a little buff and raced out to pick her up.

I had driven by her place a few times in the past week just to see if I might catch a glimpse of her. I wasn't that lucky, but I knew I could be there in fifteen minutes with ease. While I drove around to kill some time, the first sprinkles of rain landed on my windshield and reminded me of the morning forecast. You could feel the wind wanted in on the bidding or maybe it was just asking the rain to continue their endless dance.

I parked by her place and sent her a text.

> *Your chariot awaits.*
> *I'm outside but don't let me rush you.*

She replied:

> *I'll be five minutes.*
> *All good*

She was quicker than all that and I shivered with joy when I saw her. I got out to give her a hand as the wind was boldly taking the lead. She had a couple of small bags and when we got them in the car, she hugged me and gave me a kiss.

"Nice to see you," I said.

"Same here. I just have two suitcases to grab inside—can you give me a hand?"

"What?"

"I'm just kidding," she said with a flirtatious smile. "I'm not moving in, but you seem a little punchy."

"Very funny. Is that it then?"

"Yes, that should do. Thanks a lot for picking me up. It's starting to get a little nasty out. Do you know if we're getting a storm or something?"

"I guess it's something like that," I said as we started driving away. "We're supposed to get a lot of rain and some high winds right through the night. It'll be a good night to stay in and get under a blanket."

"Well, that sounds cozy. How was your day?"

"It was good—better now, of course. Doug and I went for some groceries, I cleaned my flat and made a few plans for food, which I hope you'll like. How was your own day?" I asked.

"It was really good. I wasn't all that sharp when I got up but I shook it off pretty quick and I'm better now as well. I had a really good sleep and was in bed by midnight so it wasn't as bad as if I'd stayed out all night."

"Yeah, I know what you mean. I wasn't much later than you going to bed."

"I had a lot of fun last night. Did you go for another drink?"

"Yeah, we went just around the corner and had a couple of shots and then grabbed a cab. Doug was looking for the scoop on Clair—is there anything else you'd be willing to share about her?"

"I think I told you most of it last night. She's been single for a few weeks and she's ready to move on. I always thought her old boyfriend was strange and they were unhappy for a while so it's over. I think she's a great girl and we've become good friends. She was there for me when I needed her a few months ago so I'm trying to be there for her now."

"Oh, that's nice. She seemed nice and she's very attractive. I'd say she won't be single for long."

"Yeah. Doug seems nice and she was looking for more info on him, as well. Something's cooking."

"That's interesting, I told Doug to call her and see if something happens— you know, let them figure it out themselves."

"I told her the same thing." And we both laughed.

We stopped for wine and picked up a few bottles of McManis and a couple of others, as well, so we wouldn't run out.

By the time we got back to my flat, the showers had changed to a light rain and the wind was right beside her. We got settled inside and I went straight for some glasses and asked, "What colour will we start with?"

"Let's start with the one that brought us together," she said.

I opened the red and poured two glasses. She came over beside me and pretended to pinch me again.

"I'll give you ten minutes to stop that," I said.

She kissed me and we held each other so close I felt every contour of her body and more. We were locked together in a frantic, heavy way. It felt like we were finally alone together and both of us knew we wanted it this way. We eventually backed away and I said, "I knew the wine tasted better off your lips."

She smiled and said, "I think I'll have to try it a few more times to be sure but you can help yourself any time you like."

"So, are you hungry?" I asked.

"Yes, I am, and what sort of delectable treats have you lined up for us?"

"Well, I would like to share it a bit at a time if that's OK with you."

She was happy with that so I asked her to slice some bread and I cut into the block of old cheese. I grabbed the strawberries, whipped cream, and butter from the fridge and she grabbed some plates and we had our first little feast.

"Well done and I love it all. So quick and easy.

"So I have some fairly big news to tell you," she said as she slurped on a strawberry.

"Oh, what is it?"

"First of all, these berries are the best."

"You're the berries," I said with a grin.

"You're only saying that 'cause it's true." She coyly smiled back at me. "So, here it is, are you ready?"

"I think so."

Not having a clue what was coming next.

"I put in my notice to leave the clinic and I got a full-time job at the hospital."

"Holy wow, that's a lot. How did that all happen?"

I raised my glass and congratulated her.

"Thanks a lot and there's a bit of a story, so here it is. I was pretty much full time at the hospital without the pay or the security for a few years now. I was also working at the clinic to fill in the holes and make a few extra bucks. So then about a month ago I applied for basically the same job I was doing, only it's full time and I got iiiiiiit. There's a nice big pay raise, more vacation, and security, that's the best part."

"Well, that's awesome. Is there any downside?"

"Well, yes and no. I have to work most weekends for the next few months but then I go on a regular rotation and do the same number of weekends, just like everyone else. So it's great and it doesn't really matter since I was working at the clinic most weekends anyway. Now I can get out of there!"

"Wow, Maggie, I'm really happy for you and I want to hear the rest of it but I think this calls for a special toast. Do you like scotch?"

She said she did so I went for the bottle a friend of mine had given me for doing him a favour. I thought of the moment in the shower that morning and wondered if there was any connection.

"Here it is, a nice single malt that came from the Glenora Distillery near Inverness. It's kind of ironic because it's called Glen Breton."

"Is it any good?" she asked.

"We're about to find out."

"On the rocks or straight up?"

"I like a little ice."

I poured two the same and said, "Here's to good things happening to good people, here's to you and your future. Congratulations."

We tapped our glasses took a small drink, and she said, "Glen Breton, eh? That's really nice, it just warms the cockles of my heart. Thank you, it's a big move for me and I want to tell you something else."

"Sorry, Maggie, I didn't mean to cut you off, I just wanted to make a little deal out of it."

"No, that's fine, but I also wanted to tell you about the clinic and that whole story."

"OK."

"So I told you I had been dating Barkley up until about two months ago."

"Yes, I remember."

"You see, his father owns the clinic and for a long time now I've been feeling trapped by it all. So last Sunday, after our trip to the country, when I went to work I had this terrible feeling and Barkley was there. He was trying to get me to go for a drink with him and get together and I'd had enough. On Monday, I wrote his father and told him I was giving him my two weeks' notice. I didn't really need to do that but I feel better for doing it that way. So, I'm done!"

"That's huge, Maggie."

"Oh, there's more. You see, I applied for a different position there a month ago and they gave the job to someone else, and, let's just say, I think I was more qualified."

"Well, that's a heavy week, for sure," I said.

"Yeah, well, it's been brewing for a long time and after our trip and the experience we had I just knew the time was right. So I was a little scared doing it but then on Tuesday, I had an interview at the hospital for the new job and they called me this morning to offer me the position. Crazy, eh?"

"It's kind of wild, that's for sure. I wish I'd known you were going through all that."

"Well, I didn't think there was much you could do and I didn't want to jinx anything with the new job, so I just kept it to myself. I nearly told you a couple of times last night but I caught myself and said no, not here in front of everyone."

"Well, I'm glad you saved it especially for me."

I leaned over and kissed her and said, "I'm thrilled for you."

"Thank you. I'm glad for me, and I'm glad for us. As I said, even though I broke up with Barkley I still felt like he controlled me a bit. Zoe works at the clinic, as well, and I always felt like she was working undercover for him.

"So, I'm so glad to be out of there, you wouldn't believe it. I took all my stuff from there today and don't plan on taking another shift."

"Is that why you took the shift today?" I asked.

"That was part of it. Plus, they were stuck. I wanted to say goodbye to some of the ones that work there. You know, there are good people everywhere."

"Yes, I know. Unfortunately, there are just about as many assholes."

She agreed and I finished my scotch, which tasted like another. I poured myself another shot and asked Maggie if she wanted more but she was happy with the wine. We'd been munching on the bread and cheese while we talked, and the berries were over the top. They exploded in my mouth and I said, "Do you want something else to eat besides this?"

"This is hitting the spot but I am kind of curious what else you have in mind."

"Well, I have a number of choices to choose from next and only one requires a bit of work."

"Let's hear them," she said.

"Starting with the easiest is a shrimp ring with seafood sauce."

"I love shrimp. What else?"

"We could make baked mushrooms stuffed with feta cheese and spinach, or scallops wrapped in bacon either baked or pan-seared. What do you think?"

"Oh, my gosh, it all sounds great."

"I would say something hot would be nice, so let's go for the scallops. I haven't had that in a long time."

We fried the bacon till it was pretty much cooked and then wrapped it around the large, fresh scallops and held it in place with toothpicks. We seasoned them with a little salt, pepper, and paprika, and seared them in a frying pan with butter and lemon juice. We were done in about twenty minutes and I learned more about her job, her friends from work, and the girls who were at the bar the night before.

Maggie was pretty impressed with the ease of making our delicious treat and I was more than pleased with how they turned out. I'd made them several times before but I'd often overcooked them. These were perfect!

I filled up our wine glasses and we proceeded to enjoy our little creation. We finished them in short order and Maggie got up and said, "We've been talking about me since I got here and I've been looking around at all your drawings and pictures. I'd like to know more about you and who all these pictures and places are.

"And, by the way, these drawings are really well done. Have you been drawing forever or what?"

"Yes, pretty much as long as I can remember." We got up to walk around.

I took her through most of the sketches of the places I'd lived, like my old family homestead, my favourite place by the brook when I was a kid, my other favourite place on top of the mountain where I thought you could see forever. Then it was on to my new life in the city with the busy streets and the harbour with the huge container ships and pleasure boats.

"So, this must be your parents," she said as she stopped in front of their old wedding picture.

"Yes, that's them. I'm pretty sure they'd like you. They were hard-working, honest people who didn't have much time for the bullshit in the world."

"Your mother was beautiful and I think you look like her. What were their names?"

"Stephen and Annie MacLean. I've thought about them quite a bit since our trip up the country. I kept remembering things about them that I'd sort of let slip away and I feel good about that, so, thank you."

"So, are these your siblings? Oh, my, that's you there, isn't it? How old are you in that picture?"

"Yes, that's the whole family, and I was around ten there."

"Well, you were too cute. You must have been beating the young girls off back then, were you?"

"No, not really, I did have a few admirers, but it wasn't like I couldn't leave the house without security. I was never all that interested in chasing them around and, besides, we were usually working pretty steady at home or trying to make a buck someplace else."

"Well, I'll find out more about that at another time. And it looks like two sisters and a brother and you were the youngest, is that right?"

"You are correct. That's Monica, Theresa, and Hughie."

"I've hardly seen them since my parents passed on and they've all moved away across the country. I talk to my sisters regularly, but haven't talked to my brother in ages."

"So, who are the children right here? I assume they are your nephews."

"Yes, you're right, those are Theresa's boys, Kenny and Rick. They must be ten and twelve by now, I guess. They're nice kids—at least they were when I saw them last, pretty cute."

"How about Monica and Hughie? Are they married?"

"Well, Monica is, but Hughie isn't, as far as I know—again, we were never very close.

"Monica's married to Peter and they've tried to have children since they got married but haven't had any luck. She's the oldest and I think they've pretty much given up on having children. I guess if it happens, it happens."

"Ah, that's too bad. I think they look like your mother, as well."

"Yeah, pretty much the spit right out of her mouth."

"So, tell me more about your drawings."

"Well, I will, but I need a topper first. How about you?"

"I think I'd like another shot of that scotch. I'm feeling kind of full from the food, so I'd prefer that."

"OK, you keep looking and I'll get the drinks. If you see anything you really like, I'll get you a good price," I said jokingly.

As I stepped back into the kitchen area I could hear the rain coming down much harder and the wind was matching its every move.

I started thinking of the poor little birds that just yesterday were pouring their hearts out as I played with the stereo effects of the window going up and down. I wouldn't dare open it at this time for fear of being soaked.

I returned with the drinks and knew it was a good time to give Maggie the little sketchpad. I handed her glass to her and said, "I have something else for you."

"What is it?"

I took her hand and led her over to the chesterfield, where I picked up the small pad and gave it to her.

"This is for you. I hope you like it."

She opened the front page and read the inscription and saw my sketch of herself and looked at me and said nothing, for a moment. Then she looked at it again and looked at me and leaned over and kissed me and said, "It's beautiful. Thank you so much."

"You're welcome. You're beautiful. There's more, keep looking."

She turned the page slowly to Mungie and just looked at me. Then to Sadie and she looked like she was about to cry. When she got to Malcolm on the hill she was in tears and closed the book.

I offered her a napkin that was on the table and said, "I didn't mean to make you cry. I thought you'd like them."

"Like them? I love them. No one has ever done anything like this for me in my entire life. Aside from what Mam did for me, this is the first time I've felt like someone really cared."

She was still crying and looking at the sketches and she said, "Last weekend was just such an important thing for me, and then meeting Jackie…I'm starting to figure out who I am and you did all that for me and now this. It's just beautiful and I'm sorry for crying."

I reached over to her and we held each other for a long time as only the rain on the windows had anything to say. She kissed my cheek as she pulled away and I said, "There's a couple more in there, and I don't think you'll cry when you see them."

She turned the next page and it was the picture I had sent her of the strait before time and she loved that, as well.

When she turned to Donald she burst out laughing and kept pointing out all the things that were wrong with it. She made a game of it, like when you have to find all the things that are out of place in a picture, and then she said, "I'm going to send it to him to see what he thinks of it."

"That's fine with me but I was going to drive up there and pin it to the bulletin board at the café."

After a lot of laughter, we both agreed it would be better to just keep it to ourselves.

"So, all this drawing stuff, you didn't tell me the whole story. You could be making a living at it, I think."

"It's funny you say that because I went to art school for two years before deciding to go into engineering."

"Why did you switch?" she asked.

"Well, I really enjoyed it and learned a lot going there, but I was broke all the time and most of the people there were broke unless their parents were rich and mine certainly were not."

"I can see your point," she said. "But if you wear a hat you'll cover it up. But seriously, you don't have to have a lot of money to be rich."

"Well, that's very true, and funny. Speaking of hats, what did one hat say to the other?"

"I don't know."

"I'll stay here, you go on a head."

She chuckled and said, "I hope you don't mind my asking, but do you think you could do a sketch of Mam for me, if I gave you a picture?"

"Yeah, sure. I'd love to know what she looked like after all this investigating we've been doing. Do you have a picture with you?"

"No, I don't, but I have a couple of nice ones back at my place."

"Well, I could do that any time, tomorrow or something. I could do it in no time or we could do it together."

"What do you mean?"

"I could make the outline or base and you could do some of the shading or texture stuff. I'm assuming you don't really draw."

"You're right, I don't, and I don't want to mess it up on you."

"Not at all, we could do it ten times if we had to. Besides that, I have erasers and I know how to use them. I think you'd be pretty happy looking at it knowing you had a hand in it."

"Well, if you're willing to share your talent, why wouldn't I accept the gift?"

"Speaking of working together, do you want to tackle the mushrooms now or wait for a bit?" I asked.

"I'm not very hungry now, but I'll have some more wine. Can I get you some? I need to go to the bathroom anyway."

"Sure, I think I've had enough scotch for now. Maybe I should stay with the wine for a while and can you find your way OK?" I asked.

"Yes, it's bigger than my place but I don't think I'll get lost. I'm pretty sure the bedroom is there and the bathroom is over here and the wine is right where we left it. Is that about right?"

"You got it, Pontiac."

While she was in the bathroom I thought about going to the common deck for a change. It was a neat little deck out by the stairs that I shared with the other tenant on this level. I thought the wind was blowing from the east, which would make the deck protected and it had a roof over it so it might be a perfect little refresher from my flat. I kind of needed to do something if we weren't going to cook anything.

When she returned with the wine, she complimented my place and asked how I'd found such a cool spot. I told her about my last place and the roommates I needed to get away from. It happened so fast and I was so lucky when this guy from work had a baby and had to get a bigger place. I don't think he wanted to give it up but knew he had to so they bought a house and it worked out pretty well for me.

She thought it was a very unique place and I asked her if she would like to see another part of it. She protested a bit when I said she needed her shoes and sweater. I told her not to worry, took her hand, and opened the door to the deck by the stairway. It was sheltered from the storm and we sat beside each other on the two old chairs and I asked her what she thought.

She loved it and with the storm slashing around us she slid her chair closer to mine, put her arm over my shoulder, and whispered in my ear, "Are you on any kind of birth control or have you had a vasectomy or anything like that?" as she touched the bottom of my ear with her tongue.

I was a little bit startled and it gave me a horny shiver, but I looked at her and rubbed her jean-covered leg with my hand and said, "No, I haven't had a vasectomy and the only birth control I'm practising is abstinence. How about you and why do you ask?"

"Yes and no, and it's because I want you." She pulled me a little closer.

You could feel the dampness from the rain and the strength of the wind pounding all around us as we put our drinks down and embraced each other with both arms. Our lips and tongues collided in a frantic feast of passion and desire as our hands searched for any part of our bodies that were at all accessible. We stood up and pressed against each other as if we had nothing in between us. The wind and rain raged around us and within us as our mouths searched for air. She pulled back and said, "I think you should show me your bedroom."

I reached down for my drink and she for hers and as I reached for her hand she pinched me again on my bum cheek. She smiled, stuck her tongue out, and licked her perfect lips. I did the same but I don't think it had the same effect. She took my hand when we entered the flat and I led the way to the unity chamber.

I closed the door and we embraced again but this time we removed the thin layers that separated us, one garment at a time. I touched and stroked every inch of her and searched for more as she responded the same. We managed to get under the blankets as I caressed her breasts and kissed every inch of her I could get to. She guided me into her and we moulded our bodies together like two lost souls that had finally found their mate. We made love to each other as the storm beat its jealous eyes on the window.

We passed the next two hours exactly the same way, finding different ways to pleasure each other and release our caged desires. I loved her back as much as her front and wondered if I should have a favourite. We stopped on occasion to slip to the bathroom or refill our glasses and maybe grab a strawberry or a piece of cheese.

The wind and rain kept up the pace right along with us and, eventually, our stomachs started to sound like the thunder that was missing from the party. We talked about getting up and making the mushrooms and decided a little kitchen time would be good for us. She slipped on one of my T-shirts and I put on my comfy clothes and we headed for the kitchen.

I took out the shrimp ring and sauce and we nibbled on that as we started preparing the next grazing treat.

We chopped up the stems of the mushrooms and tossed them with chopped spinach, a little garlic and feta cheese. Mixed it all together and stuffed it back into the mushroom cap and sprinkled it with parmesan cheese. We put that in the oven to be baked for fifteen minutes, then stood back and kissed each other as if we'd just sent our children off to school.

She opened a bottle of white wine, poured two glasses, and gave one to me as she tipped her glass to me and said, "To a great night."

"To a great night."

"Do you feel like you saved yourself for the right woman?" she asked.

"Without a doubt. There's no one else I want to be with but you."

She leaned over, kissed me, and said the same.

"So, I'm ready to hear the rest of your story if you want to share it with me."

"About my parents and Mam?"

"Yeah, I'm kind of curious. After all, you've met my battered family, albeit through pictures on the wall."

"Well, there's not much to tell. Well, that's not completely true. My mother's name was Katie Campbell, and Mam had a sister named Anna who looked after me after Mam died. She died not that long after Mam died, so I kind of went from Mam to Anna to being on my own.

"How they were able to raise me and leave me some money to get an education, I'm not really sure, but here I am today. Then I ended up with a good job and some friends and you. I'm a pretty lucky girl, maybe a miracle."

"Well that's quite a journey, but I think you would have landed on your feet anyway. You strike me as a very smart woman."

"Well, maybe, but they kept me alive."

"So what happened with your parents?" I asked.

"Well that's a little bigger train wreck, and the truth is, I don't really know. But here is some of what I have—maybe all of what I have.

"Mam described Katie to me just like the girls from Rear Iona described Mugsie. Not that I think she saw fairies or anything like that, but she may have. She was a bit like those pictures you see of the flower child in the hippy-dippy days. Just didn't care if she was connected to anything and eventually she was...was...what was the word they used in Iona Rear for pregnant?"

"Oh, *trom*," I said.

"Yes, that's it, heavy with child. Now, somehow she was hooked up with this Archie MacKinnon, who is supposed to be my father, although Mam said she didn't think that he was at all.

"Whenever I asked Mam about my mother and Archie, she used to say, 'They were like the cheeks of my arse. They're together but they're not.'

"So he was around for a few years when I was really young, but then he went away sailing and I haven't seen him since."

"Wow, that must have been pretty tough."

"Yeah, it was, but I knew kids that had it worse. Anyway, to stick with him for a minute, Mam said she knew him, and his people were from the country. And now after being there and all the talk of MacKinnon's Harbour, I just wonder if he came from there."

"Well, there's a pretty good chance. Did you mention that to Jackie?"

"No, I didn't get into that with him but the other story was that his siblings moved up to the Cape North area of Cape Breton, and there are quite a few MacKinnons up there, so that's another adventure of a different type."

"Are you still glad you kissed me?" she asked.

"I'm going to kiss you again, regardless," I said, and I leaned over and kissed her softly on the lips.

She slowly smiled and said, "Mom took off about two years after Archie did, and we only heard from her a few times. By then Mam was raising me as her own, kind of like Sadie, I guess. So that's pretty well it."

"That's a lot and you've been carrying around a lot of questions for a long time, haven't you?"

"Well, only for the last few years, I think. It was just the way it was when I was growing up. Once I was on my own and started thinking of Mam's old stories, I knew I needed to do something to heal myself. I think it's an age thing, as well—at least it was for me."

"I suppose, and I bet we'll get to the bottom of it all, or most of it, anyway. Now let's get to the bottom of those mushrooms—they look like they're done to me."

With that, we removed them from their broiling womb and began to enjoy our sizzling treats.

At that time, I noticed the night was upon us and the lamp in the corner was providing most of the light in the room. The wind and the rain were still dancing but now in the dark and I wondered if they would take a break or continue through the night.

"These are delicious. How did you learn how to make these?"

"They were in an Italian cookbook and sounded so good I just tried them."

"I'm not sure I can eat anything else," she said.

"I'm getting full, as well. They're pretty rich and they don't have a cent." Maggie chuckled.

"I guess it just depends on how long we stay up but I had a couple more things on the menu."

"What are they?"

"Well, I bought chicken to have as a stir fry with rice but that seems kind of heavy right now. And for dessert, I thought we could try to make Sadie's biscuits and make a strawberry shortcake. Have you ever made biscuits?" I asked.

"Oh, geez, no. I should have learned from Mam but never did. All that sounds delicious, just like everything we ate tonight. But can we save it for tomorrow?"

"Sure, it will be just as good then."

"I would love to try to make the biscuits with you. That would be fun."

"So, what next? Do you want to watch a show or something?"

"Well, how 'bout this plan? How about we clean up the kitchen and you show me where a few things are that I might need for the morning?"

"And then what?" I asked.

"Well, then," she said, as she slyly came toward me. "You and I go back into the bedroom and listen to the wind and the rain. You can pretend you're the wind, and I'll pretend I'm the rain."

With that, she reached around me and squeezed both of my cheeks.

We kissed and held each other tight, and I asked her what was on the menu for the morning. She coyly looked at me and said it was a surprise. And with that, I showed her what she asked for and she went to the bathroom.

I cleaned a few last things up and turned off the light in the kitchen. When she'd finished in the bathroom, I washed myself and brushed my teeth.

I noticed she didn't really have a lot with her but she was fully prepared, just like on our first date.

I entered the bedroom and she was lying on the inside against the wall looking gorgeous. I turned off the light, got into bed as she rolled over beside me and her naked body fell upon me again.

We made love, but this time it was gentle and slow as we savoured every last moment of the evening we had. We said nothing else to each other as we listened to the weather outside and fell asleep.

I woke sometime through the night and could feel Maggie next to me and I didn't want to move for fear of waking her. She was soft and warm against my skin and smelled like a greenhouse in springtime, earthy and sweet. The rain outside had a soothing, gentle feel to it and the wind had left the dance floor.

I spent the longest time looking at her and couldn't believe how fortunate I was to be here with her. I couldn't remember the last time I felt so comfortable with myself and someone else, let alone a beautiful woman like her. I guess good things do happen to good people more than we know.

The next thing I heard were noises in the kitchen and I saw Maggie was not beside me in the bed. I heard pots moving and she was humming a tune softly and sweetly but I couldn't place the melody. I saw her moving intermittently as she went back and forth in my sightline. She was wearing my white T-shirt from the night before, and I wanted to go be with her but she seemed so content I didn't want to disrupt her own time.

I decided to get up, but before I did, I stretched an intense stretch under the covers and it felt as though my whole body was charged and ready for the day. I was able to quietly slip into the kitchen and wrap my arms around her without her hearing me. She turned her head toward me and kissed me gently on my lips. My hands pressed against her stomach and chest and I said, "Good morning, you feel good."

"Thanks, and good morning to you. I'm feeling great. And how are you?"

"I couldn't be better. What are you making?"

"Well, it's eggs Benedict, I hope you like it."

"I love it, but I've never made it before. Isn't the sauce hard to make?"

"Not when you use this little packet of hollandaise sauce mix. It's dead easy."

MAGGIE NORA LIZA MHÓR

She turned around and wrapped her arms around me and kissed me long and hard as I felt my desire rising inside me again. We held each other tightly as our lips and tongues resumed the alliance they had started the night before.

Jesus Christ, I had half a soup on. We could have easily made love right there but she pulled back and said, "You better let me finish making breakfast or you might not have me back. I can't back out of our little arrangement now."

"I suppose not. Do you need any help?"

"No, I think I have it covered, but thanks."

"I might grab a shower if it's going to be a little bit."

"For sure, it'll be around fifteen minutes. How do you like your coffee?"

"Like a double-double," I said.

"I'll have one for you when you get out."

I hit the drops and images of the night before raced through my mind. It was pure magic and excitement as the hot water reminded me of the wild weather that tried endlessly to enter our world. I returned to the kitchen all buffed and ready for my morning feast, which smelled delicious.

She placed the plates on the table and it looked like something out of a magazine or a high-end restaurant. The plating, as they say, was perfect, with the sauce falling off the sides of the eggs, and a slight garnish of mint and the flecks of pepper and paprika on top, and I said, "It looks too good to eat."

She smiled and said, "Try it. I'll make it again if you mess it up. Try the coffee, I made it the way Mam used to make it."

"It's really good."

It was creamy and smooth but with a nice little zing to it.

"How did you make it?" I asked.

"Well, it's a secret, but I'll tell you just because I like you. But don't go sharing it with everybody you sleep with."

"I think it's safe."

"Well, it's hot milk with instant coffee and sugar."

"Really?"

"You just boil the milk in the microwave for two minutes and twenty-two seconds. While you are doing that, you scoop the double, double of coffee and sugar into a glass with a little water to make it dissolve and mix it. Then, when the milk is done, you mix the two together, and there you have it. Pretty easy, really."

"It's great," I said as I dug into my Eggs Benedict. "The dish is delicious, as well."

"Well, thank you, sir, I'm glad you like it. Does this mean I can come back?"

"You don't have to leave," I said as I leaned over to kiss her.

"That's sweet," she said with a smile. "But I didn't really pack for any longer than a night."

We finished our breakfast and made some plans for the day, which included the little market down the road and a walk in the public gardens. We talked about the food we didn't make the night before. I offered to clean up the dishes and she decided to grab a shower while I was doing that. As she entered the bathroom, I said, "Do you want any company or help?"

"Maybe another time," she said, winked at me, and closed the door.

The day was sunny and warm and we spent it together doing things that young couples falling in love do with each other. We went to the market where we saw the sketch guy and Maggie told me my drawings were much better. We went to the beach and did some shopping at the waterfront market and the day passed like something out of a movie and I eventually had to take her home.

We reached her building and I wanted to go up to her apartment and make love to her again but didn't. We stayed in the car and enjoyed our final moments together as we fraughtfully kissed each other. We made plans to stay in touch more closely in the coming week and talked about all sorts of things that we could do together.

I wished her luck with her new job, which started the next day, and we talked about making plans that would work around her new schedule. We talked about going to Ginger's again on Friday and we held each other tightly before she left.

I watched her walk up the stairs as she turned toward me, forcing a smile. She faintly waved and closed the door.

I drove away and missed her immediately.

A 'Dèaneamh Ìm

Reel

Paul K. MacNeil

CHAPTER 10
Bridges

Another Monday arrived again with all its glory. At least the memory of the weekend was fresh in my mind and would carry me through the first few difficult hours of this week. I had no reason to complain when the birds were singing, the sun was shining, and there was always another Friday waiting to be opened.

My phone was chirping like the birds in the trees as I drove to work. I knew something was happening that I'd need to attend to as soon as I got there. I parked the car and checked my phone. It was my boss, Jackie, times three, and Maggie. Tough choices, but Maggie finished first.

> *Good morning.*
> *Hope you have a great day.*
> *This is me on my first day at my new job.*

She sent a selfie in front of the hospital and she was glowing. I quickly wrote her back as I walked into the office.

> *Have a great day.*
> *So happy for you.*
> *You look incredible.*

The boss, Butch, wanted to see me as soon as I got to work so I was glad to be early. Jackie wanted me to come to his office after I saw Butch and I wondered how he knew I'd be there. Jackie's other two texts were a lot more fun sounding.

I got the bikes sorted out.

And right after it was:

When can you guys come up?

Well, that was great news and my morning had done a complete 360 in about five minutes. My feet were moving quicker and the glow from my face was much brighter. I wasn't sure what was going on but there was only one way to find out.

I stopped at Butch's office and he told me about a big project that was starting right away. We needed to examine all the bridges on the 200-series highways in our district. There was a lot of work and it needed to be completed in the next three months, so we'd be going pretty hard.

The best part was that I could hand off most of my current projects to other guys and I'd be working with Jackie until it was completed. Jackie was the lead on the project and he'd asked for me to work with him, which was a pretty big deal for me and I felt pretty good about everything.

My next stop was Jackie's office and he was pumped to see me and get started on the project together.

"How was your weekend?" he asked.

"Just about as good as it could be. How about you?"

"Ah, it was good, kind of quiet on the home front, so I got a few things done around the house. You know, homeowner shit," he said with a smile. "Were you talking to Butch this morning?"

"Yes, I just left there. Butch said I was going to be working with you on the bridge project."

"And are you up for it?"

"Well, of course. It's a great opportunity and Butch said you asked for me, which was very kind. Thank you."

"Well, I think it'll be fun working together and getting out of the office for the summer. Now with that, there's a lot of work to do as well and you'll probably have to take it home with you. Are you OK with that?"

"Oh, yeah, for sure."

"OK, and what do you think Maggie will think of this?"

"Well, I'm pretty sure she'll be glad for me and support the opportunity."

I wasn't really sure what to tell him since he thought we were a couple and I didn't know what we were for sure. I was confused and doing a balancing act again but I went for it anyway and said, "You know, she just started a new job at the hospital today so her work schedule is going to be a bit erratic for the next little while. I'm pretty sure we'll find a way to make it work. We don't have children to move around so we can handle it."

I couldn't believe I was talking about children and Maggie and trying to explain it to Jackie. I realized I had more conversations about children in the last ten days than I had in the last ten years. What was it Dylan said, "The times, they are a changin'." How true.

"I thought Maggie was the cat's pajamas and what's the story on her new job?"

"Well, it's the same job, really, but it's full time, better money, and a bit more shift work, so she's really pleased about it. She'd been working part-time at a private clinic as well so she put her notice in there to leave. It's all coming together for her."

"Sounds like lots of changes. Change is how I got this job and change will put me out the door, as well. It's usually easier to go along with it than to struggle and fight with it. And you know what, for the most part, it's better for everyone.

"Anyway, I got some bikes sorted out for us and a couple of others want to go on a little rip. Any idea when you can go?"

"In a word, aahhh, no. We're both dying to go but I'll need to see what her schedule is going to be and go from there. I assume a weekend is best for you and the others."

"Yes, for sure, and I was thinking of two weeks' time, if that would work. There's a wedding that weekend in Iona so we can do the bike run during the day and catch the reception that night. Would you be up for that?" he asked.

"The reception, too? Do you think the couple would mind?"

"No, jeez, no, they won't care. It's my cousin's daughter so the more, the merrier. Half of the community will be there and most of them don't get an invitation, they just go. It's open, as they say."

"I love the idea but let me send Maggie a text and see if she can get that weekend off. So when is that, like July ninth?"

"Yeah, that's it, and I've got a spot for you to stay as well if you want. It's close to the hall so you won't have to drive."

"Well, it sounds perfect and Maggie was really glad she met you, said you clarified a lot of stuff for her, so thanks again."

"*Ach*, no problem. I enjoyed her a lot, as well. Cat's pajamas, I tell you. The cat's pajamas.

"So let's meet this afternoon about the project and I'll send you some stuff to look over and we'll get after that."

I left his office and felt like everything was going my way. It was like I was a gambler at a high-stakes card game and I knew what every unturned card was. As if every card was the one I needed and every bet and hand were perfectly played.

I wondered if this was all going to come crashing down on me and if this run of good luck would somehow leave me bruised and bleeding on the side of the road. I thought of my mother again and how she could never accept the good things that were happening to her when they did. To just enjoy the moment for what it was and let the chips fall where they may.

Deal again, I thought. *Deal again.*

I needed to get some work done but I needed to talk to Maggie as well, so I texted her.

> *Can I call you?*
> *I have a lot of news.*
> *How is the new job?*

I didn't expect her to get back to me very quickly because of her job and she didn't.

I zoned into my job as I looked over the documents and the plan that Jackie sent to me. It didn't take long for me to realize there was a pile of work to do in a short amount of time. I couldn't believe the number of bridges in the district and was delighted to see I was going to be travelling to a number of places I'd never seen.

Just around lunchtime, my phone rang. It was Maggie.

"Well, hello there. How's the first day going?"

"It's great. Well, it's kind of the same, only different, but so far so good. Tell me, what's the news? It must be kind of big when you needed to talk."

I told her all the things that happened and she was thrilled for me and for us. She was over the moon about the bike trip and said, "I won't start working weekends until July sixteenth. I'll get a four-day weekend on the ninth and then work the next one. This is going to work out perfectly."

"How about staying up there and the reception plan?" I asked.

"Easy, peasy. From what Jackie said at Ginger's the other night, I don't think we should be driving back to the city anyway, so let's just stay there. What kind of place is it?"

I told her I had no idea and she said it didn't matter. We both figured if Jackie lined it up it would be perfect for us. I said I'd nail it down and I could tell she was coming out of her skin thinking about it.

I shared my own good fortune from work and told her I'd be on the road for a few weeks. I said I'd have more details after our meeting and she asked me to thank Jackie for all he'd done.

When I let her go, I was rattling like a druggie in need of a fix. My mind was racing and I felt like I was being given electric shocks in just the right amount to keep me alert and frightened.

Jackie, Butch, Mike, and I met in the afternoon to discuss the project and we were indeed going out on the road the next day. We'd be gone for the week and would be back in the city on Friday. We decided we should plan on working the following weekend just to get ahead of it.

I called Maggie that night and told her we were leaving the next day and suggested we meet at Ginger's on Friday when we got back. She was OK with all of it and, besides, what choice did we have? It was only four days and she was excited about seeing me at the end of the week.

The next day we met at the office and headed out in Jackie's truck. We had clothes, gear, tools, food, and equipment stuffed in as we drove away and Jackie said to me, "You told me you were out in Iona Rear at the Rory G's, right?

"Well, I was at Mungie and Sadie's house," I said.

"Yes, that's the same place, and you met Joe there, as well? Joe MacKinnon."

"Yes, we did. Why?"

"Well, he landed in the hospital on Saturday. They said he had a heart attack."

"No way."

"Yes way, but they think he'll be OK. I guess they almost lost him."

"Where is he now? And what will Mungie and Sadie do?"

"He was in Baddeck but I think he's coming to the city today or tomorrow, I'm not really sure what's next for him. The ladies will be looked after by someone nearby, they have some good neighbours and family around."

"Well, that's the strangest thing, I could have sworn I saw him at Ginger's on Friday night."

"What? When was that?"

"Well, it was around midnight and we were coming back from the dance floor. I thought I saw him down the back smoking a cigarette having a beer and a shot."

"Well, he used to smoke, and he likes to drink."

"It kinda caught me off guard and when I turned to look at him again he was gone."

"Well, that's strange. You might have had a little vision there, you know, with all the talk of spirits and little people," Jackie said.

"Do you think? Do you think that's what it was?"

"I don't doubt it for a second and I think it's a bit of a blessing, really, to see something like that."

"Well you know, I might've seen things like that before but I just didn't realize it at the time."

"That's part of the mystery of it all I guess. We don't realize it's happening until it's past."

"I guess, I just never knew I was experiencing it before."

"Well, you know that the whole area around MacKinnon's settlement had a little vibe to it that was different than other places nearby. Just beyond Joe's house is a little place called *Stumpa Na Bhòcain* that has spooked people for years."

"Really?"

"Yes. In the light of day, it was just another turn along the wooded road. But at night, it was like a hangout for spirits on the campaign trail. You may need to see it so you can feel it."

We firmed up plans for the weekend of the ninth as we spent the rest of the day driving, laughing, and getting a ton of inspections done. There were so many bridges, most of them beam bridges, and I realized this was the best job I ever had.

Later that day between stops I texted Maggie to tell her about Joe and told her about seeing him at Ginger's. Or at least, I thought I saw him.

She texted me later that night.

> *I called Mungie to ask her about Joe.*
> *I had a few other questions for her.*
> *She and Sadie might come to the city on the weekend if Joe is here.*
> *She sounded sad for him.*
> *How was your day?*
> *Do you really think you saw him at Ginger's?*

I replied,

> *The day was great and, yes, I think it was him.*
> *Lots of laughs and work.*
> *Look forward to Friday.*

The week went by like a bolt of lightning in a thunderstorm and I saw a hundred places I'd never seen in my life. We went around the Cabot Trail and looked at every bridge and stayed in several small towns along the way. As strange as it was for me to say I'd never been there before, I met people who said they'd never been to the city and didn't care if they ever went. It seemed as though they felt like they weren't missing a thing.

We'd seen some beautiful territory as we travelled through the Highlands, made our way around to Baddeck, and I saw the lake again—the lake Maggie and I had travelled beside a few weeks before and Jackie pointed across it as Washabuck stared back at us. I realized where I was, how close I was to the ocean, and it was all so much clearer to me.

The story of Mugsie and Boronia raced through my mind. The water touched everything and I thought of the stories I read of the mythical water horse and how true they could be. They could be everywhere if they so desired, and why wouldn't the Vikings have sailed right up through this gentle waterway centuries ago?

It seemed rather strange, but every time I went near a bridge I kept getting little stings in my legs and back. They only lasted a few seconds before going away as if nothing had happened at all. I checked my body every night for marks, but never saw anything and thought I must be losing it.

Most every time I went under a bridge, I thought of little people and wondered if they were watching us. Were they inspecting us without us even knowing, as if we were the bridge and they the humans? As the week wore on, every time I heard a noise in the bush or the rivers gurgled in a certain way, I felt like I was being observed. I grew more and more convinced that they were there. Not to mention the birds under everyone, they seemed to be everywhere.

It was all rather ominous at times and I wasn't sure I could share it all with Jackie and Mike. We had a number of conversations and I kept nibbling around the edges looking for one of them to bite, but no one did.

On Friday we drove through Skye Glen, which was the place that Maggie thought we might be going to on our first date. I couldn't believe how much I'd learned in a few weeks—mind you, spending a week on the road with Jackie was a crash course like no other.

We drove by the Glenora Distillery as we headed back to the city and I thought of Maggie and our time together. I thought of the cockles of my heart and I couldn't wait to get back and see her again.

We were heading back around two p.m., and Jackie and I were in full discussion about the small-town tour we had planned for the next weekend. We talked about the route, who was going, how long it would take, the reception and the food and drink, and then he said, "Do you want to swing by the Washabuck Falls?"

"Yes, for sure."

Then I said no.

"I think I should wait for Maggie. It wouldn't be right for me to get there ahead of her."

"I get it," he said.

"I'd like to see them," Mike said.

"Another time," we both said.

"Do you want to see where you are staying?" he asked.

"Sure, that would be great."

As we drove through Iona, he pulled into this little cottage that was right there beside the lake and Jackie said, "It's not much, but it'll get you through the night.

"It's perfect," I said. "Where are you staying?"

"I'll drag my camper up to my parents' place and park her there."

He pointed to their house as we drove away and when we crossed the bridge I felt like I was in complete control of the next weekend. I thought of when Donald asked me if I'd turned pro, and at that time, I felt like one.

Mike and I got Jackie to stop at our places and we dropped our stuff off and kept on to the office to wrap things up for the week and I said to Jackie, "We're heading to Ginger's for a couple of drinks, do you want to join us?"

"Do I want to? Yes. Can I? No. But thanks for asking, I need to get home and give Donna a break. We'll make up for it next weekend."

We tidied up a few things at the office and he drove us to Ginger's like he did the week before and said, "Let's say noon tomorrow at the office, OK? You can let a little steam off tonight but we need to stay on it tomorrow and Sunday. Probably hit the road again next week, but we'll figure that out tomorrow."

"Sounds great," we said and he drove away.

"What a week," Mike said as he ordered two pints. "He gets stuff done, doesn't he?"

"Yup, he sure does."

I'd been texting the usual suspects on our way back and Maggie was on her way with a friend from work and Joey was coming, as well. Doug and Clair were going out to supper and a movie. They wanted to come by for a drink and say hello, but planned on doing their own thing.

Mike and I grabbed a table and a few minutes later Maggie and her friend showed up. I got up to meet her and we embraced and kissed each other. She looked amazing.

"You look great," I said. "I think I underdressed again."

"Thank you. I treated myself and bought some new clothes. Do you like them?"

"Of course. It's very summery and it looks like you've been getting some sun. Your skin looks so dark."

Mike rolled his eyes at her friend.

"I have been, thank you. I needed a little lift through the week and new clothes will do that for a girl most times."

She introduced us to her friend Lisa and I went to the bar and grabbed the girls a drink. I started to get the story of her first week in the new job and she told me how much better she felt being full time. She compared it to her connection to Liza *Mhór* and where she came from. She felt like she truly belonged and asked me about my week on the road.

"It was pretty darn good, and I saw a lot of places I'd never seen before. I saw Washabuck across the lake from Baddeck and I can totally see how the whole story of Boronia might have happened. You have to see it."

"Did you go there?"

"No, we didn't. I need you to see it first or with me or something. I wasn't there—mind you, Jackie offered to take us to the falls but I knew I couldn't go there without you."

She was glad that we'd see it for the first time together. I told her about seeing the cottage and how I thought it was going to be perfect for us. She talked like I had it all sorted out but I gave the credit to Jackie.

He had the cottage, the bikes, and the trip all planned. It was a small-town tour in the day and a country party at night. We were both very excited and couldn't wait for the weekend to arrive.

I felt as though we were leaving Mike and Lisa out a bit but they seemed to be finding things to talk about and entertained themselves for the most part. They were coming in and out of the conversation with us and Mike was able to fill Lisa in with some of the pieces he picked up from me and Jackie during the week.

Lisa left after one drink and we moved in to play some pool at the vacant table. Mike had gone to the bathroom when Joey showed up and he joined us at the table and ribbed us a bit with stuff like "When did you two lovebirds land in the nest?" and some cheesy pick-up lines—all in fun, of course. I thought he was just jealous and Maggie pretty much chilled him out when she told him she had her eye on me since the spring. I had no idea and wasn't about to ask. With that, she took her shot and sliced the ball straight in.

Mike came back and the two of them had other ideas, like the week before, and headed off to another bar. Mike told us through the week that he was working on something and she was not at Ginger's.

We understood completely and wished them the best. That left Maggie and me by ourselves so we played a couple of games and decided we'd had enough pool for one night and looked for a table.

We found a table all right. It was the same one I saw Joe sitting at the week before. We went to it and sat down and I said to Maggie, "This is where Joe was sitting last week."

"You're kidding me—are you sure?"

"Right here and I had a couple of dreams that he was connected to, as well."

"What do you mean?"

I told her all about my dreams. I was sure I was in his car with a girl with soft hands and pretty face. I told her about sensing the little people when we looked under the bridges and knew there had to be a connection.

"I bet there is," she said. "Those people, my people, have been in my head every day since we went there. I told you I was talking to Mungie, didn't I?"

"How are they?" I asked.

"They're OK. They're praying for Joe and they think he'll be all right. They might be down to see him tomorrow or they'll go see him in Baddeck later next week. If he's moved back there it's a good sign he'll be OK."

"Well, that's good," I said.

"I also asked her about coming by next weekend to see them again. Mungie was delighted to hear that and she hoped you were going to be there, as well."

We figured the best thing was for us to drive there on our own on Sunday. Jackie had been so helpful to us but we knew he'd want to see his own family, so that was our plan.

"So then, what about Malcolm on the hill? How are we going to find that house he talked about? You know, Big Neil's."

"Well, it was more like a foundation or a cellar or something. I don't know. Do you want to ask Jackie if he has any idea what we could do?"

"Sure, I'll ask him and if I know him he'll work something out. Do you want to call Malcolm and see if this weekend will work for him?"

"I'll do that and I bet it just works out for us. If I don't get to see the old place this time, we'll go back and try again."

"That's the spirit. Now if I get a chance this week, do you want me to ask Jackie about the MacKinnon connection or do you just want to leave that for now?"

"I guess if it's convenient, you could see what he says. I'm more interested in seeing where Mam came from and the whole area around the falls. I'd love to meet some people that might have witnessed something around there. You know some sort of magic or miracle or something."

"Well, you're not asking for much," I said jokingly. "He did say he knew someone who lived nearby that might have a story or two."

"I can't wait to go there and see all the back trails. Have you ever driven one of those bikes before?" she asked.

"No, I haven't, but it can't be that hard. Have you?"

"Well, yes, I have, and it's a lot of fun. I caught on pretty quick, if I do say so myself."

"Well, I guess you're driving then."

"Oh, you'll have to try it. That's half the fun."

"Yeah, it looks like fun. And speaking of which, are we staying for another, or do we want to go somewhere else?"

"Somewhere like where?" she asked, as her light blue eyes lit up to match her smile.

"I don't know. My place, your place. What are you thinking?"

"Well, either place works for me. I'd like you to see my place, but you haven't been in your own bed all week so I think we should go there."

I was happy with that so we paid our bill and headed for the door.

We hailed a cab, drove back to my place, and when we got to the top of the stairs, the door to the little shared deck blew open. There was no real weather outside and I looked toward Maggie and said, "Come on in, Joe, welcome to my flat."

"That's a little creepy," she said.

"No harm in Joe, I just hope he's OK."

I was home and we made some food, had a couple of drinks, and went to bed. We talked for a long time about the weeks we'd had and the excitement that was building toward the coming weekend. We made gentle love with each other and drifted off to sleep.

We slept like babies all night and the morning came in its own sweet time. Maggie and I explored each other as we were in total comfort and knew our time together was short.

That was our weekend. I'd be working well into the night and Sunday was a write-off, as well.

I drove Maggie home and watched her leave again. I was having more and more difficulty with that part and thought about a time when we might be together forever. I kept on to the office and returned to my other life.

Farewell to My Glen

Waltz

Paul K. MacNeil

CHAPTER 11
Small-Town Tour

I spent most of Saturday afternoon cleaning my place and thinking about the whirlwind I was in and how could it have happened so quickly. I felt like I was working on a puzzle—and, in many ways, I was. My world was dropping pieces in front of me and every piece had found its spot.

I was humming all afternoon as I worked and thought of the songs and airs that Mam had sung when she busied herself around the house years ago. There was one in particular that kept coming back to me time and time again and I felt, for the first time in forever, that Mam was there with me.

I thought of my new job, how nicely it had worked out for me, and was looking forward to Monday. I thought of Patrick and somehow all of these good things seemed to be connected to him.

At least he was connected to all the good things that had just happened. I thought about him working today, tonight, and leaving again tomorrow. I knew it meant we would be together all next weekend, but I missed him now.

It was then that a knock came to my door that surprised me a bit. I hoped it was Patrick but somehow knew it wouldn't be, and I was correct. It was Clair from next door and a bottle of wine.

"Can I come in?"

"Of course," I said. "Are you starting early or was I working late?"

"Oh you're working way too late," Clair said as she came into the kitchen. "I heard two things today."

"What's that?"

"Well, I heard you working all afternoon and I heard Patrick was buried at work so I thought you might want some company."

"And how did you hear about Patrick?"

"Well, I was talking to his friend Doug," she said in a giddy sort of way.

"Oh, yes, how was last night?"

"It was nice, nice and easy. Food and a flick, you know."

"Anything else?"

"No, but I was tempted, I can tell you that. He made me laugh and that always feels good. I think he's a nice guy and we both said we should try and go slow."

"Slow and steady wins the race," I said.

"Yeah, I know. But he's kind of stoking my coals, if you know what I mean."

"Oh, I know what you're going through." I chuckled, thought about myself, and said, "The bigger the mound, the hotter the fire."

"Well, I guess I have that to look forward to, but I feel like I need someone right now, and then I don't want to mess it up either."

"Just take your time. You've been through a lot lately and I'm sure it will all work out."

We drank her bottle, one of my own after that, and talked about all the fun things that were happening to us. We were both a little needy and made great company for each other as our conversation flowed with great ease.

I told her more about myself and my past than I'd ever told anyone besides Patrick. She was thrilled about my story, at least the part that was happening now, and by the end of it, she wanted to come with us on our bike trip. Maybe another time, I told her.

She had her own story of a miracle baby in her family that had always made her wonder about the magic of it all. Her cousin, a single woman in her mid-twenties, was told she was going to die. She wanted to leave something behind in this world and was determined to get pregnant.

Her parents agreed to raise the child if she died and when she did a few months later they raised a healthy baby girl. The child was a grown woman today and people always think of her and her mother when they see her. She'd heard a few other stories as well but the details were getting a little cloudy by the end of the night.

Clair went home before it was too late and I went to bed and slept like a rock. I dreamt of waterways, streams, bridges and what Patrick told me of feeling watched when he was under the bridges. In every dream I saw a young-looking woman in a white gown and long white hair decorated in flowers. Small birds were singing, chanting some sort of song or melody that seemed familiar.

I woke up with a jolt and a shiver as I remembered seeing her in every dream. I thought about Patrick seeing Joe at the bar in his dream and the door blowing open Friday night. I thought it was all very mystical and somehow eerily related.

I thought about Patrick and where he was right now. They were leaving that morning and wouldn't be back until Friday. That was the one thing that wasn't going my way right now and I needed to keep reminding myself the travelling wasn't going to last forever. I missed him and I felt, to some degree, incomplete without him.

I thought of the morning before and how we just rolled around in his bed all morning and enjoyed the loving start to the day. We needed to be nowhere but there. And we were.

For some strange reason, the week went by very quickly and smoothly. When I wasn't working I spent my time preparing for Patrick and myself to fly out of town on Saturday morning. I was packed on Wednesday and had the contents for our cooler sitting in my fridge waiting to leave.

I talked to Patrick a few times throughout the week and things were going well for them on the road. From what he told me they were very busy and ahead of the schedule they had set for themselves. They'd be back on Friday and were taking a few days off that ran right into the weekend and Monday. On Thursday night, he called and said, "Are we all set for the weekend?"

"Yes, I have everything packed and plenty of food ready to go."

"Were you talking to Malcolm and the ladies in the Rear?" he asked.

"Yes, we're going to visit the Rear on Sunday after lunch. Mungie asked us to have lunch with them, but I didn't want to put them out."

"OK, and what about getting to see your old place and hooking up with Malcolm?"

"Well, listen to this. Malcolm told me he was talking to Jackie and the two of them had worked out some sort of plan. You must have said something to Jackie—did you?" I asked.

"Well, I mentioned it to Jackie and he said, 'We'll figure it out.' He didn't tell me that he had it figured out."

"Well, that's OK with me. I thought we'd go exploring on Sunday after Mungie and Sadie's, and see where it takes us."

Patrick was cool with everything and was sure it would all work out. He asked about hooking up at Ginger's on Friday and I was non-committal. He needed to do some laundry and get prepared for our next adventure so he decided to go home. He would get sorted out and come to my place when he was packed and ready.

I wanted him to spend the night at my place where we'd leave from in the morning and everything should work out OK. He said that was the best offer he'd had all week and I said it best be the only one. And then I asked him for a little favour.

"Of course, what is it?"

"Can you take some of your sketching equipment with you? I wanted a sketch of Mam, but I also thought it would be nice to do one of Mungie and Sadie and leave it with them."

"Oh, that's a nice idea."

"Do you mind? Because if you do, it's no problem."

"I think it's a great idea—consider it done."

"Oh, and one more thing before I let you go."

"What's that?"

"Barkley called me and asked me to work this weekend at the clinic."

"And what did you say?"

"I said, 'Not even at gunpoint and told him not to call me anymore.' It felt pretty good."

With that, we let each other go, I did a final check on everything and went to bed.

I slept pretty well but when I woke it was with a start. I'd been dreaming of the young lady with the white hair and this time I was with her in the forest and I heard lots of water. I heard little voices and chanting, but it wasn't really chanting, it was monk-like music or something like that. I couldn't quite put my finger on it but it was familiar and yet unknown to me. There were birds, all kinds of small birds and they chanted and sang their songs and flew around us in circles.

I thought all day about my dream, the weekend, and seeing Patrick again. I wished he was there in the morning when I woke but there was nothing I could do about that. The day went by and he texted me around 6 p.m., and said:

I'm back and working on laundry and packing.
Should be there around 7:30.
Can't wait to see you.

I was waiting by the phone, as they used to say, and texted back:

Can't wait to see you, too.

I guess I could have done a couple of things to pass the time but I decided to pour a glass of wine and make one of Mam's old recipes. It was an old bonnach recipe that I'd made with Mam but I'd never made on my own. It just seemed to be the right time and if it turned out I'd add it to our weekend supplies.

I remembered souring the two cups of milk with two tablespoons of vinegar and thinking it was so gross. The longer it sat, the lumpier it got. I whisked up two eggs and had the molasses ready to dump in. Mam never measured it, she'd just go by the colour and texture, but it was about a cup.

Three cups of white and three cups of whole wheat flour and a quarter cup of brown sugar. One tablespoon of baking powder and one teaspoon of baking soda and salt.

I mixed the dry and dumped in the wet and married it all together. It was much like regular bread dough, but a little wetter. I sprayed the cookie sheet and revved the oven up to 400 degrees. I divided it into two loaves about an inch thick and formed them like an oval.

I used to call it bomb bread when I was really small because it looked like a torpedo. I slid it in the oven, turned it down to 375 degrees after five minutes and then baked it for forty-five minutes in total. It would be ready by the time Patrick got there, and I hoped it turned out like Mam's. The raw dough sure tasted good.

Now that called for another glass of wine and I ran the water for the tub. I decided to lie back and enjoy the last bit of my time alone. I thought it just as well to take the bottle with me rather than have to get up in twenty minutes if something changed.

I slid into the hot, soapy water and thought about my week at work, and what might happen in the next few days. I thought about being alone, but knowing I was enjoying it because I wouldn't be alone in a very short time. I thought about how good that made me feel and I thought about the people who don't have someone they really like coming over. I thought about being with him all weekend and I felt so...felt so...pleased.

The wine was delicious and I topped up my glass. I knew I should get out but decided to enjoy it for five more minutes. My phone chirped and it was Patrick.

> *Running a few minutes behind.*
> *I'll be there by eight.*

Like I thought to myself earlier, I knew he would be here soon so I stayed in the tub a little longer and enjoyed myself.

I almost drifted off or maybe I did. Oh my God, I did. My whole body shook and my mind started racing as I checked the time and I was OK. I must have just slipped away for a minute or two and I thought of our little nap in the church in Iona on our first date. Or was that our second date? It was all a little confusing but I smiled to myself and then remembered the bonnach in the oven.

I jumped out and grabbed a towel and my robe and I suppose I was like the blacksmith's dog and ran to the kitchen. I smelled it right away—it was beautiful and amazing. Ok, breeeeaaathe, I gave it a poke with a skewer and if it came out clean, we were in business.

Clean as a whistle. It was like giving birth to a child for me and the memories of Mam came rushing back again. I was very proud of myself! I had raised my knife to cut it open when the buzzer rang from the front door. Oh no, was it Patrick? It couldn't be.

"Hello."

"Hi, it's Patrick."

"Ah, come on up."

I was thinking as fast as I ever had and wondered what I could do. And there was nothing I could do. This was not the first impression I wanted him to have of my apartment and I hoped he liked my old bathrobe.

I just went to the door and met him before he knocked and said, "Hi, you're early."

"And overdressed again," he said with a clever grin.

His arms came out toward me and he pulled me close and we kissed like we hadn't seen each other in a week. It felt so loving, I didn't want it to stop. But he backed away.

"You taste good. Is there any more?"

"There's lots more where that came from," I said and took his hand and led him into the kitchen.

"I just love that perfume you're wearing. It smells like sweet bread."

"It's a little family secret," I said, as I poured him a glass of wine.

"Feast your eyes on this." And I introduced him to the bonnach.

"Wow, and thanks," he said, taking the wine.

"OK, don't say anything."

I sliced the bonnach and covered it in margarine. I let it melt and then covered about half of it with molasses.

"Try that."

"Oh, my. This is just amazing. It's so good."

"Help yourself, I'll be right back."

I went to get changed and heard him oohing about the bonnach as I tried to decide what to wear. I had no interest in going out so I slipped into something silky and soft. Although makeup wasn't my usual routine, I put on a little and a splash of perfume and took a quick look at myself.

I liked what I saw and thought I looked pretty darn good. I spent more time looking at myself than usual but I looked happy and felt good about myself. I felt good about us.

Patrick was staring at a picture of Mam when I quietly came back into the living room. I snuck up behind him and pinched his butt cheek and said, "Come here often?"

He jumped, turned, and stared at me.

"I'm going to start. You look beautiful," he said, and he leaned toward me and we kissed.

I grabbed his cheeks again and said, "You feel good."

We just lounged around my apartment for the evening and I introduced him to the pictures of family, friends, and my life on the wall. We talked about Doug and Clair, our weeks at work, and the weekend in front of us.

We had a couple more glasses of wine and firmed our plans for the morning and headed off to bed. I was the last to bed and, before I shut the light off, I stared at him in my bed and wished he was there all week. I thought of my dreams and the young lady with the white hair and I wondered if she would pay a visit tonight. I slid in beside him and felt his masculine body against mine and he felt so good. We held each other close and caressed each other as we made love and fell asleep.

I was awake early and ready to get rolling. Part of me wanted to lay there with Patrick for hours but this was the day I had been waiting for all week. I was up, dressed, and putting bags by the door and cracking the whip on my slumbering companion.

"We'll get a coffee and a breakfast sandwich on the way out of town—let's get going," I said.

"No shower, no coffee, no anything."

"No, not now. It's a large day and we need to get after it."

It was a beautiful day and we were out the door and heading for the country bright and early. When we stopped for coffee Patrick suggested I drive so he could work on the drawings and finish up some stuff for work.

I was happy to drive his little red Honda that had so much power. It was a sharp-looking rig and I played with his head, acting a little crazy behind the wheel.

"Am I driving OK?" I asked, jokingly.

"Just great, you have driven before, right?"

"Oh, yes, lots of experience, can't wait to drive the bike," I said, shaking my head from side to side and smiling.

Patrick grabbed the Jesus handles and pretended to be scared until I told him I'd stop.

I continued to drive and we didn't talk that much as Patrick did his work and then started doing the sketches. It was effortless for him and fascinating to watch as the faces came together every time. I looked over from my place behind the wheel and had to concentrate very hard to not be hypnotized by it all.

The time flew and the trip seemed so much shorter this time compared to last. It could have been because I was driving, or knowing the road or where we were going. I kept seeing things that now looked familiar or not as foreign as the first trip.

I knew we were almost there when I saw the turnoff for the café and the next thing we were crossing the bridge. I smiled and said, "Do you remember this place?"

"Yes, I think my heart is over there on the beach."

It seemed a little awkward for a minute and then he said, "I meant that in the nicest way possible. Never mind, I withdraw the statement and replace it with this one. I have great memories of us being here together. Better?"

"Yes, better now. Where is our little spot?"

"Right there, down by the water."

"Oh my God, it's perfect."

The cottage was not at all small and had a gorgeous deck on the waterside that looked out over the strait. The only thing between us was the railroad tracks and I had every intention of going for a walk on them if only to be able to say I did it.

"It should be open," Patrick said.

And it was! It was cute as can be on the inside. It had a nice open kitchen and living room, two bedrooms and a nice big bathroom. It was terrific. We took our stuff in and I started putting a few things away in the fridge but also sorting out what was going on the bike.

Jackie had told Patrick they were leaving by 10 a.m., and we were well ahead of that as we heard bike engines in the distance. The sound itself was spiriting as the anticipation of getting out there was rumbling in my mind with the gentle roar from the distant motors. I needed to pee and the thought of a dog popped into my head.

Toilet paper: I thought of that as I was making my water. I was sure this would be a day of nature peeing and having toilet paper would be darn handy.

I wondered what else I had forgotten and didn't really care. We had all we needed and then some. Food, drink, friendship, transportation, and a glorious day—we needed nothing, but I was glad I remembered the toilet paper.

When I went outside I heard the bikes heading our way and seconds later, two bikes were at our door. It was Jackie and his wife Donna. Donna was driving a Yamaha side-by-side and Jackie was driving a huge Honda with a seat on the back. Donna stayed on her bike and turned it around and waited as Jackie jumped off and said, "Is everything OK here with the cottage?"

"Oh, God, yes, it's perfect," I said.

"OK, are you ready to go?"

"Yes, for sure."

"OK, throw what you're taking in the back of Donna's rig and we'll chat down at the wharf. There's a tradition that the last one to the wharf has to chug a beer and take a belt of rum before we can leave, and I don't want that to be me."

Patrick got on the back with Jackie and I sat beside Donna and we took off. Donna said hello and asked about our drive but I couldn't see her face with the helmet on. I wondered if we needed them or if we should have brought them. I was strapped in a seatbelt and my hair was flowing in the hot morning air and Donna was flying. She was no rookie with this machine as she left Jackie and Patrick in the dust.

We passed by the little store and got down to the wharf and there was a barrier up to keep vehicles from driving down to the end. It was a very large structure and there were three bikes already parked there. The other bikers had walked out onto the wharf and were looking at what looked like a house floating beside the wharf.

We got off the bike and Donna removed her helmet. She gave me a hug and said, "Welcome to Iona, I've heard a lot about you and Patrick."

"Oh thank you, it's really nice to meet you, as well."

She was a tall woman with thick, flowing brown hair, a gentle smile, and a soft voice that was welcoming and full of love.

Jackie and Patrick were pulling up and Donna said, "I hope you don't mind but I'm going to have a little fun here."

I figured this is where I should stand back and watch, so I did.

Donna pulled out two beers and handed them to the boys and said, "Suck 'em back, boys. You're last, the way I see it."

Jackie protested a bit and took his helmet off and said, "It's nice to see you, Maggie," as he reached for a hug.

"The same."

"Drink up, boys," Donna said.

And the games were on.

"There are others coming, but let's go look at the house over there while we wait for them," Jackie said as he opened his beer.

We strolled down the wharf and, sure enough, there was an old house on a barge floating beside the wharf. Jackie explained that they'd barged it from the other side of the island from a place called Troy and they were going to haul it through town and take it to the Highland Village.

The Highland Village is a museum of sorts that tries to depict the life of the early Scottish settlers to Nova Scotia. He told us we should go up just to see the beauty of the place if nothing else and then he told us the journey of the house.

He said they moved it by truck from its cellar in Troy and loaded it onto a barge and tugged it through the canal at the Canso Causeway and down around the bottom of Cape Breton to St Peter's. They kept going through the canal there and up the big lake to here. They had to wait for high tide to bring it through the bridge here and land it at this wharf.

As we looked at and talked about the house, other bikers showed up and most came down to see the floating spectacle. We headed back to the bikes and Donna said, "How 'bout the shot, boys? Who's having one?"

"I have this nice scotch, if that counts," Patrick said as he pulled out the Glen Breton.

"Oh, that counts," said Jackie, as he took the first drink.

Patrick took his drink and Donna said, "Single malt, eh? I'll try some of that."

So Donna took a shot and then she said, "Come on, Maggie, try a blast. We're all in this together."

"Well, I know I like it. It's just a bit early for me. But what the hell."

I tipped it back and took a healthy shot. It went down smooth and warmed my chest and calmed my anxious feeling. It lit the cockles of my heart and I felt great.

There were about a dozen bikes and all different occupants from couples like us to single guys and single girls driving a wide assortment of bikes. Jackie talked to the lead guy and we were all going to meet again at the end of the Rear Road before going through the wooded area and one of the trickier sections.

Jackie had helmets for us and we could talk back and forth among the four of us if we wanted or we could shut that down. Patrick and I could also talk on our own if we wanted.

"There's a little spot I want to show you that they call *Stumpa Na Bhòcain*," Jackie said. "It means stump of the ghosts. We'll catch up to the others after that at the end of the Rear Road."

I was driving with Patrick in the side-by-side and Jackie and Donna were on the Honda as we took off up the beach along the lake we so admired. Patrick was delirious, hooting and hollering, screaming from ear to ear as we roared away. It was a fairly impressive sight, with most of us in a line and some of the younger ones trying to pass each other. All the while the lake sparkled like the crown jewels beside us.

Jackie gave us some play-by-play along the way and we came to the end of the beach and turned up by Mic Frank's cottage, which was stunning. We carried along a narrow driveway and came out halfway down what they called the graveyard hill. I recognized the pond and plaster island from our first time there a few weeks earlier and let out a little hoot myself. It was brilliant, exhilarating, and I felt so cool.

We turned onto the highway and drove for a short distance until we reached the plaster peninsula and we drove up. We stopped there for a few minutes and enjoyed the view before going back down onto the twisty highway. Just a short distance later we made the left turn onto the Barra Glen Road, leaving the lake behind like we had a few weeks earlier. The bikes were kicking up quite a bit of dust as we drove along and then everything pretty much came to a stop.

We came up behind a wine-coloured Nissan and followed them until the Iona Rear Road, and the car turned down there, as well. We passed right on by while the other bikes followed the crawling car. A short distance later, Jackie pointed out Joe MacKinnon's place as we went by. We were just on the western edge of MacKinnon's settlement when we stopped the bikes and Jackie said, "They saw and heard a great number of *bòcains* and ghosts or mysterious things around here over the years. It would be darker than a miner's lung out here and they'd be hearing noises and meeting things on the road that people couldn't explain. Everything from people being pushed and pulled as they walked along, to people hearing teams of horses and wagons."

"It looks innocent enough," I said.

"Yes it does, but it's ten a.m. See what you think if you come back at ten p.m., and have to walk any distance through here."

"Come on, let's catch up to the others. I don't really like it here in the daytime," Donna said.

We wheeled around and picked it up a bit and were back on the Rear Road in no time. As we drove by Mungie and Sadie's driveway, we saw the wine-coloured Nissan climbing the hill to their house. As we dipped by their driveway and climbed the next hill we saw the forest and the last of the bikes pulling up to the tree line. We caught up to them and it was decided we'd stop at Red Neil May Ann's for a drink.

We all headed into the woods on what was now very much a four-wheeler mud trail and Jackie said, "When we hit the mud holes let the bike ahead of you get through so you don't both get stuck. And once you get in there don't slow down, keep going hard."

As we waited for the other bikes to go through, Jackie said, "You know, Mickey Red Neil built his new house here and moved it into Iona years ago. Little-known fact."

"That's three houses in this little area that were moved," Patrick said. "Mungie and Sadie told us their father moved their house across the pond when they were children."

"Well, I didn't know that," Jackie said.

The trip through the woods was daunting at best but eventually, we got to a beautiful old farm that was losing the battle with nature. You could see where the barn was but it was now just bushes and weeds. The house still looked pretty straight but vandals had smashed in the windows and it was just a matter of time before its life would come to an end. The good thing was that the road was improving.

All the bikes stopped as we walked around and enjoyed a beverage. We were introduced to a few of the other bikers as we basked in the tranquility and beauty of the place.

Jackie told us there was said to be a fairy hill in that area many, many years ago. He told us that Mickey and May intended on spending the summers here and the winters in the new house in Iona. Right after they left, pretty near everything in the house was stolen and, a week later, the windows were smashed.

How anyone could do that to such beautiful people in such a peaceful place was beyond us all. We were all thinking the same thing and perhaps worse about the people who did that. Maybe someday something would happen to them and they'd feel some of the pain and loneliness they caused that elderly couple.

The younger crew were ready to move pretty quickly so the next call-out was for Gillis Beach, in Jamesville.

The speed picked up as the old driveway was long but still in pretty good shape. We turned onto another dirt road and came out at the pavement and Patrick said, "That's where the beach is, I remember this from our last trip. I almost went down there the first time we were here."

We crossed the pavement and right back onto the other dirt road, passing several cottages along the way. We'd driven for about ten minutes and we came through this funky little tunnel and, TADA!

An amazing beach. It was about a kilometre long and was shaped like a horseshoe as the road travelled along beside it with only sand and wild grasses between. There was no one on the beach, but a small cottage stood about halfway down and bordered a large pond on the other side.

It was amazing and it was like it magically appeared out of nowhere.

"We used to come here all the time when we were young and the place would be packed. The water was so warm and we'd dive for quahogs and cook them up on a beach fire with beach potatoes," Jackie said.

All the bikes stopped and it was time for another beverage. The scotch came out again and I was feeling warm all over and Jackie said, "You know there were many sightings of the ghost of Darby right here along this beach."

"I assume Darby was a person?" I asked.

"Oh, yes. And he was seen here over the years by a lot of people. People chased him and tried to talk to him but they never caught him and he never harmed anyone."

"Don't be scaring them," Donna said.

"I'm not trying to. Maggie's really interested in this sort of thing and other powers that we may not understand as normal. Isn't that right, Maggie?"

"Well, yes, I am."

Donna and I started talking on our own and I explained a bit of my story to her and she found it captivating. We walked along the beach for a short distance as Patrick and Jackie talked to a couple of the younger guys. Three or four others stripped down to very little and went for a quick swim.

We stayed there quite a while and had a beer, while a couple of the bikes went off on their own, and, eventually, the next stop was announced as MacKinnon's Harbour.

We decided to switch rigs and Patrick got the quick tutorial as he took control of the Honda. He was a little skittish at the start but after a few moments when he was comfortable he was ripping through the gears and yahoos and said, "This is so awesome, I can't believe I've never done this before."

He was squealing like a stuck pig as I wrapped my arms around him and hugged him so tightly. I kissed the back of his neck and told him how awesome the day was so far. He felt the same.

Jackie pointed out some old farms and old names as we continued down this nice dirt road. After about ten minutes we came out again at the pavement and he said, "We're in your territory now, Maggie. This is MacKinnon's Harbour."

"Where's the harbour?" I asked.

"Well, we needed to go in the other direction to see the water but this is the main settlement—or 'the interval,' as they say. If you look across there, it's the way to Highland Hill where Big Neil and Peadair Custie lived."

"This could be where my father came from," I said to Patrick.

He rubbed my leg with his free hand and said, "We'll come back here tomorrow."

I looked around. The area was very flat with most of the homes a long distance from the road. Most of the land was kept up to some degree but none of it looked like it was seriously farmed. It was the same story—it had seen better days and I sensed there was quite a difference from years ago.

We crossed the pavement and headed up a long driveway that swung into another dirt road that was lined with new power poles and wire. We climbed the mountain for the longest time and eventually got to a plateau at the top and turned to the right. There was a tower there and Jackie told us it was for the internet. It was a wireless signal they sent out to areas that couldn't get high speed over the usual copper wires.

I felt something inside me that was completely unfamiliar when we stopped at a large opening that looked like a blueberry field. We were back into the beverages and Jackie talked to the lead guy again and took off on the side-by-side by himself.

Donna looked at me and said, "He'll be back in five minutes and he has a little surprise for you."

"What is it?"

"Well, it won't be a surprise if I tell you."

"How 'bout another little shot?" Patrick asked.

"I'd love one," Donna said, as she raised the bottle toward me. "If this is where you came from, then this must be your mountain?"

I didn't know what to say as she handed me the bottle. I felt a bit stunned as I took a small drink. I felt a bit like crying and laughing at the same time when I heard Jackie's bike returning. I saw him with a man seated beside him on the side-by-side. It was Maxie.

Everyone said hello to Malcolm as if he was famous and he looked at Patrick and me and said, "You found the place," and he reached his hand out to greet us again.

"Is this it, for real?"

"Come with me," he said.

The five of us started out through the field and a number of the younger ones came along with us. We walked for quite a while through the vast blueberry field, down through another little opening in what was such a stunning place. You could see for miles with the lake in sight and calling to us the whole time. In the distance an old cellar was appearing as Malcolm talked about how busy the place used to be. All sorts of names and stories of *Céilidhs*, Gaelic singing, house parties, and work. There was no end to the work and it sounded like they enjoyed it all and we arrived.

"This is where Big Neil's house was, and just over in the woods back toward the road is where *Peadair Custie* lived. Now I can remember full well being here when I was young but I don't remember *Peadair Custie*. I can just remember being at that house. It hadn't quite fallen but it had a pretty good bend to her. Of course, there were so many stories, so many stories. I always smile when I think of this but they used to say the old lady could knit behind her back."

I reached toward him and hugged him and said, "Thank you for being here and showing me this. You don't know what this means to me."

"Oh, I have a pretty good idea. You know, I lived away in Toronto for years and it took me a long time to realize I should be here. I know it's not the same, but I can remember what I felt when we decided to come home and I never forgot it."

"Well, I've never felt like this anywhere in my life so I'll try not to ever forget this moment. Thank you again."

"It was my pleasure and I'm glad it means so much to you," he said.

"How long since Big Neil passed away?" Jackie asked.

"Oh my, it must be fifty years, at least. Sure, it could be more."

"Was this whole mountain full of farms?" Jackie asked.

"Oh, yes, all across here and over to St. Columba Mountain, even back toward Cain's Mountain. Logging and farming mostly in these parts. You know, a lot of MacKinnons settled in Cain's Mountain first and then moved to MacKinnon's Harbour, but that was before my time."

"I didn't know that," said Jackie.

"Well, you know, this place is cleaned out, Cain's Mountain is pretty well cleaned out and St. Columba Mountain is pretty well gone, too. Jimmy is out there with Gail Lake's crew, but he has a hard time getting around, so he won't be there long."

"I've seen a lot more people leave than arrive and with that, unless you have any more questions, I should head home. There's supposed to be someone coming to look at the mill."

"It could be that foolish Frankie calling and saying he's someone else and with no intention of showing up."

"He wouldn't do that, would he?" said Jackie.

"I guess he would. He used to torment poor Martin, his neighbour, you know."

"How's that?"

"He'd be watching him from his own place and as soon as he saw Martin outside going to feed the chickens or split some wood, he'd ring the phone. Martin would go back in the house and Frankie would hang up. And then as soon as he saw him outside again, he'd do the same thing."

"That's kind of funny," said Patrick.

"Not if you were Martin. He'd do that three or four times in a row and then wait and do it a day or two later."

We were all kind of laughing at the end of it.

"I tell you, you could hear Martin cursing up here and that's two miles away. The air would be blue with him spitting sparks, 'Bunch of sluts,' he'd say. 'GD sluts.' Now pardon my language."

"That's OK, I've heard worse," I said with a treasured look.

As we walked back to the machines one of the young guys offered to take Maxie home as he was separating from the group. We were doubling back and, before he left, we thanked him again and he drove off with the lad.

The next stop would be Washabuck Bridge, but before we mounted up to leave this glorious place we all had another shot of scotch. The rumble of the machines cut through the stillness of my mountain and, as much as I wanted to stay, there was something else that needed to be seen.

This was a long stretch of mud roads, old logging roads, and some government roads that needed work. We were very much surrounded by forest and heading downhill the whole way. Patrick was whooping it up and I hugged him from behind and squeezed him tight. We were having a blast.

I thought of Mam and Mary Fiona and what it was like for them to be living out here and how they could have possibly survived. I thought of my own job, apartment, and when I worked at the clinic and none of it seemed anywhere close to the work they must have done in their lifetime.

It really was two different worlds and I wondered how so much could change in such a short period of time. As all of this and a hundred other things washed through my mind, we came out of the woods and stopped at the end of that road.

We turned right and headed back up a mountain and, as we did, we passed a small man and a dog on the road. I found it strange that no one turned their heads or waved except me, but we kept on going and, not too far up the mountain, all the bikes stopped.

When the machines stopped you could hear them, and that was pretty much it. We were there—we'd made it to the falls. You could hear the mystic cry from the forest and most of the riders headed straight for it.

We weren't far behind and as I headed down the hill I realized my phone was in the bike and I wanted pictures. I told the others to go on and when I returned to the bike the man I saw on the road was standing there with his little brown dog sitting right by his side.

"Hello," I said.

"Good day to you, ma'am," he replied.

I don't think I'd ever been called ma'am in my life until that moment.

"Are you here to see the falls?" I asked him.

"Well, yes, I am, but I've seen them many times before."

He was an older, thin man with a very narrow face, sunken eyes, and long, skinny hands. His clothes looked to be a little big on him and he wore rubber boots that were rolled down at the top. He seemed to be watching me pretty closely and he said, "You look familiar to me. Do I know you?"

"No, I don't think you do, but my name is Maggie MacKinnon and my grandmother was Liza *Mhór*. What's your name?"

"My name is Murdoch, Murdoch MacInnis, and I knew Liza and her mother, as well. Fine women, they were—pretty, like yourself."

"Well, thank you, yes, she was. Do you come here often?"

"Well, I come here more often than most people. It's a very special place for me."

"I've heard that and I was just about to go down to see them. Can you tell me what you've seen here?"

"Oh, I could tell you all sorts of things, but you'd have to believe that these things can happen or it wouldn't really matter. Do you believe?"

"Well, yes, I think I do, I've heard about these things from Liza *Mhór* and I'm trying to find out for myself if they're true."

"Well, it depends on what you believe."

"I'm not sure what part you are asking me about. I believe this place has special powers, even though I've not seen them yet and I believe that little people have magic powers. I believe the ancient tales of Boronia and the Vikings being here thousands of years ago. Is that what you are asking me?"

"Most of that, yes."

"Do you have reason to believe?" I asked him.

"Yes, I suppose I do."

"Why now is that?"

"Well, because I know they're around me and they're as much a part of me as I may be of them. I believe they have certain powers that we can't always explain and most don't understand."

"And what do you think it all means?" I asked.

"Oh, they see life differently than we do and they can cleanse souls so others can have a new beginning. They see the true beauty of life that most others take for granted. But you need to believe these things to have any chance of seeing them happen. Now, I think we should go down to the falls and you may see something you haven't seen or felt before."

We started down a pleasant path at first and then along a steep bank. Thankfully, there was a rope to hang on to as we carefully made our way toward the falls. All this time it was hard to hear anything but the roar of the water.

I remembered the sounds from my dreams with the little birds flying about in a circular direction and drifting upward through the canopy. I had no doubt I had seen and heard this all before and when I turned around to ask Murdoch about the birds, he was gone. It was at that moment I felt a little sting in my leg that left as quickly as it arrived.

I walked closer to the falls and it was as if time had stood still. I was right behind them in line on the rope and when I asked if anyone had seen Murdoch, they all looked a little confused.

When I caught up to Patrick, I said, "Did you see the little man down here?"

"Who do you mean?"

"Murdoch, an older, short little man with the rubber boots turned down."

"No, I'm sorry, I didn't see anyone, but this is exactly the way I feel when I'm under the bridges at work. I feel like someone is watching me."

"What do you think?" asked Donna.

"Oh, it's just beautiful," I said. I was scrambling to understand what had just happened.

"Isn't it, though? We came here after we were married and I just felt so fertile when I left. My whole body felt different."

"And did anything happen?"

"No, not really, but we had no trouble getting pregnant once we decided to start a family. I heard of other couples coming here to get a little magic when they were having troubles and with some I've heard that it works."

"And do you feel any differently?" Donna asked.

"I feel something different and I've had dreams about this place. I don't see the falls but it sounds exactly the same with the birds singing like they are now and the steady roar of the water. There is more going on, but there is something very special about this place."

"Lucky girl."

We stayed for quite some time and walked around the stony banks that lined the area. The falls dropped around sixty feet from the top to the pooling water at the bottom. It looked as if the top may have shifted over the years as there was a large indent in the rock face that must have taken thousands of years to form. The rock at the bottom near the pool of water looked like the face of an enormous sleeping reptile that was frozen in time.

The mosses and foliage had somehow found a way to survive and make a home for themselves in this challenging environment. There were all kinds of outpourings of rocks and what looked like tiny caves on the banks. The shading and sunshine seemed to share space like I'd never seen before. The trees, branches, and leaves reached and stretched to capture the precious rays of sunshine they could hold.

There was no denying we were in an amazing place and, after some time, we decided to keep going.

The day was wearing on as we all headed up the bank to the road to our next location, Jimmy Calaman's, on St. Columba Mountain.

We climbed and climbed for at least five minutes and then turned up a narrow driveway and climbed again. We passed the remains of an old barn and saw another old house that had seen better days but still had smoke coming out of its chimney. It was another old farm that was once again being reclaimed by nature.

We passed the house and I saw an old black truck parked in the tall grass, half buried, waiting to be devoured by the earth. We went to the top, the highest place on this peninsula, where two cell towers and a coast guard tower reached higher and higher into the sky. You could see everywhere.

The bridges that spanned the Barra Strait looked like engineering marvels you'd see from outer space. It felt like I was seeing everything, from the small end of the lake we drove by from the city to the big lake the floating house had been barged on. The lake was now more exposed than I had ever noticed before and it was spectacular. It was, indeed, the massive and mighty Bras d'Or Lake.

I turned and looked to the north and saw the Washabuck side where the Highlands and the mountains we'd been travelling on blended into one. I saw a part of the lake that would have turned into the Washabuck River that would have been fed by the water from the falls. It was overwhelming in many ways and I had never felt so embraced by nature as I was at that moment.

We decided to break out some food as we were all getting a little hungry and our stomachs needed a little mopping up. We had plenty and I was very pleased when everyone praised my bonnach in particular. There were only a few bikes left besides us and they were calling it a day. It was a straightforward trip on dirt roads back to Iona and Jackie and Donna were sticking with us to the end.

Jackie explained the meaning of the name of the lake as being *arm of gold*, which was given to it by the early French explorers, most likely because of the reflection of the sun on the water and the blazing effects on the trees and shoreline. He also said there were some references to the name Labrador, which made us talk of Boronia and the Viking settlements in Newfoundland.

When we went to leave, Jimmy was standing by the road so we stopped and Jackie introduced us and told him Liza *Mhór* was my grandmother.

He kept his eyes on me the whole time and said, "I knew your grandmother, I did. She was a lovely woman. You know, she looked a lot like you."

"I've heard a few people say that around here."

"Well, they should. I knew her mother, as well. I can remember her being here when I was a boy. They used to travel back and forth through here a long time ago, in my mother's day. You know, Liza *Mhór* lived down the road here for a few years and you could go right through the woods there to MacKinnon's Harbour and Highland Hill, but it's after growing in now."

He was kind of a gruff old man with grey, scraggly hair and a bushy grey mustache. He seemed a bit wobbly on his feet as he kindly spoke of his mother and the faith she had in the old beliefs and customs.

"You know, my mother had great faith in the fires of the *Bealtaine* and the May morning mist. Do you know about these things?"

None of us knew anything about them, which surprised me a bit as Jackie had been our go-to guy for any of this stuff and he was not informed on this one.

"Well, I'll tell you of the morning mist and the dew that would be on the ground on May the first. The women washed their face with it for it was said to enhance their beauty and keep them looking young forever. Some men would do this, as well, but it was mostly the women who treasured that day. My mother always followed that custom and all the old people around here did the same."

"And what about the fires?" I asked. "I have dreams about fires and dancing and chanting that I can't explain."

"Well, it was a bonfire really and you would light it on May first as long as the weather was OK—if not, the *Bealtaine* fire would be set any time in May. We used to extinguish all the fires in the house and relight them with the embers from the *Bealtaine* fire. The ash was thrown around the house and property, for it had protective powers. We would dance around the fire and there would be lots of food and music, as well.

"You know the cattle would be let out to pasture and we would decorate them. It marked the beginning of summer for us and old Rory, my horse, would be covered in flowers with his braided mane, that's hard to explain. Now that was quite a sight, I'll tell you."

"So, do you think some of these things are connected to the old tales about the Vikings coming here and the little people and their magical powers?" I asked.

"Well, yes, and at certain times of the year I can hear them chanting and singing and they're all around but I don't feel at all threatened by them. It scared me the first time but not after that. You know the wind can be very powerful up here and it comes from every direction and they travel with it. Some of the sounds I hear up here you wouldn't consider normal."

"When do you hear them?" I asked.

"Oh, I could hear them anytime, but they are nearly always around late in the fall, you know, what used to be our New Year. You know the spirits were free to travel back and forth between the worlds. Not many people believe that these days but the old people were very faithful to these old, old traditions."

He continued to talk about the power of the place and his life living there. He was another person I thought had only one address all his life. He kept returning to his mother's faith in the old customs and her belief in the spirit world. It seemed she felt that you needed to believe before you could see.

I completely respected what he was telling me and it was a conversation like none other I'd ever had.

I told him about the bonnach I'd made from Mam's old recipe and I gave him what was left in our basket. And, with that, Donna said, "I believe we better get going because this day was fun, but there's dancing to be done."

It was another one of those times I didn't want to leave but we drove away and travelled on another dirt road. I was driving again and my mind was just spinning from the day we'd put in. Then again it might have been the beer and the scotch, but I think the experience was what made my head spin the most.

We came to the end of the Fraser Road and stopped at a crossroads and Jackie said, "Do you know where you are?"

"Not really, but I know we passed this before and it looked familiar."

"Straight to the pavement to Gillis Beach, right to MacKinnon's Harbour and Maxie, and left back to Iona Rear and Iona. It's kind of the holy cross of the dirt-road tour."

"OK, it makes sense."

"That's Iona Rear right over that mountain and probably pretty close to where their house used to be," Jackie said.

We headed back toward Iona and met the wine-coloured car turning in the driveway at the bottom of the hill. They waved as we passed and we continued down the dirt road and retraced our tracks from the morning loop. We ended up back on the beach by the wharf and back to our little cottage.

Steering With My Elbows

Reel

Paul K. MacNeil

CHAPTER 12

I Lost You

Jackie and Donna invited us to come up for supper but we had plenty of food and chose to relax on our little deck and recap our day. I thought we all needed a little break from each other and I was sure they had other people to spend time with besides us.

Patrick had gone in to use the bathroom and I was standing on the deck watching the birds again doing the same sort of thing I saw in my dream and he snuck up behind me and pinched my cheek and said, "Come here often?"

"No, but I'm hoping to."

He wrapped his arms around me and held me tightly and, in a timid tone, he said, "I'm having feelings I've never had before."

"Oh, and what kind of feelings are they?"

"You know, like I always want to be with you and I really like being with you."

"Oh, I see. You know what they call that, don't you?" I asked with a curious smile.

"Ah, no, I'm not sure."

"Not sure, eh, I think it's a four-letter word that starts with L."

"Is it lost?" he asked, raising his eyebrows and sheepishly smiling.

"That might be it, but let's not get too far ahead of ourselves. I really like being with you as well and we just had an extraordinary day together."

He got a little quiet and I felt a little funny myself. Part of me wanted him to say it and I wanted to say it to him, as well, but I also thought we had plenty of time and didn't want to rush it.

"Do you want to do something?" he said.

I walked over to him and said, "I want to kiss you and I want you to hold me tight."

We did just that for a long time and wrestled with going to bed but decided to relive the day and all the mysteries we'd unravelled. We made some tea and sandwiches on beautiful cheese bread and rejoiced in the grand adventure we'd been on.

We freshened up, changed our clothes, and waited for Jackie and Donna to pick us up for the reception. They had a driver and when we got to the packed hall, they got us into a square set right away.

Neither one of us had done this before, so I danced with Jackie and Patrick danced with Donna until the third figure and they sent us back together. We tried really hard to limit the chaos that surrounded us for it was only confusing to us as everyone else knew what they were doing. We tried our best to follow the couples beside us and, in the end, it was a lot of fun and everyone said we did very well, but I was leaking badly.

The hall was boiling hot with all the bodies and the dancing so when the third figure was over, we went outside into the cool evening air to refresh ourselves. We were invited to a car of one of the couples who were on the bike trip that day and some cans of cold beer came out and a bottle of rum.

Donna and I stayed for a little while but we both needed to go to the washroom so we left the men outside.

After the girls went inside, another car pulled up and parked alongside us and who was it but Donald Willie. He knew Jackie and the other man and he started talking to them and then he said to me, "You look familiar, do I know you?"

"Well, yes and no. I met you a few weeks ago at the café with my girlfriend, Maggie."

It sounded nice to call her my girlfriend.

"Oh, yes, I remember you now, you were looking for Mungie and Sadie. How did that go?"

"Well, it couldn't have gone any better—thanks again for your help."

Jackie stepped in and said, "This is Patrick MacLean and his girlfriend is Maggie MacKinnon. Patrick and I work together."

"Oh, is that right? Well, it's nice to see you again.

"Oh, and Jackie, have you heard anything on Joe MacKinnon, you know, Joe Dear?"

"Well, I heard he was coming home this week. You know, Patrick met him out at the Rear when he was there."

"Oh, good, dear. Did you notice him say that, Patrick?" he asked.

"Well, yes, dear, I did."

"Did you know his brothers, Jackie?" Donald asked.

"Well, I wouldn't say I knew them, but I remember Dan Malcolm. He worked on the ferry with my father."

"Yes, yes," Donald continued. "There was Peter, Dan Malcolm, Jerome, and he had a brother that died when he was a teen. I can't be sure of his name but, I think it was Columba.

"He got caught up in the traces when he was watering the team of horses. I guess they got spooked, ran off, and dragged him quite a piece. It must have been pretty bad. They say the family never got over it and I don't think any of that family ever married or had children."

"It must have been pretty tough," said Jackie.

"Now, Joe had two sisters, Mary, who died very young, and Theresa, who was a nun. Sister Cornelius was her church name and he had another brother who went on to be a very successful businessman in the States."

"I don't think I heard of him," said Jackie.

"Yes, he went to work on the harvest trains, to Nebraska and places like that. I guess he worked on the Boulder Dam in Colorado and eventually he ended up designing and building farm machinery."

"Is that right?" said Jackie.

"Yes, that's right."

"His name was John Deere," he said, and he roared. "John Deere." And he turned and started for the hall. "I need to get to my date."

But you could hear him saying, "Nothing runs like a Deere," as he laughed and skipped toward the hall.

With that, the lifters were out and we were chasing them with pop and you could hear the music going again. We talked for a few more minutes about Donald the *Cù* and Jackie said we should get back in and catch the third figure and slide into a set.

I told him I would be in shortly as I wanted to admire the moon as it danced on the shimmering lake. It seemed to be frantically keeping time to the music coming from the hall and filling the night air.

When I walked in, I saw Jackie and Donna on the dance floor but I couldn't see Maggie. I looked all around the hall and then I spotted her and who was she dancing with but a beaming Donald Willie.

Oh, that slippery Donald! I caught her eye and headed to the bar to grab a couple of drinks.

I watched the dancers and the young girls making the music, who were tighter than a cow's arse at fly time. There were two on the fiddle, one on guitar and one on the piano. They were just rocking it out as the dancers were screaming, laughing, and having a great time. I thought of the story of the sick man in the hospital and I saw the bride and groom in the middle of the hall dancing and smiling from ear to ear. It was like I was in someone else's dream and when the set ended, Maggie came over to me and said, "He came right up to me and asked me to dance. I couldn't say no."

"You looked like you were having fun."

"Well, I was. He's a beautiful dancer and he knows exactly what he's doing," she said, with a blushing sort of grin.

I swallowed, rolled my eyes, and shook my head.

Maggie laughed and shook all over.

We spent the rest of the night on the floor and outside by the car but we kept pretty close to each other to ward off the *Cù*, which was fine by me.

We decided to leave before it was all over and we thanked our two unbelievable hosts for the glorious day. We walked back to our cottage in the air, which was cooler now, remembering everything about our day. We had nothing left in the tank as we crawled into bed together, exhausted.

We kissed each other softly and felt great contentment in each other's arms again. We lay there in the darkness and stillness of the night, with the lake rolling softly against the shore and I said, "Maggie?"

"What?"

"I lost you."

"Patrick," she said.

"Yes."

"I lost you, too."

We fell asleep.

Lost in each other.

I Know You Know

Song

Paul K. MacNeil

Chorus

I know you know I___know you_ care_____ I feel the same way

too way too___ way too. I love your lips your hips_ your

finger tips_ I love your skin your chin,_____ your fre - e - ckled grin. I love you

wild and styled___mellow mild._____ I know you know I___ know___ you care.

Verse

I woke in a Feb - ru - a - ry dream_ un sure of_where the hell_ I'd_ been

__ Co-vered in___ love as thick_ as clay_____ shoud I run or should

__ I___ stay?_____ Should I run or should_ I___ stay?

CHAPTER 13
A Mystery, a Faith

The morning came as if the night had never been there. It seemed as though we had just gone to sleep and the birds were howling already. What was it my father used to say—you can't hoot with the owls and soar with the eagles? But then again I don't think he ever put a day in like we did yesterday.

The idea of a recreational vehicle such as we enjoyed would never have been on his radar. If it wasn't a work machine it wasn't worth having. I had plenty of friends growing up that had some sort of fun craft but that was never happening in his house.

But things change and the world is a different place today than it was thirty years ago or 300 or more. The things my parents went through are a whole lot different than what Maggie and I would have to deal with. At least back then we had each other and that was worth everything at the time.

I looked over at Maggie, with her soft, rounded shoulders and golden skin and I felt for her. She'd never known a sister, a brother, or her parents, for that matter, so that had to be a lot tougher than anything I'd gone through. I thought of the joy she found yesterday, let alone the past two weeks, and I wanted to hold her forever.

She lay there so peacefully beside me and I thought she deserved so much better than the hand she'd been dealt. So I said to myself that I would never let her down and I'd love her like she'd never known love before. I just had to find the right time and place to tell her.

I lay there for a long time without moving or making a sound so I wouldn't disturb her from her own dreams. I wondered if she was dreaming about the falls and the young lady with the white hair. I wondered if someday we'd be able to do things like see each other's dreams when we're sleeping. I wondered if it would be a good or bad advancement in our world or if we were better off with them appearing for one night only.

I waited as long as I could but a trip to the bathroom was my top priority and, if she woke, so be it. I was pretty sure I wouldn't be going back to sleep and we had things to do. I slivered my way out and took care of my needs and, with Maggie in a deep sleep, went to the kitchen to whip up some sort of breakfast.

I made the tea, toasted some of the nice bread and cut up some cheese. It wasn't much, but it was plenty and there was something special about buttered toast dunked in tea. Simple and sweet, as I looked in on Maggie, who was just stirring and said, "That smells good."

"You stay right there and I'll bring it in to you."

"I need to pee but I'll jump right back in when I'm done, I promise."

I was a minute or two behind her with the tea, toast, and cheese. I cut up a nectarine, as well, and it looked pretty good and tasted better.

"You ordered room service, my dear," I said as I handed her my humble offering.

"Well, I don't really remember ordering, but I'll gladly take it. How long have you been up?"

"I've been awake for about an hour but just got up fifteen minutes ago. Did you sleep well?"

"Oh my, yes, and you?"

"I don't think I moved. I slept right through, didn't wake once."

"Nice. This is delicious, by the way. Thank you very much."

"You're very welcome but it's missing a little lip jam," and I leaned toward her and kissed her.

"Lip jam, eh, I don't think I've heard that before."

"It's better than toe jam, I'll tell you that."

"Well, I've never tried that either, so I'll take your word for it."

We were sitting in the bed enjoying our breakfast as we listened to the tender waves lapping against the shore. We talked about the day, the night, and how much fun we'd had and Maggie said, "Do you have another day in you?"

"I'm in it for the long haul. What's next on the list?"

"Well, I'd like to drive around this whole area and go out to see Mungie and Sadie, like we talked about. So that's a start. And I have to go back to the falls again, but there's something else."

"What's that?" I asked.

"Well, I thought of this last night when we walked back here. I kind of think I'd like to go back to the church."

"Really?" I said, a bit surprised.

"Yeah, is that OK?"

"Sure. You know it's Sunday morning. Do you want to go to mass?"

"Yeah, I think I do."

"Well, let's do it. Any idea what time it starts?" I asked.

"Well, I read the sign last night and it said ten-thirty on Sunday morning. I didn't want to say anything last night to make us get up for it, but here we are."

"Then we better get moving. I guess that means there's no morning service here."

"It doesn't look that way. Plus, I need to get a quick shower."

I cleaned up, did the dishes, and when she came out, I hit the drops myself. We were out the door with a few minutes to spare.

The bell tower was ringing as we walked up the hill to the church and I noticed we weren't the last to arrive. There were more cars and people arriving as the padre and his pastoral associates were walking from the vestry to the front door. We had time to spare.

We found a seat closer to the front than I would've liked but it didn't really matter. We were up on the right side not far from the choir and when the mass started, they lit the place up. It had a grooving piano, guitar rhythm, and the voices were young and strong. I felt the power of yesterday again from the choir, which was a mix of kids, teens, women, and men in their forties, fifties, and older. The seemed so comfortable with each other, like the way things were 100 years ago.

I looked over at Maggie and she smiled at me and mouthed the words *thank you*. I grinned and did the same.

The priest was young as far as priests go and he was a very fluid and graceful speaker. The readings and scriptures all sounded familiar to me, but the music was over the top. I recognized some of the girls who had played at the reception the night before and they were clearly comfortable here with their elders.

I peeked around at times and saw people who looked familiar to me but they weren't with the spouses or siblings. It was the strangest thing, but some people looked like people I grew up with, but they just weren't those people. I saw Mungie and Sadie on the other side of the church and then the strangest thing happened.

The priest said, "Let us proclaim the mystery of faith."

The choir sang it and it dawned on me that anything was possible.

"When we eat this bread and drink this cup, we proclaim your death, oh Lord, until you come again."

If all the people in this church believed, and people all over the world believed, then why couldn't all the folk tales be true? Was this not a form of folk tale? Was believing that the body and blood of Christ were right there in front of you so different than what Maggie and I had been hearing? I was now convinced it was true.

It felt good to be there and to take communion and it felt even better to have been there with Maggie. When we were leaving, I thought about our first time there and wondered if we hadn't stopped in, would everything be different? If the doors were locked, if there'd been mass on at that time, we wouldn't have stopped. There were a thousand reasons to keep right on by that day, but we didn't.

Walking out of the church I mentioned it to Maggie and she was quick to point out that Donald had put the bug in our ear and I should probably thank him. She told me she was really glad we went and wanted to know how I felt. I told her it was like most everything else when I was with her, more than I was expecting.

We'd parked by the little store near the wharf and decided to keep walking and go look at the floating house again since we were right there.

As we approached the house, we saw an older-looking man on the wharf scratching his whiskered chin. He kept taking his hat off, rubbing the top of his bald head, putting his hat back on, and scratching his chin again.

As we got a little closer, I saw him chewing pretty heavily on some gum and his bottom lip almost struck his nose on every stroke. He didn't have enough teeth in his head to chew porridge. His rubber boots were rolled down at the top and he walked toward us and said, "Is this your place?" in a funny musical tone.

"Oh, jeez, no, we just came down to take a look at it again."

"Well, I've never seen anything like it. It looks like a home for dwarves or little people."

I never thought of that but the tide was low and you could have stepped onto the roof the way it was floating now and he said, "My name is Mickey, Mickey MacNeil." He extended his rather thin arm and bony hand.

"Well, I'm Patrick MacLean and this is Maggie MacKinnon."

"MacKinnon, eh? From the Harbour or Cain's Mountain?"

"Well, I'm not entirely sure about the MacKinnon side, but I think the harbour. But now my grandmother was Liza *Mhór* from Highland Hill and the back of the harbour, I guess."

"Liza *Mhór*, is that right? I knew her and her mother years and years ago. She was a fine woman, she was. I believe she was a MacKenzie—no, no, she was one of Big Neil's, before she married Campbell out in St. Columba, and then I think she moved away. And what of your father on the MacKinnon side?"

"Well, I'm afraid I didn't really know him."

"Oh, I'm sorry, I didn't know. I wonder was he one of the boys from the big family, there was twenty-one or twenty-two of them from the harbour, I think. Now he could have been one of *Steafag's* crowd, as well."

"I'm sorry, I didn't really know. His name was Archie."

"Yes, well, I'm not sure I knew that crew very well, but now your mother, Liza *Mhór's* daughter, what was her name?"

"Her name was Katie, but it was Liza who raised me and I didn't know my mother very well, either."

"Oh, yes, Katie. I can remember meeting her but I didn't really know her. She may have been kind of special, if I'm not mistaken."

"Yes, we've been learning all about them both and it seems that might be true."

"Well, I believe it to be true."

"That's strange because we've been hearing a lot about the magic of little people and forerunners and the like. Have you any information on these things?" Maggie asked.

"Oh, I've heard them, and I've seen them, as well."

"You haven't," said Maggie.

"Lots of people in the old days saw them but nowadays no one looks for them or wants to see them."

"Well, we'd like to see them."

"Oh, and why is that?"

"Well, to know if the magic is true, I guess."

"Well, if you believe they exist then you must know they have magic powers."

"I suppose you're right, but to see them would be quite special."

"You don't normally see them, but the old folks swore they came around when the spirits would be going to the other world. Do you know about that?"

"Yes, I do. Halloween," she said.

"Well that's today's celebration, but in the old times it was known as *Samhain*.

"*Oidhche Shamhna* was that night and it was the beginning of the dark season, the opposite of the springtime. That's when the *Aos Si*, the little people, are easier to be seen and encounter. This is when the Gaelic Otherworld and the mortal world come closest together and the spirits can pass between.

"My mother used to set a place at the table or leave food outside for the departed souls on that night. They can make quite a lot of noise when they get going so you can usually hear them before you see them.

"Now I just need to just ask you about your father again," Mickey said.

"Well, his name was Archie MacKinnon and that's about all I know."

"Now, I'll tell you I think he's a grandson from the big family, and it reminds me a little bit about myself. I didn't know my father either, because he died when I was very young."

"Oh, I'm sorry," said Maggie.

"Well, thank you, but that was a long time ago now. Anyway, his name was Neil or *Neilleag* in Gaelic and my mother was known as *Bean Neilleag*, or wife of Neil, because he died. So I am also known as Mickey *Bean Neilleag*."

He continued, "A good friend of mine was John Dan Jim D. Now he was John Dan and his father was Jim D or James Donald Og, and I could go on if you wanted.

"But anyway he moved from Castlebay to Barra Glen and married Annie Catherine. Now she was from out St. Columba Mountain, and her father had died when she was very young.

"Are you still with me?" he asked.

"Yes, yes," Maggie said.

"So, Annie Catherine's mother was *Màiri*—in fact, *Màiri Sheamus Mhìchael*, so when John Dan and Annie Catherine got married, he became known as John Dan *Màiri*."

"That's very interesting," Maggie said.

"Well, it may be, but my point is that lots of people don't know their parents but you always have their names. So what if I call you Maggie Liza *Mhór*, or Maggie Archie Liza *Mhór*, or Maggie Katie Liza *Mhór*. Do any of those names sound like who you are?"

"Well, I think I should see which one I feel the best with over a little time, but I like Maggie Liza *Mhór*."

"That's probably a good idea, but then again Liza *Mhór* was born Nora Liza, was she not?" he asked.

"Yes, she was."

"So how about, Maggie Nora Liza or Maggie Nora Liza *Mhór*—do any of those sound like you?"

"Well, they all do, really, and I like both of them a lot."

"Well, you just think about that and I better get going as my wife will be wondering what happened to me. She's quite a bit more jealous than my first wife was, God rest her soul. But I need to tell you this before I go.

"There was a family of MacKinnons that lived over on the other side of the island in a place called MacKinnon's Brook. They could be your people, you know, and, by the way, were you ever there?" he asked quickly.

"No, no, never."

"Well, anyway, they were pioneer settlers here on this island around 1820 and they came with three small children to this remote area and then they had two more children over the next two years.

"So the father, I believe Hughie was his name, set off by foot to register his land grant in Sydney, which would have been a week away at that time. Anyway, when he finished his business and was on his way home, he fell through the ice on Sydney Harbour and drowned.

"Now they say his spirit can still be seen there on occasion, and I think, I think of the hardship they must have endured," as he struggled to continue.

"Well, that must have been very difficult," Maggie said.

"Well, I'll tell you, any time I felt sorry for myself over the years I thought of that story or one of a hundred more like it and I thought I had it pretty good. Now, I better go—my Rosie will be growing concerned. It was nice to meet you," as he lightly stepped away.

I turned to Maggie and said, "I can't believe the knowledge of these people we keep meeting. It's like they are professors of life or something."

"I know, what in the world is next?"

We strolled to the end of the wharf, returning to the tales he'd told us, and eventually made our way back to the car and cottage.

We packed up the car and had a light snack and sadly left our shoreline villa as we steered our way to Iona Rear.

This time, I felt as if the car was driving itself. There was no fear of the Highlands, no fear of getting lost, no fear of them not being the right people. We knew where we were going and why we were going there.

We arrived and walked toward the door and heard Betsey barking inside. But today there was no smell of wood burning as the heat from the sun had forced the windows of the house open. They had lovely flowers blooming by their door and the lilac bush was in its glory. We heard the bees working their guts out on the lilacs and the birds once again controlled the airwaves.

Mungie greeted us at the door just like the first time and invited us into the kitchen. They'd just finished their lunch and were having tea, so we joined them for tea and a sweet. There was no wood fire on and it smelled of baking and flowers. We told them of our bike ride the day before and all we'd seen and learned and Maggie said, "We just wanted to drop by and say thanks again for all of your help."

"We didn't do much," said Mungie.

"Well, you did enough to get us sorted out, and, like I said to Malcolm yesterday, 'Thank you for being here.' We brought you a little something that Patrick did and we hope you like it."

"You didn't need to do anything," Sadie said.

I handed them the sketches and said, "I'm sorry I didn't get them framed, but I just did them on the drive up here yesterday."

Both of them looked quite pleased and a little bashful when they looked at them, but they said they loved them.

"We have a niece who does a lot of painting, so we'll get her to frame them up," said Mungie. "You have quite a gift, young man. These are very well done, thank you."

"Oh, it's not much and I'm glad you like them."

We talked about a number of things and they asked many questions about our lives and our jobs. They seemed to have as many questions for us as we'd had for them on our first visit. We intended on not staying too long, but I needed to ask them something before we left, so I said, "We were at mass this morning and it struck me during the mystery of faith that anything is possible if you believe it. What do you think of that?"

"Well, that's one of the greatest parts of the mass and the faith. God is there with us and we receive Him. It's no different than if we believe in life after death and spirits living around us. You may not see it with your eyes, but if you have faith in it, who can tell you differently?"

"So you really just need to believe," I said.

"I think you have it," Mungie said.

Maggie said, "I think that might be a discussion for another day and we should get going. I promise I'll keep in touch and we'll pick up this conversation the next time."

And with that, we hugged them both and continued on our way.

We decided to go back the way we came, to drive around the entire peninsula and go where the road took us. We had no fear like our first visit; we felt like we now belonged here like anyone else.

The paved road was twisty and bumpy but the lake was never far from our sight. We passed many old farms and old places that were nestled into the forest in what must have been the style 100 or 200 years ago.

After about twenty minutes of driving, we found ourselves at the end of the road in Lower Washabuck and the beauty of the place struck us again. It was a very open area and you could see down the lake toward the Atlantic Ocean and Baddeck was directly across the channel. It looked to be two or three kilometres wide. I said to Maggie, "Did you know this is called St. Patrick's Channel?"

"No, I didn't, and are you telling me the truth?"

"I am, I just noticed it on a map recently and forgot to mention it to you until now. Crazy, eh!"

"Yeah, that's ironic, for sure."

"I know, and I think this would have been a very exciting place for Boronia to reach all those years ago. To think they were only moments away after their long journey across the ocean. Do you still think that tale to be true?" I asked.

"More than ever," she said.

"I see no reason to think it didn't happen. I see it in my mind like the night at the shore by the café. Nothing else but trees, beach, and the faith of arriving where they were destined to be. I believe it."

As we drove alongside the channel it left our sight when the forest took over again and, on the waterside, we saw a sign for Laughlin MacLean's grave-yard, St. Peter's Cemetery. We had no choice but to drive down and check it out. It was a long, narrow driveway that opened up to a clearing with a large monument nestled against the forest, and I said to Maggie, "Do you remember Jackie talking about this guy at Ginger's that night?"

"Yeah, I do. He was very old when he died."

"Old, I guess he was old—114 years old, if I remember correctly. Let's get out for a minute."

We stopped the car, got out, looked around, and saw a few houses close by. I felt like I was intruding a little bit. The whole time I was hoping no one would come out and try and sell me a mill.

We didn't say much but I had a very strange feeling come over me as if I'd been there before but I knew I hadn't. We were just about to get into the car and I felt a familiar sting on my thigh and said to Maggie, "This place reminds me of someplace I've been but I can't put my finger on it. Do you think this has anything to do with Boronia and the ceremony you mentioned when we first travelled up here?"

"I don't know if it does, but I'm glad we came in here just the same."

We drove back out onto the highway and, eventually, the channel came back into sight. We travelled beside it as it narrowed and turned into a river. And we came to the end of the road by a small bridge. It was right where we'd come out on the bikes the day before only from the opposite direction. Perhaps it was another holy crossroad.

We turned up the hill again and passed a little man walking his dog, and, shortly after that, we stopped at the falls. You could hear them calling to us like they had the day before.

There was no one else there but us that day and the place had a completely different feel compared to the day before. I was sure it had something to do with us being alone or maybe it was because it wasn't our first time seeing them.

The sun peeked in between the trees, highlighting many areas and shading many others. The water glistened in the sunlight as it fell and the depth of its power was all around us and Maggie said, "Do you see the birds and hear their songs?"

"I see them but the sound is not familiar to me."

"It's the sound I hear in my dreams," she said.

"Well, that's a little eerie."

"They were like that yesterday, it was just harder to hear them with all the people talking. And the way they are flying around in circles and up and out through the canopy of trees."

"That's also a little odd."

"It feels like a holy place," she said.

"Well, I don't doubt it is."

We stayed there for at least an hour, just walking around and crossing the overflow of the stream that meandered away down the hill. We followed the stream until it came to another sort of waterfall. It was nowhere near as dramatic as the main falls, but stunning in its own way.

It was like a little sister to the bigger falls. We walked through the forest to the top of it all and saw every angle we could. The whole place had a presence unlike anything we'd felt before and Maggie said, "We'll have to come back at night."

"Really!"

"Yes, I think so. I can just feel something happens here and I sense it happens at night. You know all those tales of spirits and forerunners nearly always happen at night."

"Do you want to see that?"

"Yup, I do, and I'm not one bit scared. I think it will only bring out the goodness in us and I don't sense any fear or pain from whatever spirits we find.

"Everyone has been telling us that we need to believe to see if these things are true. I really believe this place has something else to show us.

"So when are we coming back?"

"I don't know," she said.

"I think we'll need to do a little more digging and thinking to figure it out. I mean we could stay tonight, I guess, or come back next week but I think there's more to it than that."

"Well, what about the Halloween connection we keep hearing about? Do you think that could be it?"

"That seems to be the most logical to me and I think we should let all this stuff we learned sink in. I'll need to do some more reading about that piece of folklore and go from there. The other thing is, it's going to be difficult to wait that long, but I don't think we have a choice."

We really didn't and figured it would go by quick enough. We took a few more pictures of the place and, as we headed back to the car, a gust of wind seemed to shake all the trees in a haunting sort of way.

We drove through all the old back roads we'd been on the day before and others we hadn't seen and we always found our way. We drove back up to the top of St. Columba Mountain, where you could see everything and we saw it all again. We slowed down as we passed by the old house, but there was no sign of Jimmy.

We kept on going and went back up to Maxie's mill, but only turned around and drove away. We talked about walking back up to Big Neil's where we'd stopped yesterday, but decided to go to MacKinnon's Harbour. The place we passed through the day before.

We stopped in the old church parking lot and got out to see what the place felt like and Maggie said, "This must have been a busy little place years ago if there was a church, and that looks like an old school over there. What do you think?"

"I'd say it was. It's a strange thing that so many people would leave such a beautiful place, but they did."

"Yes, I guess they had their reasons, just like Mam. Work, money, family, wanting something better. Maybe no different than the people that left Scotland 200 years ago."

"I wonder how many people there are like Malcolm that go away and long to return, and then you have the Sadies of the world that had one address all their lives," I said. "Makes you wonder how we all end up where we do. It's a bit like you and me, I guess."

"Yes, it does," Maggie said, and I'll tell you one thing: I'm glad I found this piece of me that's been missing all these years. Whatever happens next doesn't really matter."

"So, have you been thinking of your father?"

"Yes, a little bit, more than I thought I would."

"And do you think you will search him out?"

"I don't think so. That's another mountain to climb and I'm not quite finished this journey yet."

"Well, you know, for what it's worth, I think it would be good for you when the time is right. Look at this whole puzzle and the joy it's brought you. I think finding out more information about your father would be a good thing."

"Well, thank you. You may very well be right."

I walked over to her and gave her a big hug and we just stood there like that for a long time. I sensed she was a little low and maybe close to crying, so I suggested we go back to Gillis Beach and have a beer. She thought that was a great idea and so we headed for the beach.

Maggie was very quiet as we went down the road so I left her to her own thoughts. I was busy enough with my own.

I wished I hadn't said anything about her father but I was glad I did at the same time. I felt bad that it made her sad but I also felt there'd be a happy ending if she did find out who he was. I thought about what would be going through my mind if I hadn't known my own father and mother.

How could finding out something about her father—anything—not be a good thing? He was probably a good man in his own way, and who knows what he was going through all those years ago? Maggie was beautiful, inside and out, in my eyes, and that told me she came from good people, whether her father had been around for her childhood or not. And at that moment, Maggie said, "I think I will make a little effort to find out who he is when I'm ready."

"Good for you. Whenever you're ready, I'll do whatever I can to help."

She looked at me, smiled, and said, "I was hoping you would."

"I wouldn't miss it. Just look at all the interesting people we met on this little adventure and you have to think there are just as many out there that have some sort of connection to your father."

"I'd say you are right—it could be a lot of fun."

It didn't take us long to get to the beach and we grabbed a couple of beers left over from the day before. They were cold enough and we were both in need of a little splash to push us through the rest of the day. As much as we enjoyed it the day before, I was glad we'd finished the Glen Breton.

We walked along the beach and enjoyed the sunshine and the waves, which were now crashing pretty hard on the shoreline. It was another of those times we didn't need to say much. We just held hands and the memories of the weekend blended like a great story.

We drank our beer and enjoyed the sounds before we headed back to the city.

We started on our way back and drove through the little town. We passed our little cottage and I thought about Jackie and Donna. We passed by the church and the hall and I thought of the music and the "mystery of faith." We crossed the bridge and passed the floating house at the wharf and I wondered what we would discover on our next adventure to this mysterious place.

Reflection

Slow Jig

Paul K. MacNeil

CHAPTER 14
We Talked About

We came back to earth over the next few weeks as the work world seized an unrelenting grip on our lives. It wasn't as though we were forced to spend every waking moment there, but both of us found ourselves in far more important positions than we'd grown accustomed to or expected.

Maggie's new job was paying a lot more than her previous two positions put together, but the schedule was not what you would call friendly. She had no free weekends until the fall, which meant our escapes to the country would have to wait until then.

My own job and the bridge project with Jackie was front-loaded, for sure. July was pretty much a write-off and when things started to slow down toward the end of August, another project was moving in on us so the work had more than piled up.

Still, Maggie and I were finding as much time as we could for each other and our relationship had settled into the usual trappings of boyfriend and girlfriend. Time with Maggie was always fun and people expected to see us together. We were happy and comfortable like that, but we both wanted the summer to go by as fast as possible.

A lot of people will tell you not to wish your time away and they're right, but often when a seed is planted we struggle to wait for it to grow. I don't think we were wishing it away; we just wanted to know if what we believed was going to present itself.

We weren't searching for it but we continued to find people around the city who had some sort of connection to the country or old Scotland. We met people who'd moved to the city from other areas that had similar stories and the information and opinions were endless. Conversations with Maggie often began with: *You'll never believe who I talked to today and they told me this sort of a tale.*

All of the stories added more fuel to our fire, which seemed so far from our reach in the middle of summer. But September came and went and the summer heat faded into the shorter days and cooler evenings of October. Maggie and I were itching to return to the Washabuck Falls to feel her strength and uncover her mystery.

We'd stopped making Ginger's a regular Friday night event, although we got there on occasion. We were choosing to go out for a nice meal by ourselves, with friends, or with Doug and Clair, whose fire had kept burning. Our social scene had slowed down, so most nights we stayed in and discovered a new meal, and we liked it that way.

So, on October 17, about a week before Maggie's birthday, we were enjoying our supper and I said to her, "Is there anything you want to do on your birthday next weekend?"

"Not really, why do you ask?"

"Well, I'm working on a little plan and I can make it a surprise, or I can tell you about it."

"Well, I'm not big on surprises—can you give me a hint?"

"I'll give you one hint and that's it. If you guess it, I'll tell you the whole plan and if you can't guess it, I'll just make it happen. Fair enough?"

"It sounds fair, but do you think I'll like it?"

"I'd be shocked if you didn't."

"OK, it's a deal. What's the hint?" she asked.

"Well, it will be an activity in and around Iona, and we would stay at that same cottage we stayed at last summer. That's the hint."

"It's another bike ride and I'd love to go. Book it," she said with a smile as wide as the table.

"Tooooo baaaad," I said in a long, drawn-out way. "It's not another bike ride, but I'll book it anyway," I said with a smirky grin.

"What is it?"

"I told you, it's a surprise."

I had one of those rare feelings when I was around her when I actually had her on the ropes.

"So that means we'll be there for two weekends in a row. We're still going there for Halloween, right?"

"Oh, yes, for sure. I booked the cottage months ago for Halloween, but this sort of just came up."

"So, when will we leave?" she asked.

She was just glowing.

"Well, I need to sort that out but either Friday night or early on Saturday morning. Will that matter?"

"Well, I'll need to make sure I can get around work but I don't think it will matter. I'm so excited—are you sure you won't tell me?" She rubbed her foot against my leg under the table and winked at me.

I smiled, blushed, and told her she'd have to wait.

Maggie tried very hard all week to get me to spill the beans about our weekend trip, but I didn't break. She must have guessed twenty-five things that may have been possible, but she couldn't figure it out. Of course I had as much fun with it as I could, but almost every time it ended with me saying *you had your chance.*

I kept a close eye on the weather as this event wouldn't be happening in a storm, but I said nothing to Maggie about that caveat. Everything had been working out for us and Saturday's conditions looked perfect, so we decided to go up on Friday night.

Maggie was cracking with excitement all week and was packed and ready to leave on Wednesday. Unfortunately, we were forced to slug our way through the last two workdays and arrived at our cottage around 8 p.m.

We unpacked our food, drink, and clothes, and Maggie asked, "Are you going to tell me now?"

"No, I can't until tomorrow. But I do have an idea for tonight if you're interested."

"What's that now?"

"Well, we can stay here and enjoy our cottage or we can drive down to the falls and see what they're like in the nighttime."

"Oh my, yes, let's do that," she said.

She was dancing once again and we headed off with great confidence into the depths of the night. We hadn't travelled the roads at night before and it was a lot different than the middle of the day. We passed an occasional streetlight or met a car, but it was dark. Just like Jackie said, "as dark as a crow's pocket."

We stayed on the paved road around Washabuck and turned up the St. Columba Road and, two minutes later, we were there. We pulled over, got out, and all you could hear was the roar of the water inviting us in.

The fall air was noticeably cooler on this cloudy night as we walked into the forest. We looked back toward the road and saw that it sparkled with flashing embers from the fireflies that patrolled the wilderness. We continued down the hill with a small flashlight and more than enough fear.

Maggie grabbed me and said, "Are you OK? Because I'll protect you."

"I'm fine," I said, but she was fearless.

"This is so cool," she said.

We made our way closer to the falls and I felt a sting in my leg as a glimmer of light appeared overhead.

"What the heck is that?" I cried.

"That would be the moon."

As quick as the pain came it was gone and we were left in total darkness.

"I think you need a hug," she said, and we came together and she whispered in my ear, "Bock bock, feather face, bock bock, feather face. I'll protect you, don't be scared."

"I had that feeling again, like when I was working around the bridges." I felt another sting and there was a rustling sound in the bush, and I shook.

"It's a bunny or something," she said. "Just relax, close your eyes, enjoy the sound and smell."

And, just like that, everything was better. We stayed there for what seemed like forever and I felt it in a whole different way. Beyond the steady drone of the falls, the forest was full of creaks and noises that sounded like everything from gunshots to whispers and all things in between.

The waterfall glistened when the moonlight seeped between the clouds as the spray danced like glitter, exploding on the stony ground. The whole time the shadows and darkness came and went, as the forest stumbled around us.

We found our way home and talked until midnight on the deck in our heavy sweaters, enjoying some food and drink. The moon made the odd appearance and danced on the lake when it could, but mostly pounded the back of the thickly quilted sky.

We talked about going to bed and I asked her to wait a few more minutes. I went back inside and returned with a small gift bag and handed it to her.

"Happy birthday, Maggie."

"Oh my, what is this?"

"Just a little something. I hope you like it."

She pulled out the framed sketch I had drawn and gasped.

"Oh my God, it's me and Mam together and Maggie Nora Liza *Mhór* under both of our pictures. It's beautiful. Thank you so much."

"You're welcome. I did it a while ago but decided to save it for tonight. I'm glad you like it."

"Oh, I do." And she kissed me. "This is so special to me, I hope you know that."

"I do and I think tomorrow will be better. Now I think we better get to bed because we are leaving here at 6 a.m."

The morning came quickly and I heard Patrick busy in the kitchen. The smell of fresh bread being toasted told me I needed to get up.

"Wake up, wake up," I heard him calling.

"I am," I responded.

"We don't have much time. Jackie and Donna will be here shortly.

"What? We're going with them? Where are we going?"

"It's a surprise, I told you. Now get yourself ready and dress kind of warm."

A painful blue sky was just starting to brighten in the east and you couldn't find a cloud in it. The thin pale image of the moon was waiting to hand off responsibility to the sun. I had a sense of excitement like the bike trip in the summer, but there were no sounds of motors in the distance. You could only hear the seagulls chattering and the distant call of a lonely loon.

A few minutes later they were at our cottage and we were driving down the road with breakfast in hand and coolers packed and ready for the day. I couldn't get a clue from anyone where we were going as we drove on the pavement back through MacKinnon's Harbour and past the old church.

The cars, roofs, and fields had a thick coat of frost that was starting to melt as the heat of the sun fought back against the nighttime's wicked work. We turned off under an old train trestle and arrived at a small dock in Ottawa Brook. They started singing "Happy Birthday" and told me we were going on a boat trip.

I was shocked and it felt so special, even though I was hardly awake. I felt a sense of adventure and love come over me and a large dog came up behind me and pushed his nose against my hand.

"Well, hello, there. What's your name?"

As I scratched behind his ears, a rather tall, young-looking man with thick grey hair and a beard approached, a few steps behind. He looked like a seafaring man and I thought about my father. I thought about asking him if he would have known my father as they looked to be about the same age, but I couldn't.

"Hello, there," he said in a quick, sharp, friendly voice. "That's Dylan, and I'm David. You must be Maggie." He reached out to shake my hand.

"Well, yes, I am. Nice to meet you. And what kind of dog is Dylan?"

"Dylan is part lab, German shepherd, and Catholic," he said with a chuckle.

"Catholic, how's that?"

"Well, in the summer he liked to go to church with us at the harbour. We'd all pile into the back of the truck and, with the church doors open, he'd come in and wander around. He kind of came and went as he pleased and no one seemed to mind."

"Well, that's very funny," I said.

"Yes, it was. It was even funnier to see him get in the lineup for communion," he said with a deep laugh. "I'm not sure the priest liked it though."

I was still laughing when the others returned from the boat with Phyllis, David's wife. Patrick introduced himself and I met Phyllis. She was younger looking than David with shining blonde hair, a peaceful face, and glowing eyes. She was tanned much darker but their skin looked to be aged as one.

They were old friends of Jackie and Donna's and, after Captains David and Phyllis welcomed us aboard their thirty-foot Cape Islander-style boat, we putted away slowly. They told us the plan was to travel around MacKinnon's Harbour and then head out onto the big lake. As long as the weather was good, we'd travel down to Iona and through the opening at the bridge and carry on to MacKay's Point and up the Washabuck River as far as we could go.

We could land on shore for a little while but we needed to keep a weather eye as the darkness sets in earlier than summer and they wanted to be back in their port by nightfall. If things didn't go so well, we'd tie up at the wharf in Iona. They had it covered one way or the other and I felt like a floating princess.

It was nothing short of spectacular as the fall foliage was still in bloom and basking in its own splendour. The harbour was like a sheet of glass as we cut through the stillness of the morning air. All the while, the sun crept higher in the sky with one thing on its mind.

There was plenty of fog hanging in the air that filled many of the lower areas and valleys between the rolling mountains. I noticed many cottages nestled around the sheltered haven while we were inspected by nesting eagles and their military eyesight.

I gained a whole new perspective of the hills and mountains in the distance. You could easily see the tower we'd gone past on our bike ride and I thought once again of being at Big Neil's and where Mam had been raised.

You could notice a significant change when we entered the big end of the lake but it was not what you would call rough as we passed the old gypsum pier.

Captain David told us of the struggle to keep the harbour open to the lake after years of neglect. It seemed as though it could have been let go like so much of the land if people didn't fight to save it. He pointed out several places along the way like Fiddle Head and Red Point as we passed by Gillis Beach and other locations that had become familiar to us.

We were travelling eastward and you could see Pipers Cove and Derby's Pt. as the railroad became more prominent hugging the shoreline along the Barra Strait. We passed by our little cottage and saw the Highland Village on the top of the hill at Hector's point.

We talked about the floating house and its new home as we passed through the open bridge and left it all behind.

They talked about the government wharf that hosted so many pulp boats and barges and the work it created. It was the hub of the island before the big highway was built in the late sixties. Everything travelled by rail back then and most everything around the lake was transported through Iona.

They told us there were freight boats, ferries, and more that ran out of there moving cattle, people, supplies, mail, and just about everything in between. It seemed as though the highway killed the railroad, and so many little town centres along the lake perished with it. Just as the wharf was leaving our sight they pointed out the mysterious Christmas Island to the south, but they seemed reluctant to speak of her stories.

We passed the plaster island and sandbars near the turnoff to Barra Glen, which we could now respect the depth of from our new location. They talked about the gypsum mine and the finished product that was produced and shipped from Grass Cove 100 years ago.

We passed another dirt road to St. Columba Mountain, Gillis Point, MacNeil's Vale, and other locations before pulling into Maskells Harbour. There was an old-style lighthouse that defended the entrance, a small sandbar cove, and a couple of small boathouses along the shoreline. It felt like we were tied up at a wharf as we were guarded on all sides by the blazing mountains surrounding us.

Returning to the lake, we kept going north toward St. Patrick's Channel, passing Pony's Point, Burnt Point, MacKay's Point, and Sand Point along the way. Entering the channel, we passed Spectacle Island, Bone Island, and Toothbrush Island as a tropical breeze filled the air and calmed the waters. As we headed west, the sweaters and coats came off and it seemed like we were in a tropical dream. We passed the Holy Rosary Church, MacIver Cove, Murphy's Point, and Birch Point, with the Highlands overlooking it all.

The whole time on our voyage the air seemed to become filled with more and more seagulls. It wasn't that I never noticed them before but I could clearly see there were many different shapes and sizes. So I asked if anyone knew the difference between all these gulls.

Captain David went into great detail about the five prominent gulls. The largest with a black back and a white head like an eagle was the great black-backed gull. The herring gull was medium-sized and shapely looking, with a yellow bill and pink legs. The glaucous gull resembled the black back, but it had a grey back and the ring-billed gull had a ring on its bill. The Iceland gull had a white body and grey wings and was less common. My ears perked when I heard Iceland and I thought of Boronia.

I'm not sure why I was startled by his knowledge and we tried to ID them as they bobbed and darted all around us. I felt as though they'd been following us all day.

When we entered the river, I thought of the stories of Boronia, Noron, Viking ships, and the courage to travel so far into the great unknown. I thought of the wildness of their journey and crossing the Atlantic Ocean in a boat far less sturdy than the one we were on. I thought of the magic of it all and we slowed down.

We were in a paradise not known or seen by many and we just gazed in sheer delight.

They landed the boat on a sandy shore and we cooked up some burgers on a little barbecue they had on board. We had brought sandwiches, sweets, drinks, and then Patrick pulled out some glasses and a bottle of the Glen and said, "To our fine captains, crew, and vessel, and this glorious voyage."

We all toasted and then he said, "To Maggie, on her birthday, and her dreams, which brought us here."

It was all very emotional and I had nothing to say. I started to cry but they were tears of joy and I said, "I'm not sad, I'm just overcome with all that I have. Thank you all so much."

It was another one of those times you'd want to hold onto forever. Like the moment in Iona Rear when they knew who I was and being in the field with Maxie showing me where Mam came from. It was like dancing with Patrick at Ginger's to "Ring of Fire" and of course our first night together.

We stayed there as long as we could, but eventually the time came to return to our port. The afternoon sun had stretched across the sky and was now heading for its resting place and Donna strolled up beside me and said, "Your man Patrick sure is going to have a hard time topping this next year."

"I suppose he is. It's just been so surreal. I can't really believe I'm right here right now."

"Well, love does work in a most puzzling way sometimes. You know, you remind me of Jackie and me when we were your age."

"Really? I've never really felt like this before and I like it."

She hugged me and said, "It gets better."

I stood there watching the shoreline and the reflection on the water. The water had a deep, thick look about it, as if chambers were collecting, absorbing, and mixing the water and sky as one. It was sort of like many worlds being joined together and, as she walked away, I realized how she and Jackie just seemed to move with each other, much like our two captains. I guess when you spend that kind of time with each other, you know when to give and when to take. It reminded me of the shoreline, the lake, and the trees. All being themselves but united together.

The captains said we were in great shape and should easily make it back before dark. The waters had remained calm, drinks were flowing, and all was right in the world. The return trip was just as pleasing as the morning journey as the cottages and points of land looked more and more familiar to me.

There was a distinctly different view from the waterside as newer places or camping sites became visible. Most of the old farms we'd seen from the road no longer caught our eye. It was safe to say that many people had been drawn to the water's edge for pleasure and enjoyment compared to the pioneer settlers who farmed to survive.

It was a glorious day and, as we turned back in off the big lake, they took us around the harbour again. There was still a light peachiness to the sky in the west as the pale grey tones of night crept upon us. We thanked our hosts and drove back to Iona, this time with Donna at the wheel.

Patrick and Jackie had kept a very close eye on the Glen and the bottle was pretty well finished.

They had become good friends since the beginning of the summer and I was very happy for Patrick in particular. He saw Jackie like the father he never knew, and a person he wanted to be like.

We returned to our cottage and had a drink on the deck and talked about the day. We'd spent the day together but the conversation kept flowing and they told us of numerous boat rides they'd made before having children. We hugged them and thanked them for the day. They headed back to Jackie's parents' place and Patrick said, "What was the best part of the day?"

"I'm not really sure. It was like so many of the days I've had with you— there just seems to be one thing after another."

"That doesn't sound so good."

"No, it's all good and I meant it in the nicest way possible. It was a great day, but let me think.

"The company was great, the surprise of it all was better, and getting to the mouth of the river. Those are probably the top three. How about you?"

"Well, the company was great. I liked the harbour tour, going through the bridge, and the scotch. Oh, yes, and having you guessing for a week, that might have been the best."

"Yes, I suppose it was. How did it come together?"

"Well, I was talking to Jackie and I mentioned your birthday was coming up and that I wanted to do something special. He just threw it out there and I loved the idea. Then he called his friend David and we rented the boat for the day, it was that easy."

"Well, I loved it and was completely surprised. What will you do next year?" I asked.

"Next year? Aren't you planning ahead," he said with a grin.

"Do you plan on being around?" I asked.

"Well, yes, I do."

"Well, good. I look forward to next year's surprise."

"I'm looking forward to next weekend first," he said.

"You need to know I loved the day but I was wishing every day to go by and get to next weekend. But today I wanted every minute to last for an hour. That's kind of strange, don't you think?"

"A bit, I guess. I'm pretty sure I've felt that way before."

After the early start and the long day on the boat in the fresh air, we were both pretty much spent and went to bed early. We slept all night and woke to the same sound as the summer, with the lake quickly lapping the shore.

Our love nest was a playground and there was no need or want to be anywhere but there. In our own sweet time we got ourselves out of bed, out the door and headed back to the city. We talked about driving around the peninsula but decided to save it for another time and Patrick said, "What was better, the boat ride yesterday or the bike trip last summer?"

"Tough one, but I think the bike trip."

"Well, maybe we'll do that next year," he said, smiling.

"That's too easy. You'll need to do something bigger," I said jokingly.

Patrick drove the car back to the city and we talked all the way about the boat, the lake, our friends, both new and old, and I said, "If nothing happens next weekend, how do you think you'll feel?"

"I think I'll feel just fine as long as you're there with me," he said, and reached for my hand.

"It's a bit like our first date. You know, where we didn't know what would happen or what we'd tell people and what we did?" he asked.

"I think we just let it happen."

"I think we should just let it happen again," he said.

So we agreed to and we didn't say a whole lot more until we got back to the city. We were both a bit numb and content to enjoy the peace and quiet of the drive.

Patrick dropped me off at my apartment and headed home to get some work done. We both had things to catch up on and get ahead of for our escape the next weekend. We made a plan to get away early on Friday and arrive at our cottage before it got dark.

The days went by painfully slowly in spite of the fact we were both buried in work. We knew it was just a phase and we were doing what was best for our careers but it sure sucked the fun out of life. Patrick and I talked every night, but it wasn't enough.

I thought more and more about people with families, children, single parents, and people with disabilities, children with disabilities, and I wondered how they did it.

I thought of Mickey and his tale of the man falling through the ice and I thought of how easy my life really was. I felt I needed to be something else and I thought of Patrick and wished he was there with me.

And then an interesting thing happened on Thursday evening as I was going to bed. I had started reading books about our history and the people who came before us. History had never been my thing in school but I was growing older, learning about myself, and it had changed.

This particular piece of the book was about the old beliefs and the importance of the time of day, which I had never questioned. Morning is morning and night is night and a new day starts at midnight, day after day. But not in the realm of spirits and old beliefs.

The book said the new day starts when the sun goes down. "The spirits will rise with the new day, not when it rises but when it sets." All of this had my head spinning and I tossed and turned for hours pondering what it meant until I finally fell asleep.

I woke in a start, as the light from the new day was caressing the morning sky and I texted Patrick right away:

We need to be at the falls before dark.
I read something and dreamt about it last night.
Can you leave early?
Can you pick me up at work?

I was in a bit of a dither trying to collect everything I needed, but I kept going back to reread the story and the phrase over and over.

"The spirits will rise with the new day, not when it rises but when it sets."

I kept saying it over and over and if I had a roommate, I might have been locked up. It would have scared them, at least, but I kept saying it anyway. And, finally, Patrick texted:

Sure, I'll take off at 2.
Can you explain?

I replied:

No, not now.
I will on the drive.
Don't be alarmed.

The spirits will rise with the new day,
Not when it rises but when it sets.
Gotta run.

I had to get going to work and I was now running behind. I grabbed all my stuff and packed the cooler and, Jesus! I was sweating like a hen hauling pulp as I raced out the door.

I usually took the bus, but with all the stuff I grabbed a cab and took a deep breath when I got in and the driver said, "Happy Halloween, are you going to a party?"

"Yes, I'm hoping to," and we carried on to the hospital. He had no clue!

The day went by but I couldn't concentrate and I bungled my way through everything. I had moments all day of how I wished I was someplace else and did I ever need to get out of there. It wasn't like the clinic, it was all on me this time.

Patrick was there as prompt as ever and wanted to know if I was all right. Of course I was, but we needed to be there earlier than I thought and we had to go as fast as we could. We couldn't miss it and he asked me to explain.

"I'll try. I had a dream last night with both of us in it and I'm telling you, it was as clear as my conscience. I saw it all and it was amazing. But we need to be at the falls by dark."

"OK, there's more. And why?" he asked.

"Yeah, there's more, but you need to trust me. Do you trust me?"

"Every bit of you," he said.

"All right." I knew full well he trusted me, but I had to say it.

"I can't tell you everything I saw in my dream because, if this happens, I need you to see it for yourself and not just see what I say. It's a lot like what Mungie said months ago."

"Oh, I get it. Oh, and should we take our usual turnoff right here, or do you want to take the long route tonight?"

"Take the turn," I said. "Take the turn. And that's not funny, by the way."

He found it very amusing and asked me to explain the text.

"Oh my God, I've been torturing myself all day with it."

"The spirits will rise with the new day. Not when it rises but when it sets.

"I read it last night before I went to bed and I heard it in my dream."

"And what does it mean?" he asked.

"In the old days and during the belief period, if you will, the day ended when the sun went down. So let's say 6 p.m. Do you understand?"

"Yes, I do. So this day would be almost over."

"Right! The spirits will rise with the new day, meaning at dark, like at 7 p. m. That's when this is happening! Not when it rises, but when it sets, refers to the sun. Do you see?" I asked.

"I think I do."

"The spirits will rise with the new day, not when it rises but when it sets. It makes complete sense to me."

"Well, I'm not about to turn around now. You're very smart and good-looking—did I mention I like that?"

"Did I mention that it scares most men?"

"Did I mention that I'm not like most men?"

"You certainly aren't. Now keep driving, and faster," I said, jokingly.

The sun was racing toward the waterline as we hit the Barra Strait and it felt like we didn't have any time to spare. That seemed strange as I was sure we'd given ourselves plenty of time. Something wasn't as it should be and Patrick said, "Do you want to go to the cottage first?"

"Oh God, no. Something isn't right with the time. Look at the clock, it's almost five-thirty, we need to be there *now*."

"Five-thirty, what the heck, that clock can't be right."

"Just go," I said.

As we passed the church and the hall, I was unable to speak. I don't think I'd ever hyperventilated before, but I felt like I was about to.

Patrick said something to me but I heard nothing and nodded. We came over the top of the graveyard hill and at the bottom of the hill we were halted by that wine-coloured car—again!

Now, the next half mile from my limited experience of driving through here was as crooked as a dog's hind leg and there was just no place to pass. Patrick and I were at wit's end as we followed them and he started chanting.

"Go to Barra Glen...Go to Barra Glen." And I joined in: "Go to Barra Glen...Go to Barra Glen."

Their signal light came on and we squealed for joy and Patrick said, "Nothing like a little frustration to sharpen the spirit on."

He was so right and we wondered who they were as we kept straight toward Washabuck.

We were moving pretty fast, but the sun and the clock seemed to have a faster gear. Maybe it was because our road was not nearly as straight as the trail they were racing on. We hit every hole and bump along the way and, every time, Patrick would rejoice that he didn't miss one, we didn't miss one.

When we passed the little church in Washabuck, I was pretty sure we were going to make it. We got to the end of the pavement, started up the hill, and the car started balking, as if to say, "I'm going no further."

"What's wrong?" I said, as we pulled over to the side of the road.

The car had shut off but we had lots of gas. He tried starting it a few times and then he said, "Let's just run. We'll make it."

There was just enough light to see. We grabbed the flashlight and tried it but it flickered and went very dim. We had our phones and Patrick grabbed his sketchpad and we started running.

"This is weird," he said.

"What were you expecting?"

At that moment, a crack of thunder shook the evening skyline and I got a quick stitch in my side. It hurt for a second but thankfully it stopped.

We heard the falls getting louder as we approached and then our phones went out completely.

Some fireflies threw sparks at us, and for a few brief seconds, we could see the road but then the darkness returned. All the time, the sound of rushing water grew louder and louder. Miraculously, the clouds parted and the full moon lit the road and forest like the middle of the day. Thunder ripped through the night air again.

Patrick grabbed my hand and said, "Did you feel that?"

"Quiet, and, yes, I felt something brush past me," I whispered.

"That's it," he whispered, as he squeezed my hand tighter.

We were at the path and the glory of the moon disappeared behind a blanket of clouds. It seemed as though a small swarm of fireflies were sharing their light and heading down the path and then we heard it.

It started as a light hum—like a drone—and then a chant, and not like anything I'd heard before. We saw a light coming from the ground, as we approached the bank where the rope was.

We stopped and you could smell wood burning like we had in Iona Rear. It was a fire and my young woman with the white hair from my dreams was gracefully dancing around it. Her hair was full of the prettiest flowers and the little birds were singing louder than ever.

A second, smaller fire started a few minutes after we noticed the first and the singing grew louder. We could feel a steady breeze from what had to be spirits whirling all around us. The singing was very confusing as it seemed to be just a complete jumble of words. I whispered to Patrick, "What do you see?"

"I see your white-haired woman in her white dress lightly stepping around the fire. She dances like you, by the way. I hear a song but it makes no sense, I hear humming and I feel a steady breeze like people rushing on the street. I see a smaller fire and I think those are little people over there and are they shooting little arrows?"

"Och, do you feel that?"

"Holy. Crazy. It's beautiful."

I saw Patrick start to sketch what he was seeing. I hadn't noticed the little people but then the moon lit the area and you could see them everywhere. I felt the sting of their little arrows and then the sting was gone as the arrows dissolved like they were never there.

How did they do that?

They were right beside us, as if married with the trees, branches, rocks, and surroundings. With the full light of the moon, they were easy to see, and I wondered if they were here when we visited before.

There were many different shapes and sizes but most of them were like bunnies standing on their hind legs, transforming into familiar images, with hands, feet, and kind faces.

They were mostly older looking, but some were like young children and toddlers. Others seemed to come from shapes of birds and animals, but they all morphed into a human-like image. Their faces looked like patience, kindness, caring, humility, courage, happiness, and love. They were beautiful.

The falls were drowned out by the birds as the fires grew larger and brighter. I saw my lady, who had to be Boronia, as she gracefully leapt as if floating around the larger fire.

And then over a period of time, you could slowly hear the song make some sense. The spirits were circling around her and they were all repeating their own phrases, over and over. When the phrase was in sync with the song, they would momentarily appear as a thin human image and then they'd go hazy. They were absorbed into the fire and a small puff of an explosion would create sparks and they'd shoot off in the night sky.

It seemed as though every seventh time around the fire, Boronia would snatch a spark from the little explosion, catch it, and cup it in her hand. She would blow into her open hand toward the smaller fire, where it would burst again and float into the night sky. The little people lightly danced around the small fire and let out a shriek and an *ahh* when the little spark burst and floated away.

It kept going at a steady pace for what had to be an hour—but who could tell, it might have been ten. The song became clearer and clearer until you could hear a clean melody that sounded like one Mam used to hum, but I don't think I'd ever heard these words.

The little sparks made a steady light into the sky and then scattered in all directions. As the pace slowed down and the song became softer, the breeze of the spirits slowed and the roar of the falls returned.

The moon returned from behind her blanket, and I saw most of the little people transforming back to their original images and scurrying into the forest and air.

When it all seemed to end it looked like a few spirits came back in the opposite manner to which the others had left. They briefly appeared as an image and quickly breezed away, as if to return to our mortal world.

The fires died down and the moon went behind the clouds and we were in darkness again. Then in one last gust, Boronia floated gently past us and I felt her graze my cheek on the way by.

I reached for Patrick's hand and it wasn't there. I turned toward him and he had moved a little piece from me.

"You scared me," I said, as I reached for his arm.

"I scared you! That was, that was, that was the most amazing thing I've ever seen. Holy shit."

I reached for him and pulled him close to me and we stood there holding each other up. We held each other so close we could feel each other's hearts and I whispered in Patrick's ear, "I love you."

"I love you, too," he said, and we kissed as light as flowers.

We stood there for some time before deciding to leave with only the fireflies to guide us.

We found our way to the road and walked down the hill toward the car as the fallen dry leaves rolled along beside us. The light breeze and leaves produced a rustling crescendo sound that followed us like a marching band down the road. We were holding hands as the moon made another appearance and lit the road as far as we could see. I stopped walking and said to Patrick, "I need to hold you again and remember this moment," as the dried leaves swirled melodically around us.

"That sounds good to me, Maggie."

He felt so good and I didn't want to leave, but figured we couldn't stand there all night, so I pinched him on his cute butt cheek and said, "Come here often?" and laughed back into his arms.

"No, but I'm going to start." He pulled me closer.

We were almost at the car when we saw two images and the car started. The lights came on and a familiar man's voice rang out.

"Is this your car?"

"Yes, it is," said Patrick.

"Oh, good, good, we were just checking if it had broken down but it started right away."

It was Mickey from the floating house and the man from nearby, Murdoch MacInnis. He was the same man I had spoken to in the summer that no one else had seen.

"Now you look familiar to me," Mickey said.

"Yes, we met you at the floating house last summer."

"Oh, yes, you're Maggie Nora Liza *Mhór*, and you're a MacLean."

He introduced Patrick to Murdoch and Murdoch said, "MacLean, eh? Are you one of Laughlin's crew?"

"Laughlin who?"

"Well, MacLean, of course. He looks like them, don't you think, Mickey?"

"Yes, I suppose he does."

"Well, it's nice to see you again. Can we give you a lift?" I said.

"No, no, that's all right, dear. We like to get out for a walk on nights like this."

"And did you see anything interesting on your walk tonight?" he asked.

"Well, yes, we did, and I'd say you'd believe us if we told you."

"Well, yes, now, dear, we probably would."

"You need to be true to the sanctity of these things that only believers can see. These little miracles need to be cherished and protected. Now I hope you understand this."

"Oh, I think we understand what you are saying," I said.

"Well, we're happy to hear that. Good night now and drive slowly on these roads—you never know what you'll meet or see."

The two of them walked away with their boots rolled down and you could hear them laughing and speaking Gaelic into the darkness.

Patrick turned the car around and we headed back toward the pavement and them, but we never passed them; it was like they vanished into the night.

We drove back to our cottage, just like they said, nice and slow. We were exhausted and maybe in a bit of shock but we made it and when we arrived we saw a few little trick-or-treaters wandering around. They looked nothing like what we had seen earlier, except maybe their size. We unloaded our stuff and Patrick said, "Do you want wine or scotch?"

"YES."

I went out onto the deck, leaned against the railing and stared out into the lake. Patrick returned a few minutes later with four glasses, kissed me, smiled, and said, "I need you to know something."

"What's that?"

"I love you so much, Maggie. I have since we first came here. I was just, just, I don't know."

"Six-letter word, that starts with S? Me, too."

"I'm not stupid, I just didn't want to mess it up or chase you off. Things have been so good with you and me, you know. We just seem to fit."

I was getting a lump in my throat and felt like I might cry but I smiled at him and said, "You can't scare me off after all we've been through. I'm a keeper."

"You sure are."

He came toward me and we kissed. I raised a glass to him and said, "To the words we've been avoiding for so long: I love you!"

"I love you," we both said.

We stayed on the deck for some time and poured drinks and talked about the night. We talked about loving, laughing, and our future. We talked about what we had seen and what it all meant. We talked about not talking about it. We talked about the car stopping and the phones and flashlight and I remembered the sketches.

"Where's your sketchbook?" I asked.

"It's in the car!

"I couldn't see what I was doing. It's probably all scribbles," he said returning with it in his hand.

When he opened it, he gasped and showed me the perfection inside and said, "I didn't draw this. I couldn't have, it was too dark."

"Well, I didn't do it."

There were seven pictures of everything we saw and it was just as we both remembered it.

We stayed up most of the night and continued to talk about the last six months, six weeks, six days, six hours, six minutes—and everything in between.

We talked about love and friendship, luck and loss, old people, and babies.

We talked about our parents and Mam, Mungie and Sadie, Mugsie and Baby Lou.

We talked about Joe Dear and the couple in the wine-coloured car.

We talked about Donald, Evelyn, Jackie, Donna, David and Phyllis.

We talked about Malcolm, Mickey, Murdoch, the church, and the saints.

We talked about Boronia, the spirits, and the little people with their dissolving arrows.

We talked about our friends and the souls that returned and drifted away.

We talked about the little sparks and where they were going.

We talked about the joy they would bring to the lives of others and wondered if we'd ever know their faces.

We talked about turning pro, and feeling pro and compared it to the innocence of our first date.

We talked about the roads we travelled, the lake we discovered, and the mountains we climbed.

We talked about houses and babies and a family of our own.

We talked about...love!

THE END

The Forest

Song

Paul K. MacNeil
(Music and Lyrics)

We were walk-ing in the for-est walk-ing towards our vil-lage fair. We heard peo-ple sing-ing car-ols Seemed as though they'd much to share.

Chorus Glor E A O Glor E A O **Tag**

Ending Gloir Don A - thair Gloir Don Mha - ac Gloir Don Spio - rad Naomh Saoghal Fad Saoghal Fad Saoghal A - men.

2. They were singing Gaelic worships
   As if all the saints were there
   Thunder filled the evening sky line
   It was very loud and clear.

3. Spirits wandered all around us
   Searching for their lines to sing.
   When they found them they went hazy
   Infant babies came to bare.

4. Mysterious, wonderous, glorious children
   Brought forth by the spirits fair.
   Gracious earthly ashes burning
   Conception of life returned.

Arrangement:

Verse 1
Verse 2
Chorus, Tag
Verse 3
Chorus, Tag
Verse 4
Chorus x 2
Verse 1
Chorus x 2
Ending

261

I Know You Know
Full Arrangement

Chorus 1
I know you know I know you care.
I know you know I know you care.

Verse 1
I woke in a February dream.
Unsure of where the hell I'd been.
Covered in love as thick as clay.
Should I run or should I stay?
Should I run or should I stay?

Chorus 1

Verse 2
You looked at me, I smiled at you.
You held my hand and kissed me too.
You could have left me there a fool.
Knowing what I put you through.
Knowing what I put you through.

Chorus 1

Verse 3
You held me long and strong and true.
You said I was the one for you.
A gentle fear beneath our skin.
Trust in love and trust within.
Trust in love and trust within.

Chorus 2
I know you know I know you care.
I know you know I know you care.
I feel the same way too.
I feel the same way too.
I know you know I know you care.

Verse 4
Some time goes by, December grooms.
A pricy steak, some love song tunes.
A nighttime stroll to end the day.
On the shore in Castlebay.
On the shore in Castlebay.

Chorus 2

Verse 5
A bottle of the bubbly kind.
I said there's something on my mind.
I held your hand, a ring between.
Will you spend your life with me?
Will you spend your life with me?

Chorus 3
I know you know I know you care.
I know you know I know you care.
I feel the same way too
(way too, way too).
I love your lips, your hips, your fingertips.
I love your skin, your chin,
your freckled grin.
I love you wild and styled, mellow, mild. I
know you know I know you care.

Verse 6
So here we are five girls have grown
They're roaming, roaming from our home.
It soon will just be me and you.
Trying to capture what we knew. Trying to
capture all we knew.

Chorus 3

Verse 7
Be glad of life a card did say.
Look at the stars and laugh and play.
So many dreams of ours came true.
You know I know you know it too. You
know I know I know it too.

Chorus 3

Chorus 1

You know I know I know it too.
You know I know you know it too.

GAELIC FOOTNOTES

Broch: Ancient stone structures

Johnakinns: John MacKinnon's people

Ach co-dhiù: But anyway

Jimmy Calaman: Seamus Chaluim Aoughais Chaluim Mhóir

Mór: Big

Mhór: Aspirated form of big…sounds like *vor*

Liza Mhór: Big Liza

Cheeag: Old Place name in Barra Glen or An t-sìtheag…female fairy

Cùil: Old Place name in Barra Glen…The back

Cù: Dog

Peadair Custie: Peter Christy

Màiri: Mary

Pòl Thòmhais: Paul Thomas

Seumas Mhuracidh: James Murdoch

Ciamar a tha sibh: How are you (with respect)

Móran Taing: Many thanks

Trom: Heavy (pregnant)

Bidh Modhail: Be mannerly

Thugainn ma-ta: Come along then

Nòisean: Deep interest or fancy

Stumpa Na Bhòcain: Stump of the ghosts

Bòcain: Ghost or spirit

Bonnach: Type of bread

Smùid a mo Rùin: Love smoke

Céilidh: Visiting and sharing of music and stories

Bealtaine: May 1st…spring festival

Samhain: Oct 31st…fall festival

Oidhche Shamhna: Night of Oct. 31st

Aos Si: Fairies or elves (supernatural race)

Steafag: Little Steve

Neilleag: Little Neil

Bean Neilleag: Wife of Little Neil

Màiri Sheumais Mhìchael: Mary James Michael

Glòir don Athair: Glory to the Father

Glòir don Mhac: Glory to the Son

Glòir don Spiorad Naomh: Glory to the Holy Spirit

Saoghal fad saoghal: Life everlasting

TUNE STORIES

Keltic Drive...This tune was written in July of 1996 during a labour dispute on an eventful day on Keltic Drive.

The Girls of Rear Iona...This tune was written in 1992 after playing for a funeral in Iona. It is meant for the lovely ladies I so fondly remember.

Helen's Hymn...A tune written for my mother who enjoyed going to church as much as going to the garden. Ten years in the making, it was completed at her funeral in August 2013. It is intended to be played like the famous Johnny Cope where the first two parts are played slow, with the next three parts picking up the tempo. The tune returns to the first part once through, where it slows to its original tempo.

'Càit A Bheil Nora Liza?... *"Where is Nora Liza?"*...This jig was written in 2002 for my second daughter Nora Isobel. I would go to retrieve her from her naps and call to her Càit a Bheil Nora Liza and pretend I couldn't find her as she delightfully squealed her whereabouts. Although Nora Isobel is a lovely name she will always be Nora Liza to me.

The Barra Glen Road...A slow jig or 6/8 march that brings an earthy feeling to my bones. It was written in 2000 for the place I was brought up on, grew up on, and threw up on in my passage through life.

Tha Mise ag Iarraidh Pòg..."I'm looking for a kiss"...A jig written for my third daughter Orianna around 2005 when she was very young. As a small child, I would ask her for a kiss and she would turn and try to squirm away.

Marching Orders...A strathspey written for Joan MacKenzie after her passing in April of 2020. She was a lover of music and a second mother to many. Joan invoked and cherished many pot-banging marches at the infamous Washabuck gatherings.

A Thousand and One Wishes...This waltz was written in 2005 for Dan E. MacNeil, who passed away far too young following a battle with cancer. One of his sayings from his time in the hospital was when you're healthy you have a thousand wishes. When you're sick, you have but one.

A 'Deaneamh Ìm... *"Making Butter"*...A tune written around 1990 after an entertaining night of music and courting on Main Avenue in Halifax.

Farewell to My Glen...A non-standard waltz for the end of an era in 2010. It wasn't supposed to end that way.

Steering With My Elbows...I have done a lot of driving over the years and on many occasions, I would prepare for a gig by playing my chanter while driving; it's not like texting because my eyes were always on the road.

I Know You Know...A tune and song written for my wife of twenty-five years, Tracey.

Reflection...A slow jig that was somehow conceived in 1994. The base of the tune came out of an old book and I rearranged the notes, tempo, and rhythm, creating this piece.

The Forest...Written as a song with my oldest daughter, Jessie Helen, around 2010. This song is the genesis for this book as we pondered and questioned the existence of miracle babies.

RECORDINGS & CONTACTS

All recordings are available on iTunes & Spotify

Jamie MacInnis & Paul MacNeil 1992
Fosgail an Dorus (Open the Door)
Bagpipe Music from Cape Breton

Tracey Dares 1993
A' Chording To The Tunes
Cape Breton Piano Accompaniment Instructional Video

Tracey Dares 1995
Crooked Lake
Cape Breton Piano Stylings

Tracey Dares & Paul MacNeill 2001
CASTLEBAYMUSIC.COM
Piping and Piano music from Cape Breton

NicNeil (Daughter of Neil) 2019
Back Current Jam
Fiddle and song (English and Gaelic) from Cape Breton

All tunes and songs are registered with SOCAN.

Contact:
E-Mail: paulkmacneil@gmail.com
Website: www.paulkmacneil.com

Pages of My Life

SPRINGING FROM THE THINNEST IDEAS TO FORM A THOUGHT, THEN GLUING THOSE THOUGHTS TOGETHER TO CREATE A PAGE, A CHAPTER, A STORY, THIS NOVEL HAS BEEN CREATED FROM THE PLEASURES OF LIFE AND LOVE.

The list of people who have had some form of contribution to this project would go on for pages but a number of people deserve special attention in recognition of their guidance, support, and talents.

From the community, island, and country in which I was so fortunate to have been peacefully raised, the seed was planted early and freely grew.

It begins with the old rural Gaels that stretch a smile in my ripened soul when I think of them. So much has changed, but the memory of them ignites the present in me.

Childhood and lifeworn friends, musical brothers and sisters, co-workers at Bell Aliant, and my extended family with its many branches, roots, and warts, part of this is you.

From the original primitive words to the completion of my first draft I constantly mulled if it should go to print. I reached out to some people I respected in search of an honest and fresh perspective.

My cousins, Barry and Glenda MacNeil. It was a treat to connect with both of you again. Glenda's vast knowledge and memories of Iona Rear were a reason to continue on their own.

David, Phyllis, Jackie, and Donna for allowing your personalities and love to grace the pages of this book.

Susan MacFarlane and Billy MacNeil for letting me hear your father's voice again.

My sisters Rosemary and Myrna. Their husbands Alfred and Randy who harboured only positive thoughts and suggestions, insisting I continue.

Doug and Joanne Boyd, the first friends I called to see if "this was anything" and our friend Danny Gillis, fellow author, for their advice and support at every turn.

All of us connected through the love of music, family, history, and a good laugh. To you all, your time and encouragement were monumental. Be it the least or the most, you kept me going.

Neila MacLellan and your cover shot from Ceitag's on the Fraser Road at midnight is brilliant…Your love of the Island is crystal and your photos are just part of the proof.

Bob Martin took a hundred photos of me, making it difficult to decide which one to use. You are awesome at what you do.

Vince MacLean, friend and fellow Gael, was quick to give me permission to use the map of Central Cape Breton from his book, *These Were My People*. I have read this book multiple times and it was part of the inspiration for me to finish my own project.

My neighbour and friend, Bernard Cameron, for reading the original draft and proofing the Gaelic spellings. Your lifelong commitment to our language, music, and culture is greatly admired.

Andrea Beaton who is a treasure and gift to our lives…A master performer/composer of fiddle, voice, and piano. The hours you spent writing out the tunes is like finish work on a home that has added so much to this story. As a young mother and businesswoman, you are an inspiration to our family.

The team at FriesenPress who helped this old rookie pull it all together. You are very, very good at all the things you do and a pleasure to work with.

To my beautiful family.

I can't imagine this happening without the gift and good fortune of my life with you all.

Jessie Helen, Nora Isobel, Orianna Madelaine, Eliza Katie Agnes, Floragael Mary Evangeline, and for better or for worse Tracey Elizabeth. You are the best things that will ever happen to me…Keep it up…The future awaits us all with open arms.

In memory of my father, Roddie John Dan Jim D, who spun many a yarn. Stories and song have been in my life forever and I am forever grateful.

Last but never least, to the memory of my mother, Helen Dorothy. The sacrifices you made, the life you embraced, and the mark you left on your community and family shall be treasured and remembered forever.

I will never forget you telling me, the importance of the power of words.

Thank You All So Much!!!

Paul K.

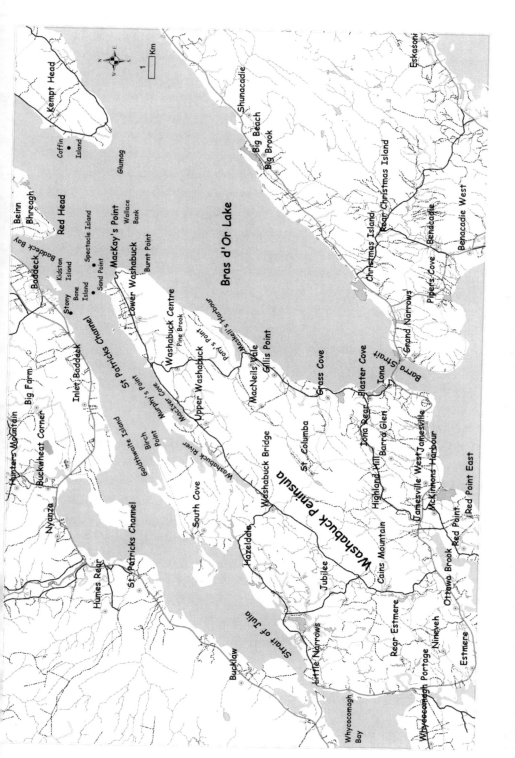

273

Printed in Canada